SQUIB

THE COLDSTREAM CHRONICLES
BOOK ONE

HELEN HARPER

For Scout, my brave calico fuzzball

CHAPTER

ONE

The stone steps leading from pavement level to the dark maw of the basement of the narrow, terraced house were the stuff of nightmares for anyone with even the mildest of vampire phobias.

Or, Mallory reflected, anyone wearing high heels.

There were glistening patches of dark, wet blood in several places; they looked fresh, as if at least one unsuspecting victim had dribbled their last drops of the red stuff as they were being dragged underground, but that was an unlikely scenario despite the location.

Doubtless the blood had been there for months, kept slickly moist by a handy flash of witch-induced magic. It was a clever trick because a good number of people, whether they hailed from Coldstream or elsewhere, would steer clear. Two things that vampires universally despised were nosy parkers and cold callers. The steep claustrophobic steps and the puddles of sticky blood would discourage both.

Fortunately, although Mallory owned two pairs of devastatingly sexy heels, they were reserved for more congenial occasions than this one. Currently she was wearing grubby high-tops which had seen better days. It was just as well.

Avoiding the blood, she descended carefully; flat shoes or not, this wasn't the time to rush and end up on her arse. She was a professional conducting a business call and there were standards to maintain.

Mallory knew there would be at least one pair of eyes watching her from behind the shuttered door at the foot of the steps, whether via magical means or through a more mundane peephole. There was a lot to be gained from the five-hundred-year-old vampire she was due to meet and first impressions were important. He wouldn't care what shoes she was wearing but he *would* care if she appeared clumsy or nervous.

Remember to breathe. Relax. You've got this. She had lived in Coldstream for more than ten years, but annoyingly she still found anxiety got the better of her at times. It was a good thing she was adept at masking her true feelings; compensating for her negative emotions with a display of ebullient confidence usually worked well.

Once the danger had passed and Mallory reached the door, she lifted her chin and allowed herself a moment to prepare. She inhaled deeply and tightened her toes, an old calming technique she'd learned years before. Then she relaxed, raised her hand and knocked.

From the other side of the door there was a shuffling sound followed by a scraping thud as the square grate in its centre was slid open and an irritated face scowled out.

The doorman wasn't vamp. Judging by his clammy, grey pallor he was merely a thrall, a servant who willingly yielded to the vampires in all things in the hope of one day being turned.

That was quite a gamble to take with your life. Mallory was well aware of the statistics: typically, only one in every thirteen thralls was allowed to become a full-blooded vampire.

Three or four people came to her every year requesting her services in return for a leg up with the vampires. Although plenty of vamps didn't bother with thralls, she could help someone become one if that was what they desired, but she had no control over what happened after that. Vampires were notoriously mercurial. People lined up to join them, desperate to partake in the dubious delights of an unnaturally long life. Some remained in thrall until their dying days, others abandoned the enterprise after a month or two of unrelenting servitude. Very, very few were turned true vamp.

None of Mallory's clients had ever made the full-fanged leap. Although it would be beneficial to her if they did because she'd have a direct line to all things vampish, she was secretly pleased. Foregoing sunlight forever and drinking blood would be bad enough, but vampires were cold creatures and the longer they lived, the worse they became. Every passing decade stripped them of another streak of humanity until they were little more than unfeeling husks on legs. When you lived for hundreds of years, everything quickly became boring – and, in Mallory's opinion, bored vampires were dangerous vampires.

She wasn't one to judge the life choices of others, however, so she gave the grumpy thrall a friendly smile. 'Good evening.' She nodded politely. 'My name is Mallory Nash. I have an appointment with Chester. He's expecting me.'

The thrall's scowl deepened. 'You're early.'

By three minutes. Mallory didn't allow her smile to dim. 'Shall I wait out here?'

He rolled his eyes expressively, suggesting that her question was completely unreasonable, then sighed heavily. 'You may come in.' He sniffed wetly. 'I suppose.' He slammed the grate closed and there was a clink as he slid back a bolt. The door creaked and, finally, Mallory gained admittance.

It wasn't her first time walking into a vampire's lair and it likely wouldn't be her last. A lot of Mallory's job involved keeping schtum about her clients; she would never admit who she had worked for in the past and the thrall would never learn how many times she'd walked into a vampire's house under similar circumstances. She knew enough to look awe-struck as he led her into the grand hallway with its flocked red wallpaper and stern paintings lining the walls.

Vampires liked it when the hoi-polloi admired both them and their surroundings. Much like the rest of the society, they wanted their life – or rather their *undead* – choices to be validated. As a mere squib, Mallory was supposed to be more impressed than other Coldstream citizens and she reacted accordingly; she knew the game and she knew her place.

The thrall gestured to an uncomfortable looking wooden bench elaborately carved with gleaming fleur-de-lis along the back, and grizzled lions with bared teeth on each arm. Sadly the carver's skill hadn't extended to making it a pleasant place to sit. In Mallory's experience, comfort often took a backseat to beauty, more's the pity.

'Sit there,' the thrall instructed. 'When Lord Chester is ready, I shall return and fetch you.'

Both the thrall and *Lord* Chester were exerting their power in an unnecessarily showy manner, and they'd doubtless leave her waiting for at least an hour before she was allowed any further into the building. Mallory checked her watch. She'd cool her heels for seven minutes but, as much as she wanted this contract, she wouldn't demean her reputation by waiting any longer than that. The vampires weren't the only ones with appearances to maintain and she had another appointment to meet before the night was out.

The easiest way to hurry things along and get what she wanted would be to ingratiate herself with the thrall. 'Thank you so much. What's your name?'

His eyes narrowed. 'Why do you want to know?'

'You seem like a nice fellow,' she lied. 'And it's always good to put a name to a face.'

His suspicion lessened a fraction but he was clearly still wary. 'Most people who come here don't care what my name is.'

Mallory felt a flash of sympathy. 'I'm not most people.'

He gave her a long look. Finally, with palpable reluctance, he said, 'It's Eric.'

She beamed. 'Nice to meet you, Eric.'

'You still have to wait.'

'Not a problem.' Still smiling, she sat down while the thrall vanished down the hallway.

As soon as she'd placed her hands on her lap, a low hiss filtered through the air. 'You're going to die.'

Mallory raised an eyebrow but didn't otherwise react.

The voice tried again. 'He will drain your blood. He will sink his fangs into your neck and suck every drop from your body until you are nothing more than a dried shell. Your skin will be parchment. Your hair will be straw. Your body will be dust.'

Uh-huh. Presumably the voice was referring to Chester, who certainly wasn't a real lord regardless of what the thrall had said. Four hundred and thirty-two years ago, Chester Longchamps had been a Yorkshire farm labourer who'd had the misfortune to get a landowner's daughter pregnant. He'd fled the county when it became clear that his offer of marriage was unwelcome and that he'd more likely find himself dangling on the end of a noose than waiting at the end of an aisle.

He'd found his way to Coldstream and ingratiated himself enough with the local vamps to be turned. Mallory hadn't been able to discover what had happened to his erstwhile girlfriend or their child, though she could imagine.

'Nobody will remember you,' the voice whispered. 'Nobody will find you.'

Although she possessed no Preternatural powers, Mallory was certain that she was the only creature capable of breath in the hallway, so she raised her eyes and examined the paintings along the far wall. There was a rich seascape deftly painted in amber hues that could well be an original Turner. Next to it was a portrait of a moustachioed man in funereal black holding a skull in one hand and a glowing poker in the other. Beyond him, she spotted a farm scene replete with stocky ponies with dead eyes.

She returned her attention to Moustache Man and was rewarded when he blinked. 'Hello!' she said cheerfully.

The Cursed Portrait didn't respond. Mallory dropped her gaze.

'Your death will be painful. You will…'

She looked at the portrait again and the voice fell silent abruptly. Mallory gave him an encouraging nod. 'Go on.' He glared at her. She waited but it appeared nothing more would be forthcoming.

She shrugged and leaned back, ignoring the petals of the wooden fleur-de-lis that were jutting into her spine. Some Cursed Portraits were chattier than others; this particular example was clearly a less verbose type, at least when he was under direct scrutiny.

She crossed her legs and continued to gaze at him. His tense expression, obvious despite the cracked eggshell paint, indicated that he was enjoying the experience far less than she was.

A high-pitched scream sounded from somewhere in the house, too far away for Mallory to discern whether it was born of true fear or merely a playful shriek. Perhaps it was nothing more than another attempt to throw her off-balance. She pursed her lips and checked her watch again, then smoothed down her skirt, stood up and started walking towards the front door.

'What are you doing?' It was Eric, the thrall, who'd appeared out of nowhere.

Mallory turned her head and glanced at him. 'I'm leaving.'

'But Lord Chester hasn't seen you yet.'

She waved an airy hand. 'Unfortunately I can't wait here all night. I have other appointments to keep. If he'd like to reschedule, he knows how to reach me.' She reached for the door.

Eric began to splutter. 'But … but … but…'

A mellifluous voice interrupted. 'But I can see you now, Ms Nash.'

Mallory paused and squinted. Towards the end of the hallway was a tall dark figure. She couldn't make out his features but there was no doubt that this was Chester Longchamps. Excellent: her display of brash confidence had paid off. She didn't say anything; the ball was in his court now. He understood the game as well as she did.

'I apologise for keeping you waiting,' he went on.

Mallory couldn't tell if the loud snort came from the Cursed Portrait or Eric, but she was betting on the former. It didn't matter. The vampire had acknowledged his tardiness and apologised and now she could be gracious.

'Very well,' she said. 'Would you like to discuss your business here?'

'No, we'll retire to my drawing room. Please, come with me.' He melted into the shadows beyond the hallway leaving Mallory little choice but to follow.

'You're going to die,' the Cursed Portrait hissed again as she passed it.

'Not today,' she murmured in response. And not by vamp. Chester Longchamps had just proved that he needed her far more than she needed him.

CHESTER'S DRAWING room wasn't any cheerier than his hallway. Mallory was unsure what design aesthetic he was aiming for, but there was certainly an eclectic array of furniture. The room contained everything from a Jacobean sideboard to a 1920s' art-deco mirror to a Brutalist coffee table that she was sure she'd seen only the previous month in a glossy magazine featuring the home of a premier league footballer and his glamorous wife.

She couldn't stop herself checking to see whether Chester's reflection appeared in the mirror. He caught her looking and smiled. 'Look,' he said and waved at it. 'No hands!'

Mallory found she was smiling back at him. 'Sorry, I didn't mean to be rude.'

His response was genial. 'I understand such curiosity. I can offer you a canapé – which most definitely will not contain garlic. You will find that all the windows in this property have been boarded up for the past three centuries. And,' he added, with only a hint of smarminess, 'I do sleep in a coffin.'

She blinked.

'It provides a more restful sleep,' Chester explained.

'Good to know,' she murmured.

She looked him over. For a vampire of his age, he was remarkably well-preserved. His eyes didn't contain much warmth but there was little evidence of the sunken skin she'd noticed on other aged vamps. His pallor told of centuries of avoiding the sun, but he'd been canny with make-up – either that, or he had a sunbed hidden away somewhere. Could vampires use sunbeds? She pondered the question. She genuinely had no idea.

Sunbed or not, Chester Longchamps was clearly someone who cared a great deal about his appearance and was keen to avoid looking like death in the way that some of his kin enjoyed. His rail-thin body was clad in a light-blue jersey fabric as if he were relaxing after a long run.

The notion that he was attempting to appear casual to put her at ease dissipated quickly when a young woman – another thrall – came into the room with a small dagger in her hand. She sliced open her wrist with practised ease and raised it to Chester's mouth. He drank greedily, slurping her blood while maintaining eye contact with Mallory. When he was done, he licked the thrall's skin so that his saliva would heal her wound.

It was considered passé for vampires to use their fangs to pierce skin, probably because it suggested a lack of consent on the thrall's part. Nevertheless, the act made Mallory shiver. Despite her many encounters with vampires, she'd not witnessed any of them feed. It was an intimate deed and watching it made her feel like an unwelcome intruder.

'I am not long awake,' Chester said by way of explanation. 'I find I require considerable refreshment before I can attack the night.' He nodded at the thrall, dismissing her.

Mallory suddenly had the thought that the act hadn't been intended to throw her off-balance but to indicate that he had vulnerabilities and needs. Regardless of the initial lack of welcome, Chester Longchamps didn't want her to feel intimidated. That was ... interesting.

He dabbed at his mouth with a light-blue handkerchief that perfectly matched his athleisure attire then beckoned Mallory to a nearby chair. Good: he was prepared to get down to business quickly. She might still make her next appointment in time.

'You are a squib, Ms Nash,' he said. It wasn't a question. 'When I first heard of your services, I admit I was sceptical. However, you come highly recommended.'

Mallory certainly hoped so; she'd worked hard to develop her reputation as somebody who got stuff done.

'What is your success rate?'

'Near perfect,' she answered without missing a beat. 'The

last time I didn't manage to fulfil a client's request was more than three years ago.' And that had been because the client in question – a troll called Bertie – had provided false information. It could be argued that the failure had not been hers.

Chester stroked his chin. 'And you deal solely in secrets and favours? You do not require monetary compensation for your efforts? Because frankly that would be far easier and, I suspect, far less costly in the long run.'

'My terms were made clear to you before my arrival.' She kept her tone pleasant.

He tilted his head and examined her. 'You present yourself as flowers and sunshine, Ms Nash, but in truth you possess a core of steel.'

'Titanium,' Mallory told him. Coated in radioactive nuclear waste. She didn't add that last part; it would have been overkill.

The vampire barked a cold laugh. 'Yes. Ha! Titanium indeed. Very well.' He leaned forward. 'I can count on your discretion?'

'Absolutely. Whether we proceed with an arrangement or otherwise, I will reveal nothing about this meeting.'

'Strangely, I believe you. Very well, then.' Chester paused for a moment before continuing. 'What I am seeking is an object. I would like to get my hands on ... the Clouded Map!' he finished with a dramatic flourish.

There was no accompanying drumroll although Mallory sensed that he expected one. If she'd known what the Clouded Map was she might have agreed, but alas she'd never heard of it. She knew better than to say that aloud, however. 'I see,' she said, keeping her expression studiously blank.

Oblivious to her ignorance, Chester went on. 'I appreciate it is a mammoth task. If it helps, I do not wish to retain the Clouded Map permanently. I would simply like to borrow it for a short period – twelve months at the most. Then I will happily return it to the Witches' Council.'

Well, at least now she knew who owned the map. Now the vampire's reasons for approaching her made sense: the witches didn't lend anything without good reason and considerable compensation, and they wouldn't strike a deal with a vampire under any normal circumstances.

'Why do you need it?' she asked.

'I am not at liberty to say.' Chester responded smoothly.

Mallory shrugged. 'I don't require specifics, but if I am to approach the Witches' Council on your behalf I need to know if your temporary possession will help you harm another sentient being in any way. And I am certainly not willing to participate, even indirectly, in any criminal activity.'

'I can assure you,' he said with a stiffness that suggested he was affronted by her suggestion, 'that there is nothing criminal or underhand about this venture.'

He hadn't answered her so she pressed the question. 'Will you use it to harm another sentient being?'

His eyes shifted. Oh dear.

Despite her earlier statement about criminality, potential violence wasn't necessarily a deal breaker for Mallory – this *was* Coldstream after all – but she wanted to know what she was getting into so she could make an informed decision.

There was a short silence before he replied, 'Not without provocation.'

She sighed; he was being deliberately obscure. 'I'll need you to elaborate on that.'

'Titanium,' he murmured. 'Very well. Before we proceed, I require your spoken vow that you will not repeat anything I tell you to anyone else.'

'I've already told you I will not reveal what is discussed here to anyone else and, as we've already established, I am a squib. I do not suffer the same consequences for breaking my word as a Preternatural does.'

Chester nodded. 'I'm aware that is the case, but I would still like your word. In the unlikely event that you break your vow, there will still be consequences.' His cold eyes gleamed and for a second Mallory had a glimpse of the predator lurking beneath his artificially enhanced skin.

'Consequences that you will carry out personally?' she enquired lightly, pretending that her heart rate hadn't suddenly ratcheted up.

His only answer was to curl the corners of his thin mouth into a half-smile.

Despite her reputation as a trustworthy broker of secrets and favours, Mallory was often presented with similar promises of violence; it was par for the course in her line of work and she wasn't offended. She certainly had no doubt that Chester Longchamps would carry out his threat if she talked. She'd probably be disappointed if he didn't.

'Very well,' she said. 'You have my spoken vow that I will reveal nothing of what is discussed within these four walls to any soul.'

Chester leaned back and relaxed slightly. 'Thank you.' He drew in a quick breath. 'I require the Clouded Map to locate a creature who has been attacking vampires. This creature has caused several deaths.'

'Vampire deaths?'

'We are not truly immortal, Ms Nash. Nobody is.'

Mallory knew that, but she was still surprised because killing vampires wasn't an easy task. Yes, it happened from time to time but it was rare. 'You want to kill this creature?'

'I want to prevent any further deaths among my kind. If killing the culprit is the only way to achieve that, then that is what will happen. If an alternative solution presents itself, then that will be acceptable.'

Mallory eyed him. She could be mistaken but she was certain she saw a glimmer of fear in the old vamp.

'Ms Nash,' he said quietly. 'Mallory. We are desperate.'

Every client presented a gamble in some way but Mallory suspected that everything Chester Longchamps had told her was the truth despite the aggression lurking beneath his calm facade. The fact that he'd now switched pronouns and was referring to all vampires rather than himself sealed the deal as far as she was concerned. 'Okay,' she said.

His eyebrows shot up. 'That's it? You will procure the Clouded Map for us?'

She smiled slightly. 'I didn't say that. What I will do is find out whether I can achieve what you are asking and what it will require from me. Then I will present you with my terms.' She thought about it. 'Twenty-four hours should be long enough for me to gather enough information to determine what is and isn't possible.'

Before Chester could express any gratitude, she added, 'I expect my fee will be high.'

He didn't flinch. 'Whatever it is, we are prepared to pay it.'

If that were true, Mallory could reap rewards from this venture for many moons to come but she knew better than to count her chickens. A lot could happen between now and the blood drying on a contract between them. However, she'd maintain her customary attitude to life and remain optimistic.

TWO

As soon as she left the building after promising to return in a day's time with her terms to seal the deal, Mallory turned smartly right and walked to the end of the street where Boris was waiting.

'You're still alive then?' the yellow-eyed spriggan called out as she approached.

She twirled and held out her arms. 'As you see. Vampires are not to be feared, Boris. I keep telling you that. As long as you are not a threat to them, they will not harm you.'

He shuddered. 'Any creature who spontaneously combusts at the first sign of a sunbeam is to be feared. You're as afraid of them as I am.'

She patted him on the back. 'You're being melodramatic.'

'I most certainly am not.' He sniffed and gave her a long look from beneath his blond eyelashes. 'What did he ask for?'

'I'm not going to tell you that.'

'What are you going to give him in return?'

'I'm not going to tell you that either.'

'But you *are* going to deal with him?'

She took some time before answering. 'It seems likely. Can

you set up a meeting for me tomorrow morning with Nicola Sturgess?'

'The witch?'

'Yep.'

'She's on the Council.'

'All the more reason to meet with her,' Mallory said mildly. 'Besides, it'll be good to get her favour off the books. There are only a few weeks before the time runs out on it.'

'Less. You only have ten days remaining on that contract.'

Oh. Mallory absorbed that news, then shrugged and gave her assistant a sunny smile. 'Then this is the perfect opportunity for her to repay what she owes.'

Boris sighed heavily. 'Okay.' He reached into his waistcoat and drew out a small leather-bound diary. Gripping a nub of a pencil in his green fingers, he scratched a reminder to himself before tucking the pad away again.

Not for the first time, Mallory told herself that she should start doing something similar to remain organised and on task. The minutiae of her life tended towards haphazard chaos which caused more problems for her than she cared to admit. Her strengths lay in remembering people, not dates and numbers.

'I should tell you that your meeting with Kit McCafferty was due to start five minutes ago,' Boris said. 'You're going to be very late.'

Mallory grimaced; it was never a good look to arrive late to an appointment. Fortunately, she doubted McCafferty would mind. The cat lady presented a benign front to the world even though Mallory suspected there was far more to her than met the eye. 'We should get going, then.'

Boris nodded, raised his thumb and forefinger to his mouth and whistled. There was a moment's silence followed by the thundering of hooves along the cobbled streets. There were many benefits to having a Fae spriggan in service to her, and the ability to magically summon transport at a moment's notice was one of them.

'I don't know what I'd do without you,' she said.

His tone was dry. 'I'm certain that you'd manage. In two years, nine months and fifteen days' time, when my favour to you is complete, you *will* manage.'

'Not that you're counting the days or anything.'

'I'm counting the days, the hours and the minutes. But you're not bad for a boss. I've had worse.'

'I'm a *great* boss,' Mallory retorted. At least she tried to be. 'And just to prove it, you can head off for the night once I get to Vallese.'

Boris swept a bow. 'Your wish is my command, my lady.'

VALLESE, an expensive Italian restaurant in one of the smarter suburbs of Coldstream, was the sort of place that you were supposed to dress up for. Mallory's grubby shoes and casual clothing might not have raised eyebrows at Chester Longchamps' place but she knew she'd feel out of place at the restaurant. If there'd been time she would have gone home to change, but it was what it was.

She patted down her colourful clothing, which at least didn't look *too* creased, but there was no point attempting to do anything with her hair. Her springy brown curls had a mind of their own and past experience had taught Mallory that it was better to let them be.

As she approached the restaurant door, she mentally reviewed the information she'd retrieved for Kit McCafferty. The cat lady had wanted to know what the Witches' Council were discussing in their daily meetings that week. In theory, that information was restricted to council members only but

Mallory hadn't needed to approach the likes of Nicola Sturgess to find it out. Late last year she'd helped a young witchling find a job at the grand council headquarters and he was still paying off that debt in small incremental favours.

It had been an easy matter to ask him to find out what was top of the council members' agenda. He'd recently been tasked with serving coffee and cake during their breaks and eavesdropping on their conversations took no effort on his part, though some mysterious shenanigans concerning a particular Fetch who'd been arrested for murder earlier in the day had delayed matters somewhat.

Obviously Mallory wasn't planning to tell Kit just how easy it had been to get the information; those sorts of secrets were hers alone.

The scent of red roses tickled her nostrils and she was mindful of the small candles dotting the fringes of the red carpet that led to Vallese's interior. The skirt she was wearing was beautiful but cheap and she'd likely flare up like a vampire in sunlight if the hem caught any of the flickering flames.

She nodded appreciatively at the tuxedoed violinist at the entrance and smiled at the maître d' who appeared mildly panicked at her approach. She delved into her memory for his name – John? Jack? Something like that. She chewed her lip and concentrated. *James*. That was it.

He'd worked for Vallese for years and was a loyal employee. She'd made an approach to cultivate him as a useful source of information about the guests who passed through the restaurant's hallowed doors but he'd refused immediately. He took his job seriously and considered blabbing to be a betrayal of the highest order, regardless of what information his boss passed over to her with loose-lipped ease. James was one of the good guys. He'd not even taken any offence at her approach, just declined politely and changed the subject.

Mallory held up her hands to forestall any polite remark he might voice at her lack of a dinner reservation. 'Good evening! I'm not here to eat,' she told him. 'I have a meeting with one of your guests. I just need a moment of Kit McCafferty's time.'

'Mr Vallese did not mention that you would visiting us tonight, Ms Nash.'

'He doesn't know, and there's no need to bother him. As I said, I'm here on business. I'm not looking for any food.' She paused. 'Though a glass of wine might be nice.' Vallese's cellar was extensive, and if there was one thing of which Mallory heartily approved it was a wide selection of wine.

James continued to fret. 'Mr Vallese will want to know...'

This was the problem when you'd worked for a lot of different people in the city: you often rubbed up against them when you were dealing with other clients. Not everyone was as circumspect as James, and Mallory doubted that Kit would appreciate the restaurant owner overhearing their conversation.

'Please,' she interrupted. 'I am sure he's busy in the kitchen. Don't bother him.'

She craned her neck so she could peer into the well-lit restaurant. Kit was in the far corner – at the best table of the house, in fact. The purple-haired woman was staring into the distance looking vaguely bored. Opposite her sat a werewolf.

Mallory blinked. That wolf was Alexander MacTire, alpha of the MacTire pack. Huh. She'd learned a lot about him from a potential werewolf client only a few weeks earlier who had told her that MacTire was yielding to the demands of his pack and actively searching for a mate.

Mallory wouldn't have put Kit and MacTire together as a couple; in fact, she was certain that Kit was involved romantically with Thane Barrow, who was a far better match for her. Unless the cat lady was hedging her bets, which seemed unlikely, this was probably a business meal and not a romantic interlude. It was a strange venue for an official meeting but perhaps Alexander MacTire wanted to show off; from what little she'd heard about him, that seemed a distinct probability.

'I'll just nip in and out,' Mallory told the maître d'. 'Five minutes, tops.' Before he could protest further, she slipped past him and went inside. Sadly, she only managed a few steps before she was accosted by a frowning waiter whom she didn't recognise.

'Can I help you, ma'am?' he asked in a polite clipped tone that was only one degree away from gazing up and down derisively at her somewhat dishevelled appearance.

Mallory pointed at the table. 'I need to speak to one of your guests for a few minutes. Kit McCafferty. She's over there.'

'You can wait outside until they've finished their meal. Then, if Miss McCafferty wishes to speak to you, I am sure she will do so.'

Mallory held her ground. 'She's expecting me.' The waiter wrinkled his nose. 'I *am* going over to speak to her,' she told him softly. 'Unless you want to throw me out and ruin everyone's evening, it is going to happen.'

James was gesturing vigorously from the other side of the front door to attract the waiter's attention and tell him that Mallory was more than welcome. Unfortunately the poor man didn't notice. 'Fine,' he sighed at the apparently shocking imposition on his time. 'Wait here for one moment.'

Mallory smiled. As the waiter went to speak to Kit, she turned to James and waved him off through the glass. She'd got what she wanted and his involvement would only complicate matters.

She watched as the waiter nodded to Kit, and Alexander MacTire stood up and headed for the restroom. Excellent. Without waiting any longer, she strode forward. 'Hey, Kit!'

The cat lady offered her a friendly smile that was definitely tinged with relief; it appeared her intrusion was more than welcome even though Kit had clearly dressed up for the occasion. She looked good; Mallory hoped that Alexander MacTire appreciated her efforts.

She sat on the chair he'd vacated before offering up a white lie to excuse her tardiness. 'Sorry I'm late – it took longer than I expected to get the information you needed. The Witches' Council has been in disarray all day.' She raised an eyebrow. 'Something about one of their own getting arrested for murder, which I believe you know about?'

Kit also raised an eyebrow. 'You're well-informed.'

Mallory's smile stretched wider. 'That's my job. Anyway, I'll knock a month off your waiting period because of the delay. If I don't come to you for the return favour within the next eleven months, you are released from further obligations. Is that okay with you?'

'Sure.' Kit looked delighted at the suggestion.

Pleased that she'd been right about Kit's relaxed attitude, Mallory leaned forward, took a slice of bread from the basket and started munching. The last thing she needed was for her conversation to be interrupted by her stomach growling. Although she'd told James the truth about not wanting any food, now she was inside the restaurant with its delicious aroma of garlic, tomato and oregano she realised she was desperately hungry. Far too often she became so absorbed in her work that she forgot to eat.

'So,' she said. 'You wanted to know what was top of the council agenda this week. Despite the spanner in the works with the murder arrest, there's one topic that's been consuming the witches.'

She swallowed a mouthful. Yum. Thank heavens for focaccia – it would keep her going until she managed to get home and heat up a proper meal. 'This is great bread.' Without thinking, she leaned forward and picked up the nearest wine glass, drinking from it and swirling the goodness appreciatively around her mouth. 'Good wine, too. A Tuscan merlot?'

'So I've been told.'

'Tasty. Very full-bodied. I like the notes of fig.'

A tiny frown marred Kit's forehead. 'The council?' she prompted gently.

Mallory jumped guiltily: it had been a long day but that was no excuse for getting distracted by good bread and even better wine. 'Oh, yes. They're preoccupied with silphium. In fact, the witch who's been arrested for murder – Fetch Daniel Jackson? – had been tasked with retrieving it.' She paused and watched Kit, whose expression suddenly displayed studied nonchalance. 'Interesting, wouldn't you say?'

'What the hell is silphium?' Kit asked.

Before Mallory could explain, a male voice answered. 'Silphium is the most desirable, most potent, most magical herb that has ever existed.'

The werewolf had it in one. Mallory flicked a look in MacTire's direction. He was dressed formally, in a navy suit and pink shirt that perfectly set off his tanned skin. There were a few glinting silver hairs visible in his dark locks that indicated his growing maturity, though she knew he was only in his early forties. His sculpted cheekbones, brief shadow of stubble and arresting amber eyes added to his appeal.

Alexander MacTire was an incredibly handsome man but Mallory wasn't fool enough to fall for a pretty face. The werewolf alpha was definitely dangerous. Even if she hadn't been aware of his standing, she'd have recognised him as someone who was used to being in a position of authority. Brooding masculinity rippled off his skin as if in dark waves directed at her alone.

Mallory glanced at Kit, who didn't appear perturbed that MacTire had joined the conversation. She shrugged and nodded at him. 'What he said.'

'It's also been extinct for the last two thousand years,' he added.

Mallory winked. Alexander MacTire didn't know everything, and that was surprisingly satisfying. 'Supposedly. Although perhaps "dormant" would be a better word. Whatever – it's priceless. If it existed today, Preternaturals would kill not just for its power but for the money a tiny silphium cutting could command.'

'Kill for it?' Kit asked.

'Oh yes.' Mallory noted the agitation that was now visible in Kit's twitching fingers. She didn't blame her; from what Mallory had learned, silphium was both extraordinarily powerful and extraordinarily dangerous. Still, if anyone knew how to deal with such a desirable herb, Mallory reckoned it would be Kit McCafferty.

'I'm quite certain. Rivers of blood would run through the streets of Coldstream if somebody possessed silphium.' Mallory took another sip of the wine and then, in a bid to diffuse the tension, she said, 'This really is an exquisite merlot.'

MacTire crossed his arms. 'That's *my* wine,' he informed her.

Oops. Mallory tightened her toes briefly then decided to brazen it out. It was, after all, what she did best. She drained the glass then asked in an overly bright voice, 'Did you choose it?' He glowered darkly so she doubled down. 'It's delicious!'

MacTire remained unamused. 'That's also my chair.'

'Oh.' She hadn't anticipated that the werewolf alpha would err on the side of grumpiness and that had been a mistake on her part. She was usually adept at anticipating clients' needs and analysing their emotions. Then again, Alexander MacTire wasn't her client.

She glanced around. 'You'd think an upmarket place like this could afford more chairs.' She caught the snooty waiter's eye and gestured for help.

If anything, MacTire's irritation increased. 'Five more minutes,' Kit said to him. 'I want to find out more about this silphium stuff.'

Something about her tone made Mallory realise that this wasn't a mere business dinner; she'd got it wrong and she *was* interrupting a romantic evening by candlelight. 'Oh no!' she blurted out. 'Are you on a date? Have I gate-crashed? I'm so sorry. I'd hate to interrupt a budding romance.'

There was a definite growl in MacTire's voice when he answered. 'On that count you're safe.'

Mallory felt a flash of relief that she'd not ruined Kit's evening; if she was honest, she was equally relieved for Kit's long-term future. The congenial cat lady could do better than this posturing alpha. Far better. 'Ah.' Mallory nodded at him. 'Your hunt continues, then.'

His eyes glittered dangerously. 'What do you mean?'

There was no point in pretending she didn't know so Mallory shrugged. 'Your search for the perfect mate. You've not found her yet.'

MacTire looked furious though Kit appeared amused. 'Don't look at me – I didn't tell Mallory I was having dinner with you. She had no idea who I was coming here with. In fact, I've never mentioned you to her.'

'Kit's right,' Mallory agreed cheerfully. 'I figured it out all by myself. Go me!'

The waiter arrived with a third chair and MacTire sat down. His movements were controlled and careful but when he gazed at her with those assessing amber eyes Mallory felt a shiver of discomfort. 'And who *are* you?' he demanded.

She wouldn't give him the satisfaction of knowing he was unnerving her. 'Mallory Nash,' she said. 'And you are Alexander MacTire.' She raised her glass towards the waiter. If she was going to stay for even another five minutes then more wine was definitely called for. 'Could we get another bottle here?'

After receiving a clipped agreement from MacTire, the waiter scurried off while Kit did her best to offer a more detailed explanation. 'Mallory is a broker,' she said. 'Of sorts.'

'Secrets and favours,' Mallory added, in case MacTire assumed she was some sort of financial whizzkid. 'Not stocks and shares.'

Kit went on. 'I asked her to find out what the Witches' Council is worrying about this week in return for an as-yet unspecified favour.'

MacTire frowned. 'Risky.'

Bristling at his ongoing scrutiny – and obvious judgement that she was a wrong 'un – Mallory said, 'There are caveats as to what Kit will do for me in return. There are always caveats.'

MacTire leaned back his chair, his amber eyes hooded. Suddenly he appeared less irritated and more intrigued, as if Mallory were a new species of creature he'd only just discovered. 'How do you know about *me*?' he asked silkily.

She felt herself relax; as long as he was asking questions and not growling at her, she reckoned she was onto a winner. 'Let's say that a potential client came to me not long ago and asked for a favour – she not only wanted you to notice her but also consider her for the position of First Mate. I'm only telling you because I declined to help for reasons we won't go into.'

There was too much that could go wrong when clients' love lives were involved, and Mallory had no interest in setting up blind dates. Besides, something about the woman who'd approached her for help in snagging MacTire had rubbed her up the wrong way. She'd had a cold, mercenary attitude towards nabbing one of the most eligible bachelors in Coldstream that was nothing to do with romance and everything to do with power and wealth.

Mallory had considered her options, researched how she might approach the situation and eventually decided against proceeding. Manipulating love wasn't her style. Now that she'd met MacTire in person, she was even more glad she'd refused.

She realised that Kit might be concerned about her loose lips but Mallory was more than capable of keeping quiet when a situation called for it. 'My real clients' business is sacrosanct,' she explained, 'and I'm not in the habit of gossiping. I won't go blabbing about your request to anyone, Kit.'

Unfortunately Alexander MacTire wasn't interested in her promises to Kit McCafferty. 'Who?' he demanded of her. 'Who asked you to do this?'

Mallory waved a hand dismissively. 'I'm not going to tell you that.' He could throw any number of lupine tantrums and her lips would remain sealed.

A note of triumph crept into his voice. 'You declined because you couldn't help her. Right?'

As if. 'Wrong.' MacTire was starting to irritate her now. 'I knew exactly how to achieve what she wanted, I just didn't choose to do it.'

MacTire snorted. 'How? How would you have done it?'

Kit intervened, doing her best to steer the conversation back to the real reason for Mallory's intrusion. 'If we could get back to the matter of this silphium...'

Mallory barely heard her. For reasons she couldn't quite explain, she couldn't drag her attention away from MacTire. His arrogant amber eyes seemed to penetrate all her defences. She tilted her chin and reverted to brash confidence. *I'm not intimi-dated by you,* she told him silently. *Growl all you want.*

MacTire's mouth twitched. *You can't fool me with any of your tricks,* he seemed to reply. *I'm in full control of my own life. I'm the manipulator here. I'm in charge. Not you.*

The sommelier appeared with a fresh bottle of wine.

'Thank you,' Kit said.

Neither Mallory nor MacTire broke their gaze. Fine. If he wanted to know how she'd have done it, she would tell him. 'It's the annual Wolf Ball next month.'

'So?'

This was going to be good. 'You're attending the ball with your beta wolf, Samantha, as your date.'

Out of the corner of her eye, Mallory spotted Kit's jerk of surprise. MacTire betrayed little but Mallory was certain she'd also shocked him. 'When you arrive at the steps of the Grand Hotel, it would be an easy matter to distract Samantha. While she's busy, my potential client would appear dressed in blue because it's your favourite colour. I'd also advise her to wear a natural perfume based on roses because that would grab your attention. Then she'd make her approach. I didn't iron out all the details because I didn't take her on as a client, but I expect it would have been something along the lines of a little drama where she helped an elderly guest in front of you so she appeared both strong and compassionate.' She shrugged. 'But I'm only conjecturing.'

MacTire's lips curled up in derision. 'It wouldn't have worked.'

She grinned. He underestimated her abilities. Considerably. 'I beg to differ. It definitely would have worked – up to a point, at least. Even my wiliest machinations can only go so far.' She took another sip of wine and tried not to let her grin turn into a smirk. 'There would at least have been consensual sexual congress. Beyond that, I can't say.'

The alpha's sneer vanished and his mouth dropped open. Mallory did her best not to preen.

'Okay-dokey,' Kit said loudly. 'About that silphium...'

Mallory gave an embarrassed laugh; she wasn't here to score points against Alexander MacTire. She straightened her shoulders and turned her attention to her actual client. 'Yes, of course. Sorry, Kit. We can go elsewhere to discuss it privately, if you wish.' It would be preferable to continue this discussion without MacTire's attention laser-focused on her.

'It's fine,' Kit said. 'Go on.'

Damn. Mallory smiled brightly. 'Alright.' She focused on Kit and told her everything she'd learned about silphium. There was a lot for her to take in.

CHAPTER

THREE

It wasn't long before they'd polished off the second bottle of wine. At some point the waiter reappeared with a dessert menu, his snooty expression replaced with a fawning, solicitous air. Mallory guessed that James had finally had a word with him. It had been inevitable.

She managed a smile in his direction and declined the menu even though her stomach grumbled loudly at the thought of Vallese's delectable chocolate torte. She wasn't here on a jolly, though she was certain MacTire noticed the audible manifestation of her hunger because he wordlessly handed her the remainder of the bread to finish off.

She felt a trace of guilt at her earlier irritation. Perhaps he wasn't so bad. Kit certainly seemed to like him well enough, and Mallory knew enough about the cat lady to trust her instincts.

She was amused when Kit had to drag a vow out of MacTire not to repeat any of what he'd learned about silphium. When the same request was put to her, Mallory capitulated in an instant. 'You have my word, Kit – of course you do.' She grinned.

'For one thing I'm a squib, so silphium's magical properties are no use to me. And I don't need money. It doesn't interest me.'

Unsurprisingly, Alexander MacTire didn't believe her. 'Really.' His voice was heavy with sarcasm.

Mallory didn't miss a beat. She offered him a sunny smile in response. 'Really.'

Kit interrupted before their temporary truce was broken and put a polite end to proceedings. 'Thank you, both of you. Please allow me to pay for dinner.'

'Not a chance,' MacTire growled. 'I invited you here.'

'Then let me pay for Mallory's share of the wine.'

'No.'

Before Mallory could interject, the waiter returned to their side. With his hands neatly folded in front of him and his head bowed, he cleared his throat. 'Your evening has already been taken care of.'

Mallory bit her lip. *Oh.* She would have preferred to avoid this scenario.

'What do you mean?' MacTire asked.

'Compliments of Mr Vallese.' The waiter bowed to Mallory. 'He hopes you enjoyed your evening, Ms Nash, and reminds you that you are always welcome to dine here with any of your friends.' With that, he backed away, a faint red flush staining his cheeks. He'd screwed up earlier; now he knew she was a valued friend of his boss, he was keen to avoid her gaze.

'Wait.' MacTire was clearly confused. 'What?'

Mallory had to admit that his reaction was entertaining. Maybe now he'd believe that she was far more capable than she appeared. Victor Vallese, the head chef and restaurant owner, had been a client of hers on several occasions and he'd always been delighted at the outcomes she'd achieved for him.

Kit was clearly enjoying the werewolf alpha's surprise

almost as much as Mallory. She pushed back her chair and stood up. 'I need to get home. I promised my cats that I'd be back before midnight.'

'Thank you for your company.' MacTire got to his feet. 'It's been a wonderful evening.'

'Indeed.' She kissed him on the cheek in a perfunctory manner. 'Let's never do it again.'

'Deal,' he said.

Mallory also stood up and extended her hand. 'If you need anything else, Kit, you know where I am. And if you don't hear from me in the next eleven months, you are free of any further obligations.'

'Oh, I'm certain I'll hear from you,' Kit said. 'Don't worry, I'll fulfil whatever favour you require whenever you require it.'

Mallory had no doubt that she would because she'd signed a blood contract to that effect and that was as binding a promise as could be. They shook hands then Kit raised a hand in farewell and left the restaurant.

Mallory turned to MacTire. 'It was nice to meet you,' she said politely. It was doubtful their paths would cross again. That was probably a good thing.

'You're leaving?' he asked.

Hell, yes. 'The kitchen is closing,' she pointed out. 'And I have a busy day tomorrow.'

'So do I.' He gestured to the now-empty bread basket. 'We both know that you need more sustenance in your belly than focaccia. Your tummy has been growling at me for the last hour.'

'Well,' Mallory retorted, '*you*'ve been growling at me. It's only fair.'

Surprisingly, MacTire's expression became rueful. 'I deserved that. If you have plans to meet someone, I understand.' He raised his eyebrows. 'Do you have a partner?'

'No.'

Something flashed in his eyes.

'And I'm not looking for one,' Mallory added firmly.

He laughed. 'Fair enough. Well, as it appears you're on your own, you should know that Glynn's Hot Dog Stand will still be open. Allow me to make up for my earlier rudeness by buying you the best food to keep those hunger pangs at bay. It's the least I can do. After all, I didn't have to pay for dinner.'

'That's kind of you,' Mallory demurred. 'But I ought to head home.'

MacTire's eyes gleamed. 'Are you afraid of me?'

'No.'

He raised his eyebrows.

'I'm not!'

'Methinks the lady doth protest too much.'

For goodness' sake. 'Fine.' Mallory shrugged. 'Buy me a hot dog. With extra onions. I'll eat it on my way home.'

'I have a car,' he told her. 'I can drop you wherever you wish.'

He had a car? In Coldstream? She shook her head. Of course he did. 'I'll walk,' she said emphatically.

Now MacTire looked amused. 'As you wish, Ms Nash.'

They walked out of Vallese's together. The violinist had finished up for the night but James remained in place. 'Mr MacTire, Ms Nash, please do return at any time. Mr Vallese would be thrilled to welcome you both.'

Mallory smiled warmly at him. 'Thank you.'

MacTire nodded. 'Thank you, James.'

Mallory was impressed that he knew the maître d's name. It was a small act that spoke volumes because there were many werewolf alphas in similar positions of power who wouldn't bother to find out.

They strolled down the cobbled street in the direction of

Glynn's small stand. 'That was an … interesting evening,' MacTire said eventually.

'Kit is an interesting person.'

'She certainly is.' He glanced at her. 'As are you.'

'You can drop the pretence, you know. I'm aware that you doubt my capabilities. Why shouldn't you? I'm a squib, I have no Preternatural powers and I'm the dictionary definition of ordinary.' She grinned to soften her words, trying to indicate that her lack of special magic skills wasn't something that concerned her.

MacTire was silent for a moment before he said, 'Of all the things I have discovered this evening, the one thing I'm sure about is that you are not ordinary.' He wet his lips. 'And I can't deny that I'm impressed by how much you learned about silphium in such a short space of time.'

She hadn't been expecting a compliment. 'I suppose you're not so bad yourself,' she said grudgingly.

He laughed. 'Damned by faint praise.'

Mallory pulled a face. 'I gate-crashed your date, sat in your chair and drank all your wine. You adapted to the situation with aplomb.' She paused. 'Eventually.'

'Eventually. Touché. To be fair, Goldilocks, it wasn't much of a date.'

'My hair is brown, not gold.'

'You sat in my chair and ate my proverbial porridge.' MacTire stopped walking and turned to her. 'Next you'll be sleeping in my bed.'

Whoa. Back up a minute. She stared at him. He stared at her. All of a sudden, Mallory felt very hot beneath her collar. 'Not in this life,' she whispered.

MacTire smiled slightly, then he carried on walking.

Mallory caught up with him. 'Don't go to the Wolf Ball with your beta, Samantha,' she said suddenly.

He blinked. 'Pardon?'

Abruptly, Mallory realised how her words sounded. She cleared her throat and did her best to explain. 'Samantha is great – amazing, in fact. But she's also incredibly scary and intimidating. Even if your potential Miss Right doesn't believe that you and she are a couple...'

He growled, 'We're not.'

Mallory nodded. 'She might still not approach you because Samantha is—' she searched for the right word '—Samantha.'

His eyes held hers. 'Do you know her?'

'I know *of* her.' Truthfully, Mallory knew far more about the MacTire beta, whom she'd never met, than the MacTire alpha standing in front of her. Samantha was one of those people who drew attention whether she wanted it or not.

Alexander MacTire was quiet for a long moment and Mallory started to think that she must have enraged him with her advice. His expression betrayed little but his ongoing silence spoke volumes.

Finally he said, 'I'll think about it.' He snapped his mouth shut and Mallory knew that the conversation was over.

THE FOLLOWING MORNING, when a shaft of weak winter sunlight sneaked in through the gap in her curtains and tickled her face, Mallory could still faintly taste the fried onions from Glynn's in the back of her mouth. MacTire had stayed quiet until they had parted company but he'd kept his word and bought her a hot dog, which she'd enjoyed during her solitary wander home.

She considered all that he'd said then rolled over and extracted a notepad and pen from her bedside drawer to jot down a few notes. Although she wasn't organised enough to keep a diary – more often than not she relied on Boris to keep her straight and encourage her to be punctual – she was meticulous about noting down information about the people she came across, both as clients and otherwise. Every scrap of information and every muttered whisper had the potential to become useful. As far as Mallory was concerned, information about people was worth its weight in gold. Her thick, well-worn notepad was her most valuable possession.

Mallory flicked through the pages until she reached the section marked 'Werewolves'. There was already an entry for Alexander MacTire that she'd made after the appointment with the female werewolf who was looking to make a romantic match, but the information was scanty.

Owns a car, she scribbled. She remembered what he'd said about silphium and added, *Classical education.* The hot dog he'd bought her offered more information and she tightened her grip on her pen. *Typical alpha sensibilities: domineering personality, needs to take care of others.* She paused and then wrote: *Intelligent. Observant. Thoughtful.* Finally, for no other reason than because the memory of his amber eyes continued to unsettle her, she finished with: *AVOID IF POSSIBLE.*

She took a few moments to write down a few more details in the entry for Kit McCafferty, and on Victor Vallese's page she added a note about the snooty waiter. She also updated the entry for Chester Longchamps. Then, with that chore completed, she untangled her legs from her bedsheet and stumbled through to her small kitchen to make a cup of coffee.

She grimaced when she opened the cupboard door and remembered belatedly that she'd run out of coffee – she'd meant to nip to the nearby market to get some the previous afternoon but had forgotten. Strong tea it would have to be.

'Coffee,' she muttered. 'Remember to get more coffee.'

Mallory ignored the familiar thuds from the pub downstairs; the cleaner would already be in sprucing the place up before it opened for the day. Instead she took her cup over to the window and gazed out across the expanse of Crackendon Square.

It was still early but there was plenty of activity. A tram with bright-purple sparks glimmering along its roof heaved its way out of view. A group of eager tourists were assembling for a walking tour, goggling wide-eyed at what was, quite frankly, a nondescript collection of stone buildings. Three worried looking witches, including one whom Mallory knew was a Council Fetch thanks to his pointed black hat, were huddling together in the far corner.

She wondered what it would be like if she had the where-withal to make use of proper spells; a bit of magically induced eavesdropping would make her life considerably easier. But daydreaming of what might be didn't change what actually was. It was important to remain grounded in reality.

She eyed the witches. From their expressions, something was definitely wrong. She nibbled on her bottom lip then put down her cup, grabbed her coat and shrugged it over her wrinkled pyjamas. It was long enough to cover her modesty and this was too good an opportunity to worry about appropriate clothing. There were many reasons why she lived in the central location of Crackendon Square and being able to gaze out of her window and pinpoint whose conversations were worth listening to was definitely one of them.

Mallory nipped down the narrow staircase that led to the ground floor, opened the exterior door then, with unhurried steps designed to avoid any undue attention, she walked across the square towards the witches.

They were making little effort to lower their voices and even Mallory, with her pathetic human ears, could hear every single word.

'Fetch Jackson is dead? Truly?' the tallest one exclaimed.

'Who would do such an awful thing? First he was arrested for murder and now he's been murdered himself!'

'It's a cold-blooded atrocity,' one of her companions agreed. 'The MET building is still smoking as we speak.'

The third witch, the Fetch, bowed her head. 'It's a dark day for us all. We've been told to assemble at headquarters for an emergency meeting at noon. After that, I reckon we'll be battening down the hatches. Until this matter is resolved and the killer is found, we'll be on high alert. All non-urgent business will be halted.'

Bugger. On all counts.

Mallory swerved away from the group before they realised she was eavesdropping. Although she'd have liked to stick around in the hope of learning more about what had happened to poor Fetch Jackson, she was mindful of her promise to Chester Longchamps. If the Council witches were effectively putting themselves into lockdown, she had to move quickly to get the information she needed.

She crossed her fingers and hoped that Boris had already contacted Nicola Sturgess. If she wanted to find out anything useful about the Clouded Map, she'd have to do it before that witches' meeting at noon. Suddenly time was of the essence.

She veered towards the excited tourists planning to loop around them, scurry back to her flat to get changed and contact Boris, but she'd barely reached them when she caught sight of a familiar figure watching her progress from her own damned doorway. Her steps faltered. What the hell?

Mallory didn't know where Alexander MacTire had sprung from. She certainly hadn't noticed him in the vicinity when she'd left her flat. It had been mere hours since they'd parted company and she couldn't imagine any good reason why he'd be here now. Given that he was standing at her front door, though, she couldn't avoid him. She grimaced and squared her shoulders.

'Ms Nash,' MacTire said as she drew near. 'It's good to see you again.'

She couldn't pretend to be anything other than confused by his presence. 'You know where I live?'

He smiled easily, flashing his white teeth. 'I guess you're not the only one who's good at winkling out important information when it's required.'

Mallory stared at him, more discomfited than ever. What was he doing here? 'What do you want?' she asked, dread filling her whole body. She tightened her toes but even that familiar action didn't alleviate her anxiety.

His face altered. 'I apologise. I don't mean to scare or worry you. After we parted company, I couldn't stop thinking about you. I spoke to a few acquaintances who know where you live. My intention isn't to alarm you – I only want to talk.'

He couldn't stop thinking about her? What did that mean?

'This is business,' he added quickly, reading her expression. 'I have a proposition to put to you.'

Mallory was still completely befuddled. She passed a hand in front of her eyes. 'This isn't a good time. I'm in a rush.'

'I can tell,' he said. 'You're in such a rush, you didn't have time to get dressed.' He gestured to her pyjamas, the bottoms of which were visible beneath the hem of her coat.

Ah. He was dressed immaculately, of course, in a smart grey pinstriped suit and brilliantly white shirt open at the collar. There wasn't a crease in sight. Mallory was wearing her favourite fuzzy pyjamas covered in images of strawberries and her somewhat grubby winter coat. Oh well.

'What can I say? I'm a busy person.' She sidestepped as if to move past him but MacTire wasn't budging. She couldn't squeeze past him and she certainly couldn't push him out of the way.

'I won't take up much of your time,' he said. 'It's about the Wolf Ball.'

Seriously? He'd turned up on her doorstep at this hour of the morning to talk about a cocktail party? She tried to keep her expression neutral but she knew that she'd betrayed her thoughts when she caught a glimmer of amusement in those damned eyes.

'You said that I shouldn't go with Samantha. I thought about your suggestion and I agree with you – but that rather begs the question of who I *should* go with.'

Much as she wanted to get away from this conversation, Mallory sensed that it would be quicker to engage with him. And she *had* created this situation by discussing the Ball last night in the restaurant. She tapped her foot and considered the question.

'Perhaps I should go alone,' MacTire said.

She shook her head immediately. 'No, you don't want to turn up without someone on your arm – it'll look as if something is wrong with you. You should go with someone who isn't threatening, who is obviously not a love interest and who signifies to all the single women out there that you're a good guy who's worth getting to know.'

He snapped his fingers. 'That's exactly what I was thinking.' He grinned at her. 'Ms Mallory Nash, would you do me the honour?'

Her mouth dropped open. 'Huh?'

'You're the perfect companion. I've been thinking it over and I can't imagine a better choice.'

She continued to stare at him open-mouthed.

'You're a squib, which means you're not threatening.' He gestured between them. 'We're obviously opposites and you made it clear last night that you're not attracted to me, so you're not a potential love interest. Most people will realise that immediately. But you *are* friendly and charming, so with you on my arm I'll prove my worth as an eligible bachelor.'

Mallory found her voice. 'You think you need to prove your worth? You're the MacTire alpha.'

He grimaced. 'Some time ago I decided that I wouldn't find a mate who was a wolf. I've already burned my bridges with a lot of werewolf women – that's partly why I had dinner with Kit last night. I was trying to expand my search. Unsuccessfully, as it turned out. Perhaps it's time I made a completely fresh start. You know what you're doing. You can advise me and tell me if there are any werewolf women out there who I should look at more closely. I may have judged some of them too harshly the first time around, and it could be that I need to lower my expectations.'

'Uh-huh.' Mallory swallowed. 'Look, Mr MacTire, I don't feel comfortable with this. It's not a business deal, it's about your personal life – hell, it's about the rest of your life. And another woman's life. This isn't what I do.'

MacTire smiled even more widely. 'Of course it's a business deal. I want to hire you to carry out a favour for me. I want you to come to the Wolf Ball and help me find the right woman to be my First Mate. I'm looking for someone who will understand my pack and its needs, who won't interfere with my day-to-day business dealings, and who will present herself appropriately. It's not a lot to ask.'

It sounded horrendous and Mallory was already shaking her head. 'Absolutely not. I'm sure you can find a marriage broker who'll help you. This isn't for me.'

'I beg to differ. You see the world in a unique way and you understand people. Your methods are unorthodox but I think that's exactly what I need.'

This was wrong on every level. 'No.' Out of the corner of her eye she spotted Boris walking towards her and gesticulating wildly. Clearly he'd heard the information about the Witches Council; if she was going to speak to Nicola Sturgess, she had to get a wiggle on.

Unfortunately, MacTire was standing his ground. 'Please.'

'It's not a good idea, Mr MacTire.'

His smile vanished and he looked at her earnestly. 'At least attend the Wolf Ball with me. We can negotiate matters from there.'

Boris reached them. 'Mallory,' he said. 'There's a problem.'

'I know, Boris.'

'If you want to speak to Fetch Sturgess today, you need to leave for the Council headquarters in the next ten minutes.'

She nodded. 'Yes. Thank you.' She turned to MacTire. 'I have to go. I need to get into my flat and get changed. I've got things to do.'

'One evening of your time. In return I'll complete any favour you desire,' he promised. 'No holds barred.'

The man was clearly crazy. 'You don't mean that.'

'I do. I need to find a mate, Mallory Nash, and I think you're the perfect person to help me.'

Boris was scowling. 'Mallory...'

She gritted her teeth. 'Mr MacTire, if you don't move out of the way...'

'Please. Help me.'

Goddamnit. She didn't have time for this.

'It's just one ball,' MacTire said. 'Five hours. If that.'

Mallory sighed. '*Any* favour in return?'

'Name your price.'

She made a snap – and probably stupid – decision. 'Twenty-four months' time frame. Any return favour of my choosing. If I don't come to you within twenty-four months to request repayment, you are free of any obligations.'

'Done.'

'You'll have to sign a blood contract.'

'No problem.'

'And,' she said firmly, 'once the Wolf Ball is over, we part company regardless of what happens or who you meet.'

'Fine.'

'I'm making no guarantees. I can advise you but I can't promise results.'

'I'm good with that.' His grin had returned and his eyes were dancing with delight. 'You and I will have fun.'

Mallory doubted that very much. 'I have to go. This is Boris – he'll visit you later with the contract. Until you sign it, you can back out.'

'I won't do that.'

'We'll see,' she murmured. 'You might have second thoughts.' She nodded pointedly at her door.

Alexander MacTire stepped smoothly to the side. 'Of course.' He dipped his head in a tiny bow. 'Have a good day, Ms Nash.'

'It can only improve from here on in,' she said honestly.

He laughed then turned on his heel and walked away whistling triumphantly to himself.

Boris was watching her with an odd expression. 'What?' she asked.

'You're usually better at saying no to people like that.'

She felt an uncharacteristic flush rise to her cheeks. He was right; so much for her titanium core. 'He needs my help.'

'If you say so.'

'I needed to get him out of my way as quickly as possible.'

Boris smirked. 'Sure thing. You also need to get going as quickly as possible.'

Mallory nodded jerkily before she darted inside and rushed upstairs to change.

Forget Alexander MacTire. He wasn't a stupid man but he had certainly made a stupid request. She'd worry about it later. Much later. Right now, she had a Council witch to meet and an antsy vampire to satisfy.

CHAPTER

FOUR

Fetch Nicola Sturgess was highly distracted. On the few previous occasions when they'd met, she'd taken the time to escort Mallory inside the grand Council headquarters and they'd sat in one of the sunny drawing rooms sipping perfectly brewed coffee and nibbling on little cupcakes decorated with delicate sugar work fashioned with the help of some specialised witchery. This time Sturgess insisted they stay in the garden. Doubtless there was enough chaos within the Council's sturdy walls to preclude a welcome for strangers.

'My deepest condolences for Fetch Jackson's passing,' Mallory said.

Sturgess widened her eyes. 'I shouldn't be surprised that you already know what's happened to him and yet I am. One day I'd love to find out who your sources are.'

The Fetch would likely be disappointed to learn that Mallory's knowledge resulted simply from eavesdropping. She smiled vaguely and took a calculated gamble based on the information she'd learned on Kit McCafferty's behalf. 'Did he have any silphium on him when he was killed?'

This time Sturgess paled dramatically. 'Mallory,' she said,

her voice strained, 'ask that question of anyone else and you're likely to find yourself in a freshly dug grave right next to him. If that's why you're here then I can't help you, regardless of my blood contract with you.'

Silphium was Kit's problem, not Mallory's, and the terms of her contract with Nicola Sturgess forbade asking anything that would be detrimental to the witches. It appeared that anything to do with Fetch Jackson and the matter of silphium fell into that category.

Even so, Mallory was smart enough to use the situation to her advantage. 'Well,' she demurred, allowing the corners of her mouth to turn down as if she were disappointed, 'if we can't discuss silphium, perhaps we can chat about another matter instead.'

'Anything,' Sturgess said, her kitten heels sinking into the soft earth as they paused beside a blush-pink rosebush. 'As long as it's not that damned plant.'

Mallory made a show of reconsidering the topic of discussion. 'Instead of silphium, why don't you tell me about the Clouded Map?'

The Fetch couldn't mask her relief. 'Okay.' She nodded vigorously. 'That is something I *can* talk about.' She gestured towards a narrow bench and extracted her heels from the ground to walk over and sit down. Mallory followed suit.

'As I'm sure you already know,' Sturgess said, once they were both as comfortable as they could ever be on a cold bench made out of unforgiving marble, 'the Clouded Map is part of our Alexandria Collection.'

'The five hundred or so papyrus scrolls and books that were rescued when the Great Library was burned?'

'Indeed.' Sturgess waved at the building in front of them. 'There's a warded, temperature-controlled room with highly restricted access inside the headquarters. The Clouded Map and the other rescued texts are housed there. As a Fetch, I'm allowed access although I've only been inside on a handful of occasions. Some of the texts are deadly dull. Some are simply deadly.'

Interesting. 'Which category does the Clouded Map fall into?'

Sturgess pursed her lips. 'Neither. Although it's an interesting object, it isn't lethal and it's practically obsolete in these modern times. It shouldn't even be called the Clouded Map – that's something of a misnomer because it doesn't obscure anything. Instead it provides clarity.'

Mallory tilted her head. 'What do you mean?'

'It's imbued with old magic and designed to illuminate any unknown area. It was useful two thousand years ago when much of the world hadn't been officially discovered. With the right incantation, the Clouded Map reveals an outline of anywhere you want it to –the complex maze of an unmapped souk, for example, or an unknown country and its coastline and rivers. The Clouded Map does what Christopher Columbus, Marco Polo and Ferdinand Magellan could only dream of.'

Sturgess shrugged, then continued. 'So as I said, it's virtually obsolete now because every corner of the globe has already been mapped a million times over. As long as you're not somewhere like Coldstream, you can use a smartphone far more effectively than an old magic map to find a location.'

True. 'Can it locate people?' Mallory asked.

'No.' The witch was adamant. 'All it can do is map out a particular place.'

Hmm. Sturgess's information had answered one important question: possession of the Clouded Map wouldn't enable the vampires to spark a war or cause problems. It had limited use and, although she had no idea how it could possibly help Chester Longchamps locate a vampire killer, it certainly wasn't particularly dangerous.

'I wish to invoke the terms of our contract,' Mallory said, 'and formally request repayment.'

'I figured as much.' Sturgess's expression was mildly rueful. Two years ago Mallory had helped her by providing information about several witches who were competing with her for promotion to the position of Fetch. That information had been invaluable in allowing Sturgess to rise up the ranks with such speed; even without the blood contract, there was no doubt that Nicola Sturgess owed her.

'There are only days left until our agreement is null and void so I've been expecting a visit from you for some time,' Sturgess said. 'Honestly, I'm glad you're here because it'll be good to close a door on this – but I can't just give you the Clouded Map. It's not mine to give. It belongs to the Witches Council.'

'I don't want to keep it,' Mallory told her. 'I wouldn't ask that of you. I only want to borrow it.'

'For yourself?' Sturgess asked. 'Or for a client?'

'A client. Does it matter?'

The Fetch considered. 'I suppose not. How long are we talking about?'

'Twelve months.'

Sturgess sucked air through her teeth disapprovingly. 'No can do. The entire library – including the Alexandria collection – is being audited in September. It happens at the same time every year and there's nothing I can do to stop it. I doubt the map will be missed before then but it will need to be back in its rightful place by the end of August or its absence will be noted. I can't afford to be the subject of an investigation into the loss of such a precious item.'

Neither did Mallory want to be implicated in such an issue; to maintain her business and lifestyle she needed to be a friend to the witches, not a foe. If Chester Longchamps wanted the Clouded Map, he'd have to agree to those terms. 'Very well.'

'There's more,' Sturgess said darkly. 'This is an ancient papyrus scroll. It's fragile – it's kept in a controlled environment for a reason. Some minor degradation will be unavoidable, but it must be transported and stored in a properly magicked container or it will quickly become unusable. It can only be removed from the container for short periods of time and always with the invocation of a preservation spell.'

That was understandable given the Clouded Map's provenance. Mallory shrugged. 'Sure.'

Sturgess's expression grew even more serious. 'You don't understand. The Clouded Map is an ancient, powerful object that requires delicate handling even with the use of extra magic to keep it safe. Most of the time it will have to be kept in a magicked bellarmine jug with a warded stopper. They aren't easy to get hold of, not anymore.'

Mallory frowned. She'd heard of bellarmine jugs; plenty of replicas were sold to tourists at highly inflated prices. Original functioning bellarmine jugs were far rarer and they worked on a one-in, one-out basis: each jug could only hold one fragile document at a time and as soon as a document was removed it was at risk. Nicola Sturgess was right. It would be difficult to find a bellarmine jug that wasn't already being used. 'There's no alternative?' she pressed.

'Not that I'm aware of. Even the best preservation spell can only do so much. A bellarmine jug provides better long-term protection and there's no other way to preserve the papyrus effectively once it's out of the Alexandria Room. I can't agree to release the map unless I can be assured it will be safe. It's a priceless object that belongs to the Council, so anything that harms it can be deemed detrimental to witches and will void our contract.'

Mallory nodded grimly. 'Understood.'

'I hope you do. And I'll have to pass the Clouded Map to

your client rather than to you. I need to look them in the eye and repeat this information to them myself.'

'He's a vampire.

Nicola winced. 'Alright – but I still have to meet him in person.'

'That shouldn't be a problem.'

A loud bell sounded from somewhere inside the grand building. Sturgess got to her feet, adjusted her pointy hat and sighed. 'I have to go now. I can't avoid this meeting.'

Mallory looked at her sympathetically. 'I'll speak to my client, find a usable bellarmine jug then get back to you to make arrangements to collect the map.' She softened her voice. 'In the meantime, I hope that Fetch Jackson's killer is brought to justice. And,' she added for herself, 'that nobody comes across any silphium.'

Sturgess gave her a long look. 'Honestly,' she said, 'so do I.'

CHESTER LONGCHAMPS COULDN'T KEEP the fanged grin off his face. 'The others were right,' he breathed. 'You *are* good.'

Mallory wasn't ready to start preening. 'This is not yet a done deal,' she warned.

'Yes, yes.' He waved her off. 'I'm willing to accept conditions.'

Maybe, but he didn't yet know what those conditions would be. 'You can't keep the Clouded Map beyond the end of August.'

The vampire was already nodding. 'I can work with that.'

'I mean it,' Mallory said firmly. 'It'll be written into the blood contract between us. It's non-negotiable.'

'It's not a problem.' He held out his hand for her to shake; she ignored it.

'I am not finished.' She eyed him calmly and he withdrew his hand although he was still grinning.

'Hardball, huh?'

'You may only use the Clouded Map when it is under a preservation spell.' She paused. 'A *good* preservation spell.'

'If you procure whatever is necessary, I will make sure a spell is used,' Longchamps promised. 'And of course I'll pay for it. Give my name to any reputable witchery store and they can bill me directly for anything you need.'

That was just as well because Mallory didn't work with money. 'There's more. You have to meet the witch in person to take possession of the map. She wants to remind you of the rules before she passes it over.'

He rolled his eyes. 'Witches,' he muttered. 'Honestly. But yes, that's fine.'

Mallory persisted. 'And it must be kept in a bellarmine jug whenever it's not in use. A *real* bellarmine jug.'

'Okay. Find me a jug and that's exactly what will happen.'

Bugger. 'I was rather hoping that you would have one,' Mallory said. 'I'll try, but I'm not sure how long it will take me to find one.'

Only the tiniest of frowns marred Longchamps' forehead. 'I don't possess a bellarmine jug.'

'You're a vampire – you're more than four hundred years old. You must know someone who has an empty jug you can borrow.'

'I'll ask around.' But he sounded doubtful.

'We *need* the jug.'

'I'll let you know. Hopefully you will find one but I'll search too.' He started bouncing around on his toes. 'This is fantastic. The Clouded Map will change everything.'

Mallory watched him curiously; she wanted to be sure he

knew what he was getting. 'The map doesn't locate people,' she said.

Longchamps continued bouncing. 'I know that.'

'It doesn't locate any living creatures, it only maps out places.'

'Yep. That's fine. That's what I need.'

She shrugged: he appeared to know what he was getting. The details of exactly why he required the Clouded Map weren't really any of her business. 'There's also the matter of my payment,' she said.

Now he was no longer merely bouncing, he was dancing around the room taking long elegant steps as if he were a ballroom dancer in need of a partner. He held his hand out to her, indicating that she should join him in a celebratory waltz.

Mallory crossed her arms: she wasn't here to party, she was here to do business – and her price was high. Longchamps had stated during their previous meeting that he'd pay whatever she wanted in return for the map. It was time to test whether he'd been telling the truth.

'Three secrets, to be delivered at a time of my choosing.' Normally she'd have added a time limit on such repayments and clients tended to appreciate that, but vampires were different. With their long, virtually immortal lives, time had a different meaning for them and there was little chance that Longchamps would pass away while Mallory was still alive. She could benefit from this deal for a long time to come, especially if she were careful about when she called on him.

'Done.'

Mallory still wasn't finished. 'And three favours, also of my own choosing.'

Chester Longchamps stopped dancing. 'Three secrets *and* three favours? You ask a great deal. Two secrets and one favour.'

Nope. This was a complex deal and she was prepared to

stand her ground, although she wasn't surprised that he wanted to negotiate now it came down to the nitty-gritty. Alexander MacTire had been an outlier in agreeing instantly to her demands; Chester Longchamps' approach was the norm. 'Two secrets. Three favours.'

'Two secrets and two favours,' he countered.

She considered. 'No caveats and no limitations on either and you have a deal.'

He beamed. 'And you've got yourself a happy client.'

Mallory inclined her head. To be honest, it was better than she'd expected. All in all, this had been a surprisingly successful day. 'I'll have the blood contract drawn up by tomorrow. My assistant will come around for your blood signature.'

Boris would grumble about visiting the vampire but Mallory knew that Longchamps was pleased enough to make the spriggan feel welcome. 'Make sure that you read it carefully before you sign,' she warned.

Chester Longchamps was already nodding. 'Ms Nash, I will be eternally grateful to you for this.'

For a vampire, Mallory reflected, that was quite something.

CHAPTER

FIVE

'Alexander MacTire is refusing to sign the blood contract,' Boris informed her, once she was back home with a soft cushion at her back and her feet propped up on her favourite stool.

Excellent: this day was just getting better and better. Mallory took a self-congratulatory sip from her perfectly chilled, perfectly balanced Chablis. She'd hoped that the werewolf alpha would see sense and change his mind about their silly matchmaking deal, and she was delighted that her hope had been fulfilled. 'Fabulous,' she murmured. She raised her glass in the spriggan's direction. 'Cheers.'

'He says he'll only sign when you're with him. He's asked you to visit him at the MacTire residence tomorrow.'

Mallory's shoulders immediately drooped. 'Oh.'

'If he has the option to back out of the deal, so do you,' Boris reminded her gently.

She pulled a face. 'I won't do that. You know I won't do that.' Once she'd agreed verbally to a deal, Mallory made a point of sticking to it unless there were extenuating circumstances that made her involvement untenable. She couldn't afford to be seen as flaky.

'You've worked hard enough up to this point that your reputation can take a little tarnish here and there,' Boris countered.

'Maybe that's how things work in the Summer Court, but it's not the case here. It takes years to build a good reputation and only seconds to break one. I've made the offer to MacTire. I can't back out now.'

'Of course you can. Nobody cares what a werewolf thinks.'

'He's an alpha,' she reminded him. 'He's the *MacTire* alpha.'

Boris curled his lip.

'He's wealthy, powerful and he has friends in many corners of Coldstream.'

'Whatever.' The spriggan sniffed and gave her a sideways look. 'You like him.'

'I barely know him. But he's not a bad man,' she conceded.

'You know that if you're successful, you'll be inundated with similar requests. You'll end up as Coldstream's pre-eminent matchmaker.'

'This is a one-off. I won't accept any other deals like this – I'm not a one-woman dating agency.'

Boris bobbed his head. 'If you say so, Mallory.' She sent him a mock glare. 'MacTire is very handsome.' He made no effort to mask the wicked gleam in his yellow eyes.

'All the more reason that this will be an easy contract to fulfil.' As soon as the words had left her mouth, Mallory knew she was kidding herself. If it was easy, Alexander MacTire would already be happily bound to a beautiful mate with several tow-headed children running around his feet.

'MacTire is going to make the Longchamps' deal seem like child's play,' Boris smirked.

Unfortunately, on that count she suspected he was right.

When Mallory arrived at the gate to the main MacTire residence the following morning, she felt decidedly out of sorts. She'd forgotten yet again to pick up some coffee beans so she'd been forced to go without her morning brew for the second day in a row. Tea simply didn't cut the mustard. In a bid to remember on her way home, she'd scribbled the word 'coffee' on the back of her hand.

It was only the lack of bitter arabica goodness that was making her feel antsy. Or at least that was what she kept telling herself.

Mallory had expected to be greeted by a MacTire minion but it was Alexander himself who opened the gate and beckoned her in. He was dressed more casually than last time, in loose sweats rather than a formal suit. Strangely, his choice of attire didn't put her at ease. In fact, it made her feel even more twitchy.

'Good morning, Ms Nash.' He grinned in a manner that suggested lazy predator rather than good friend. She smiled back and avoided looking into those unsettling amber eyes.

'Good morning, Mr MacTire.' She glanced around the empty courtyard. 'I was expecting more people.'

'I thought it wise to give everyone the morning off.'

Mallory raised her eyebrows. 'You don't want your pack to know that I'm working for you? Don't you trust them?'

MacTire didn't look offended; if anything, he was amused. 'Of course I trust them. I gave them the morning off because I thought it would be better for *you*. I don't want you to feel any more intimidated than you already do.'

She immediately veered off-plan and met his eyes. 'I am not intimidated by you or by any werewolves!'

'Uh-huh.' His grin stretched an inch wider. Reflexively,

Mallory tightened her toes. MacTire lowered his head towards her. 'I'm glad to hear that. We'll be working closely together and I'd hate to think that my presence makes you feel anything other than comfortable.'

She resisted the urge to move away and put space between them. 'I only agreed to help you out for the Wolf Ball,' she reminded him. 'Nothing more.'

'Of course. But we'll need to do some preparatory work, won't we?'

Mallory frowned; she hadn't agreed to anything like that.

'I took the liberty of procuring the guest list. I thought you'd want to run through it with me so we could lay some groundwork. I only have you for five hours during the ball and I want to make the most of the event.' His grin subsided briefly. 'I am serious about finding a life mate. This isn't a game for me.'

Mallory rocked back on her heels and examined his face. He waited, allowing her to gaze at him without interruption. He was right about the need for some preparatory work; she'd been letting the unsettling sensation that assailed her every time he looked at her to get the better of her. As her professional pride kicked in, she realised abruptly that this had the potential to be an incredibly interesting challenge. She'd learn a lot about the werewolf community while helping MacTire find the woman of his dreams: it was a priceless opportunity.

Besides, she'd already agreed to help him so it was important to do so. His obvious intention to approach the matter with dedicated and serious energy helped her to focus. She ran through a vague plan in her head and nodded. 'Okay,' she said. 'You're right.'

His eyes gleamed. 'I usually am.'

Mallory lifted her chin. 'To begin with, you need to do less of that.'

'Less of what?'

She didn't miss a beat. 'Arrogant alpha-ness.'

'Pardon?'

Mallory deepened her voice. '"I'm always right. I'm alpha of the MacTire clan. I always get what I want. I am amazing."'

MacTire watched her carefully. 'I always get what I want because I'm prepared to work for it. And I *am* alpha of the MacTire clan – I can't pretend otherwise.' He tilted his head and a single dark curl fell across his tanned forehead. 'But I didn't say I was always right. I said I was *usually* right.'

Mallory grinned. 'Same same.'

He gave her a flat look. 'It is not the same.'

'See?' she said. 'You're doing it again.'

'What?'

'Acting like an alpha.'

'But I *am* an alpha. How else am I supposed to act?'

'Some self-deprecation wouldn't go amiss. Neither would some vulnerability.'

MacTire looked at her as if she'd asked him to don a feather boa, angel wings and do the can-can through the streets of Coldstream. 'Vulnerability?'

'You're not posturing in front of a rival werewolf pack and you're not recruiting baby werewolves to your cause. You're not preparing for a fight.' She raised her eyebrows meaningfully. 'You're looking for the love of your life.'

He folded his arms and frowned. 'At no point have I mentioned love. I want a partner I can respect, whom I like, who understands werewolves and my position as alpha. I don't need love.'

Mallory patted his shoulder. 'Everyone needs love.'

'A relationship with the right person will *develop* into love,' he stated firmly. 'You're talking about lusty thunderbolts. That type of love doesn't last.'

'Do you want to be attracted to your mate?' she asked patiently.

'Of course I do!'

She ticked off her fingers. 'Attraction, respect, understanding. Sounds a hell of a lot like love to me.'

MacTire was already shaking his head. 'You can't define love. It's not a checklist, it's a feeling.'

Mallory hesitated. 'You sound as if you've experienced it, as if you know love.'

He dismissed her words. 'I've seen *others* experience love. I know what *they* feel like. As an alpha, I need to be more circumspect. My mate has to be someone for my entire pack.' She raised her eyebrows and he grimaced. 'Not like that!'

'Are you sure that you want a mate?' she asked carefully.

'My pack wants me to find a mate. The MacTires will be more settled and stable once I do.'

'So are you pleasing them or yourself?'

'Can't I do both?'

'I suppose so – but a little vulnerability still won't go amiss. The right woman doesn't want a hard, unfeeling man as her partner. She wants someone who can be soft with her, who can share his true feelings even if it's only with her.'

MacTire's mouth tightened. 'I'm not an unfeeling bastard.'

'I didn't say you were, but you need to show that side of yourself.'

Out of nowhere, he flashed her a grin. 'See? I knew you were the right person to help me.'

Not for the first time, Mallory hoped she wouldn't regret this. 'Just sign the contract, give me the guest list for the Wolf Ball and I can get started.' She paused. 'Any particular turn-offs that I should know about? It's important that you're honest with me.'

'Nothing comes to mind. I'm easy-going in that regard.'

'In that case, this will be a piece of cake.' No sooner had the words left her mouth than she knew it was a lie – and from the look in MacTire's eyes, so did he. He coughed slightly, indicating not only his faint embarrassment but also that he *did* possess the ability to be more than simply the arrogant alpha of the MacTire pack. Good. It wasn't much, but it was a start.

She nodded approvingly and he offered her a crooked smile. 'I'm already looking forward to working with you,' he said. He pointed towards a door at the side of the courtyard. 'Let's head inside.'

Mallory expected to be led into a drawing room or a study, but MacTire took her through the main building towards the back where there was a large, gleaming kitchen. He gestured at an elegant leather-covered stool before turning to a cupboard, taking out a bag of coffee beans and decanting them into a hand grinder. He started to turn its handle.

She ignored the stool and gaped at him. 'You're making coffee?'

'That's what you want, isn't it?' He pointed at the word scrawled across her hand. 'If you'd rather have something else, there's fresh orange juice. Milk. Water. Any number of flavoured teas...'

She shook her head. 'Coffee would be amazing.'

He grinned. 'Sit down. This will take a few minutes. Once it's brewed, I'll take you through to the study and sign the contract.'

Mallory eyed the stool before she hopped onto it. It was surprisingly comfortable; MacTire wasn't simply concerned with aesthetics and that was useful information, though she still reckoned he had a type – at least when it came to partners.

While he boiled the kettle and prepared a pretty silver coffee pot, she decided to go for it. 'What's your preference?'

'Excelsa,' he answered without missing a beat. 'But I'll take arabica in a pinch.'

Mallory stifled a smirk. 'I don't mean coffee, I'm talking about women. What attracts you? You were on a date with Kit. Is she your type?'

He considered the question before he answered. 'Not typically. I don't really have a type.'

'Blonde,' said a voice from the doorway. 'Sleek. Well-dressed. Height isn't an issue but strength and strong magic are both desirable.'

MacTire scowled.

Surprised, Mallory turned to see a teenage boy stifling a yawn. 'Are you making coffee?' he asked.

This time, MacTire's smile was wry and there was a softness in his eyes that Mallory hadn't seen before. 'Does it look like I'm making coffee?'

'I guess.' The boy paused. 'Can you make pancakes, too?'

'I'm not your personal chef.' The alpha's voice was teasing.

'You're the one who gave everyone the morning off.'

'And you're the one who wants more independence. Why don't *you* cook *us* pancakes?'

The boy thought about it then shrugged. 'Okay.' He ambled over to the marble-topped island and started looking for a pan.

'Ms Nash, this is Nicholas,' MacTire said. 'My nephew.'

Mallory had suspected as much; MacTire's sister and her husband had been killed in an accident and their son, still in his mid-teens, was now living with MacTire. She'd heard they'd had a rocky start but that things were going better now. It appeared that the gossip mill had been correct.

'Hi, Nicholas,' she said. 'I'm Mallory.'

He smiled at her. 'Call me Nick, Ms Nash.'

'In that case, my name is Mallory. Not Ms Nash.'

MacTire frowned as he extracted three mugs from a cupboard.

'You can call the grumpy one Alex,' Nick went on. 'Or,' he added with a wink, 'if you really want to annoy him, Sandy.'

MacTire growled.

Nick laughed. 'Or Lex. You know, like the Superman villain, Lex Luthor.'

'I am not a villain, Nicholas.'

His nephew only grinned.

Mallory watched while MacTire poured the coffee and Nick cracked eggs into a bowl. An impressive amount of shell ended up in the mixture. Oh dear.

'Sugar, Ms Nash?' MacTire asked while Nick added flour and milk. 'Cream?'

'A splash of milk, if you have it. Thank you.'

He handed her a cup of coffee and they both watched as Nick whisked the pancake batter then dribbled a small amount into the pan, his face etched with concentration. The first attempt went badly and the boy scowled as he scraped the burnt offering into a bin.

Mallory glanced at MacTire. It was interesting that he didn't try to help. Quite the opposite; he remained uncharacteristically quiet.

Nick bit his lip and tried again, this time with more batter. It didn't help; the pan was too hot and the pancake was quickly burnt again. He hissed through his teeth. 'Alright,' he said eventually. 'What am I doing wrong?'

'Less heat,' MacTire told him. 'It's not a race.'

The teenager turned down the gas flame. 'Is that better?'

'Give it a try and see.'

Nick spooned more batter into the pan. It sizzled faintly but thankfully this time there was no acrid smell of burning. 'When do I turn it over?'

'When you start to see bubbles,' MacTire told him.

Nick peered at the pan. 'Now?'

'Do you see bubbles?'

'Yes.'

'Then you can flip.'

Nick reached for the pan with both hands and jerked it upwards. The half-cooked pancake flew upwards into the air before arcing down and landing on the floor with a dull splat. Mallory schooled her face into a blank expression.

Nick flushed and turned to his uncle. 'I can't do it.'

'It's just practice. It's better to use a spatula until you get the hang of flipping.' MacTire slid a steaming cup across to him. 'Ms Nash and I are going to my office. Keep trying – it might be easier without an audience.'

Nick nodded. There was a glimmer of determination in his youthful face and Mallory smiled encouragingly before following MacTire out of the room. 'You didn't give him any help until he asked for it,' she said, once they were out of earshot.

MacTire seemed surprised. 'Of course not. If you don't make mistakes, you can't learn. It's good for him to try things out for himself then, if he needs support, he can ask for guidance and receive it. It means he can learn his limitations, practise independence and stretch his abilities beyond what he thinks he's capable of.' He shrugged. 'It's the same whether he's making pancakes, earning a living or negotiating werewolf politics.'

As Mallory gazed at him, several puzzle pieces slid into place. 'You're preparing him to become alpha after you retire.'

'That'll be up to Nick and the rest of the pack,' MacTire said smoothly. 'It's not up to me.'

Except it almost certainly was up to him. Alexander MacTire's influence would go a long way towards putting young Nick in that position. 'You're not planning for children of your own, then?' Mallory asked. It wasn't a given that any of his direct heirs would take his place as alpha, but it was often the way of such things.

He gave her a long look. 'You ask a lot of nosy questions for a squib.'

She held her ground. '*I* don't care if you want one kid, twenty kids or no kids – but the woman who becomes your First Mate will.'

His mouth tightened a fraction but she knew he'd acknowledged her point. He sighed and finally gave her a proper answer. 'I'd like children – two. One boy, one girl. But I'm not beholden to the idea. If the perfect woman who is the right fit for me and my pack doesn't want, or can't have, children then it's not a dealbreaker.'

He raised an eyebrow as if challenging her. 'You see,' he added softly, 'I can be adaptable when it truly counts.' He paused for a beat. 'Do you want children?'

She didn't usually give away personal information to clients but something about the tone of this conversation encouraged her to say, 'Yes, I do.'

'How many?'

One boy and one girl would be beyond perfect but she couldn't say that. 'I haven't thought about it,' she lied.

'Preternatural children?'

That was easier. 'I don't care. As long as they're healthy, they can be half-witch, half-druid, half-troll or half-goblin.'

'Half-werewolf?' he asked softly.

'Half-anything,' she told him firmly. She tightened her toes. 'We should get to work. Where's your office?'

MacTire regarded her brisk attempt to change the subject with amusement. 'This way,' he said. He pointed to an oak door and bowed. 'Ladies first.'

CHAPTER

SIX

Something about MacTire's office didn't suit him and Mallory couldn't quite put her finger on it. It was overtly masculine, but so was he. It was traditional and so was he, at least in some ways. Perhaps it was the heavy atmosphere that wasn't right, or perhaps she was sensing things that weren't there.

She looked around as she sat in the chair opposite his wide wooden desk and considered the matter. 'This room needs a woman's touch,' she said finally.

'What would you suggest?'

'Lighter curtains – cream velvet, perhaps, instead of that dark brocade. Some brighter paint – not white but something less oppressive. Maybe a rug for a splash of bright colour. And a few vases of flowers.'

'Noted.' He gazed around the room as if seeing it for the first time. 'This was my father's office – he was alpha before me. I suppose I should have changed the décor and wiped away any memory of him. He was something of a collector and most of his stuff has ended up in the basement. I've always meant to get around to changing this room but there's never been time to

63

deal with it properly. And,' he said quietly, 'I didn't want to give his ghost the satisfaction of knowing that his design choices bothered me. My father was a fucking bastard.'

Mallory blinked. MacTire grinned, but it didn't reach his eyes. 'Is that vulnerable enough for you?'

She didn't answer; instead she reached out and took his hand. 'I'm sorry,' she said. 'We don't always get to choose our family.'

His fingers tightened around hers but he didn't pull away. 'No, but I will get to choose my First Mate. And it's important that my choice is a good one because it will affect everyone in the MacTire pack.'

'Even more reason why we should get cracking,' she said softly. She withdrew her hand and straightened her shoulders. 'So while some compromise is inevitable, you'd prefer a wolf with blonde hair, considerable strength and an elegant fashion sense. What else?'

He sighed heavily. 'You make it sound like a shopping list.'

'We're talking hypotheticals, Mr MacTire. I'm not saying this is who you'll get. In your mind's eye, who is your perfect mate?'

'I think we're beyond Mr MacTire and Ms Nash now. If Nicholas gets to call you Mallory then so do I. And I'd like it if you called me Alexander. Or Alex.'

Mallory nodded; it might make their future conversations easier. 'Okay. Who's your perfect woman, Alexander?'

'Werewolf, blonde, strong and with an elegant fashion sense.' He laughed. 'And she needs to be powerful, as well. She's going to be the MacTire First Mate so she'll have to help our pack remain strong. I can't have a mate who will weaken our position.'

'Do you have an age range in mind?'

'Not particularly – ten years either side of me, I suppose. If there's too much of an age difference, I can't imagine we'll have much in common.'

'You're sure you don't want a young model with pneumatic breasts?'

'I'm not twelve, Ms Nash.'

'Mallory,' she reminded him.

He inclined his head. 'Mallory.'

She smiled. 'Do you have the Wolf Ball guest list?'

Alexander reached into a drawer and drew out three sheets of paper held together by a paper clip. 'I've marked the guests whom I've already dated so you don't waste your time.'

That was smart. Mallory scanned the papers quickly. *Oh*. 'You've marked a lot of names,' she said faintly. 'Are you sure you don't want to take a second look at any of them? Maybe there's someone on the list who you had a good relationship with—'

'No,' he interrupted. 'None of them are suitable.'

He wasn't giving her a lot to work with; at least ten percent of the women on the guest list had been scratched off before they'd even started. She thought of something else and tilted her head, trying to come up with a delicate way to broach the subject.

'Whatever it is, just say it,' Alexander ordered.

Okay, then. 'What about you? What sort of reputation do you have? I mean as a man, not as alpha of the MacTire clan? What do the eligible female werewolves of Coldstream think of you?' Of course, she'd investigate the answer for her own benefit, but it would be helpful to know what *he* thought; as much as anything, it was a test of his self-awareness.

Alexander leaned back in his chair. 'That I'm attractive. I'm thoughtful, both in the bedroom and out. And I'm a gentleman.'

Uh-huh. 'Anything else?'

'That I always put the needs of my pack above the needs of

my partner,' he said quietly. 'And I can be something of a closed book. I don't always say what I'm thinking and I tend to mask my emotions.'

'Thank you,' Mallory began.

'And,' he continued, 'I get bored easily. I can't settle.'

'Alright.'

'I take people for granted.'

She swallowed.

'Communication isn't one of my strengths.'

'Gotcha.' She waited for more. 'Anything else?'

'Those would be the main points.'

'Are you a jealous partner?' she asked.

He shook his head. 'No. Not even slightly.'

'Not ever?'

He looked baffled at the idea. 'No.'

Mallory made a mental note. 'I think I have enough for now.' She held up the guest list. 'I'll go through this and look into who's attending the ball. We've got more than four weeks to prepare so that should be plenty of time.' She paused and then asked, 'What are you doing next weekend?'

'I'm working.'

'What about in the evening?'

Alexander shrugged. 'I'm free Saturday night.'

'Perfect.'

He watched her. 'What are you planning?'

'A trial run,' she told him. 'I happen to know that the druids are holding a party for Imbolc to mark the beginning of spring. It's the perfect opportunity to see you in action.'

'I'm getting the full service, then.'

'My aim is to please.'

He looked at her for a long moment. 'I'm glad to hear that,' he said. 'I look forward to being pleased by you.'

For some inexplicable reason, Mallory's mouth dried.

'Knock, knock!' Nick called from the door. 'Who wants pancakes?'

Thank goodness for the interruption. She grinned. 'Me! I'm ravenous.'

Alexander MacTire was still gazing at her. 'So am I.'

AFTER MALLORY LEFT the MacTire stronghold with the signed blood contract and the guest list for the Wolf Ball in her bag, she took the long way home. Alexander MacTire wasn't her only client. Mystical Forces was one of the larger witchery stores in Coldstream and there was a good chance they could help her get what she needed for Chester Longchamps.

The moment she stepped across the threshold, she was enveloped in the delicious smell of sage and wild garlic. She inhaled deeply; she might not be able to use most of the contents of a witchery store but she loved looking at them.

'Good afternoon,' a young male witch intoned. 'Welcome to Mystical Forces.' He looked her up and down and his smile faded. 'Oh. You're not a witch.'

'Nope.'

'You're a shapeshifter?' he asked hopefully.

'I'm a squib.'

He reached past her shoulder and opened the door. 'I'm sorry, we're not open for tourists.'

She stayed where she was and smiled brightly. 'Lucky I'm not a tourist, then. I live in Coldstream.' He stared at her. 'There are a few of us around,' she told him gently. 'Preternatural abilities aren't an entrance requirement – in fact technically I wouldn't be called a squib if I didn't live here. Only non-magical residents of Coldstream are called squibs.'

The salesman continued to gape. Finally he said, 'If you've just come in to have a nosey and not buy anything, then...'

'There are some specific items I need, though I'm not planning to buy them.'

He puffed out his chest and Mallory started to wonder if he was related to the new waiter at Vallese. 'That's how shops work,' he said, as if she were very dim. 'We stock goods. You buy the goods. With money,' he added pointedly.

This could go on for a while. Mallory tutted. 'Tell Miss Cole that Mallory Nash is here to see her.'

At the name of the store manager, the man stiffened. His eyes narrowed as he released his hold on the door and it thudded shut. In a bid to soothe his ruffled feathers, she held up her hands. 'I'll wait here by the door. I won't touch anything.'

If anything, her promise unsettled him even further. He delved into his pocket and withdrew a small bottle filled with powder. 'Don't move,' he muttered.

'That's really not necessary,' she protested as he unscrewed the lid, scattered the contents in a circle around her and started muttering an invocation.

'I will decide what is necessary,' he said. He stepped back and surveyed his handiwork. The idiot witch had encased her within a black-salt ward: squib or not, she was trapped inside it. It was a move usually reserved for shoplifters and it was irritating as hell.

'Miss Cole will be with you shortly,' he told her before flouncing away.

Well, that was annoying, though it wasn't the first time she'd been treated like a crazed intruder and probably wouldn't be the last. There was nothing for it but to wait it out; with any luck, Alison Cole wouldn't take too long.

The door behind her opened again and a pair of witches wandered in. When they caught sight of Mallory, their eyes widened and they gave her a wide berth as if they might somehow end up trapped inside the same magicked circle if they drifted too close.

'It's not contagious!' Mallory called.

They pointedly ignored her and scurried away.

The door opened again and yet another pair of witches walked in. 'It's ridiculous,' one of them was saying. 'All of Coldstream knows that water nymphs are the best cleaners in the city but you can't hire any of them at the moment, not even for small jobs. They're not allowed to work and nobody would explain to me why. I practically had to drag the reason out of the last one who worked for me. Honestly! The thought that every single water nymph in Coldstream is supposed to maintain a damned vigil at Jacob's Well until the bloody spring equinox just because of some stupid old tradition is offensive to the principles of capitalism.' By the sound of her voice, the witch was only half-jesting.

'It's not a regular thing,' her companion soothed. 'Didn't you say it's only every twenty-five years? That's not so bad.'

'Tell that to the dust collecting in the corners of my house! Why do you think I need to come here and spend a small fortune on cleaning spells?'

The other witch laughed and they pair moved away, thankfully without glancing in Mallory's direction.

The door opened yet again and this time a werewolf strode in. Mallory flashed him the same bright smile she'd given the first two witches and instead of striding away, he paused. 'Well, well, well,' he murmured. 'What do we have here?'

She realised belatedly that she knew who he was; he'd even merited an entry in her precious notebook, although she'd not had the pleasure of meeting him in person.

That crooked nose, chiselled jaw and chestnut-brown hair had been the subject of considerable Coldstream gossip lately;

as the beta wolf to the powerful Ferguson pack, he was known as a man with considerable strength and power.

Word on the street was that he was making moves on his alpha. Werewolf hierarchy made it all-but impossible for an underling to overthrow their alpha without experiencing considerable physical pain, but that didn't stop the whispers that this man was prepared to suffer whatever it took to become the Ferguson alpha.

Without evidence, Mallory doubted any of the gossip was true but now that she was confronted with Liam Ferguson there was no doubt that he possessed a confident air similar to Alexander MacTire's.

'It's not what it looks like,' she told him. 'I promise.'

He arched an eyebrow. 'And what *does* it look like?'

She grinned. 'Like I'm a dirty rotten thief who's been caught red-handed.'

'That innocent face? I wouldn't believe it for a second.' He leaned towards her. 'Besides, I already know that you wouldn't steal from this shop. What good would a bunch of spells do a squib?' He regarded her curiously. 'Your reputation precedes you, Ms Nash.'

She sighed ruefully. 'If that were true, I wouldn't be in this predicament now.' She eyed him. 'How do you know who I am?'

'You helped a good friend of mine out last year. Zeke Simpson?'

Mallory instantly remembered the affable troll who'd come to her because he wanted to find out more about a business rival. She had supplied him with a detailed report that included various underhand dealings. Last she'd heard, the rival had been serving time at the pleasure of the Magical Enforcement Team. On all fronts, it had been a job well done.

'I remember Zeke well,' she said warmly.

Liam Ferguson's eyes crinkled. 'He still speaks very highly of you.'

Mallory dipped a curtsey, which was the most that the tightly bound ward allowed. 'It was a pleasure to help him.'

'Perhaps I can return the favour and help you now,' he murmured.

Over his shoulder, Mallory spotted Alison Cole heading her way. 'Thank you, but I've got it covered.'

'As you wish. Have a good day, Ms Nash.'

'Call me Mallory.'

'And I'm Liam.' He smiled then stepped away, leaving her free to speak to Alison in peace.

The store manager didn't apologise for Mallory's predicament though she did click her tongue. 'I'm sure I told you after last time that you should warn me before you decide to drop by.'

Mallory shrugged. 'It slipped my mind.'

'Another twenty minutes and I'd have clocked off for the day. We've been having a lot of trouble with over-enthusiastic tourists, and with a high staff turnover it's not easy to keep track of people like you.'

'Pathetic squibs with no magic to speak of?' Mallory enquired lightly.

Alison shot her a wary glance then relaxed when she realised that Mallory wasn't particularly offended. 'You're far from pathetic. As we both know.'

'You're too kind.'

Alison snorted. 'Hardly.' She reached for a broom and, with the appropriate words to undo the magical ward, swept away the ring of salt. 'This is one of the good ones,' she called out to anyone who might be listening. 'She's allowed in here whenever she wants.' She lowered her voice. 'Don't you get tired of being treated like a second-class citizen?'

'I might not be pathetic,' Mallory told her. 'But I *am* a squib. There are less than a hundred of us in Coldstream. Unfair treatment is par for the course and the situation usually resolves itself fairly quickly. It used to happen several times a day, but after ten years I'm better known. I only have to deal with situations like this a few times a week.'

'It sounds horrendous.'

'If I got annoyed about everything I couldn't change about the world, I'd spend all my days in a state of rage,' Mallory said. 'To some Coldstream citizens, I'll always be a suspicious stranger because I can't shapeshift or wield a magic spell. I can deal with minor inconveniences if it means I get what I want in the end.' Most of the time, anyway.

'Uh-huh.' Alison regarded her carefully. 'And what do you want this time?'

Mallory smiled. 'The best preservation spell you can provide.'

'Not a problem. We've got plenty in stock.'

'And,' Mallory crossed her fingers, 'a bellarmine jug with a useable seal.'

The store manager grimaced. 'Seriously? A real bellarmine jug?'

'Yep.'

'It's been more than a year since we've had any of those. They are not easy to come by.'

'Can I order one?'

She shrugged. 'You can try but it could be months before we find one.'

Mallory doubted that Chester Longchamps would be willing to wait that long, especially since the Clouded Map had to be returned to Nicola Sturgess by the end of August. 'I'll see if anywhere else sells them.'

'You'll be lucky to find one.'

'So it's a good thing I'm a lucky person.'

They exchanged amused glances, both well aware that it wasn't luck that made Mallory's secrets and favours brokerage service successful but a great deal of hard graft.

'I'll fetch the preservation spell,' Alison told her. 'You still have some leeway on your account.'

Mallory shook her head. 'I'm not paying for it, my client is. He's a vampire by the name of Chester Longchamps. You can send him the invoice.'

'A vampire came to you for a favour?' Alison looked more impressed than intimidated.

'Business is good.'

'Clearly. Next I hear, you'll be working for the likes of a beta werewolf like Liam Ferguson.' She nodded towards the werewolf who was wandering down an aisle, frowning.

Mallory wondered what Alison would say if she told her she was working for the MacTire alpha, but she smiled and said nothing.

CHAPTER

SEVEN

Mallory wrinkled her nose and gazed at the decidedly non-magical map displayed at the foot of the stairs to her small flat. Usually it was a valuable tool that enabled her to keep track of her clients. It covered all of Coldstream, with red dots marking the clients whom Mallory owed, blue dots covering those who owed her, and yellow dots pinpointing works in progress.

While it was satisfying to note that there were far more blue dots than red dots, Mallory couldn't pick out any current clients who might help her find a bellarmine jug; neither could she think of any previous clients to whom she could ask for help. Even her meticulously kept leather journal with its copious notes hadn't been of any use. Frankly, whichever way she turned she was coming up blank.

Without a jug to transport it, Nicola Sturgess had made it clear that the Clouded Map was unattainable. Mallory had already been to almost every witchery store in Coldstream during the past few days and she'd asked almost everyone she could think of. Perhaps it was time to think outside the box. They had to find a bellarmine jug from somewhere. If Chester

Longchamps couldn't locate one soon, *she* would have to try even harder.

Almost on cue, Boris pushed open the door and squinted at her. 'I've done what you asked and visited the vampire. Don't make me go there again.'

'Was it awful?'

The corners of his mouth turned down. 'Horrendous – although he did sign his contract.'

Something about his tone of voice gave her pause and her heart sank. 'Did he read it?'

The spriggan snorted. 'No.'

Centuries old and yet mince for brains. Mallory grimaced. Doubtless the vampire's lack of care would cause problems later, but she'd worry about that if and when it became an issue. It wouldn't be the first time she'd had over-confident clients who under-estimated what they were getting into.

'If you don't leave in the next thirty seconds, you'll be late,' Boris warned, re-focusing her attention. 'And I doubt that MacTire will be as relaxed about your spurious timekeeping as Kit McCafferty was.'

True. Mallory sighed.

'I'm on my way,' she said. She smoothed down her patch-work dress. Its style remained decidedly bohemian but it was definitely more tight fitting than she was used to. She wriggled uncomfortably.

'Don't twitch,' Boris told her. 'It makes you look like a squashed caterpillar if you move around like that. Stand up straight and act normal.'

Mallory plucked at the corset strings. 'Easy for you to say,' she told him.

The spriggan's expression didn't alter. 'You look beautiful when you're not writhing around. Every eye will be on you.'

She pursed her lips. 'I don't want every eye to be on me. I'm not the focus, Alexander MacTire is.'

Boris allowed himself a fleeting smirk. 'Oh,' he said with an airy wave, 'I expect every eye will be on him too.'

As long as MacTire's eyes were on the three women she'd picked out as potential mates for him, she'd be happy. She grunted at Boris, picked up her bag and headed for the door.

There were no grubby trainers in evidence tonight, it was heels all the way. Thankfully this particular pair were comfortable, even if they did make her feel as if she were towering over Boris. She lifted her chin and did her best to take his advice not to fidget. 'With any luck,' she said, 'Alexander will agree with one of my choices and I won't have to go to the Wolf Ball with him.'

'If you believe that then you're far more of a fool than I realised.'

She grinned. 'There's nothing foolish about optimism.'

He sniffed. 'I beg to differ. And there's no way *Alexander* is an optimist.'

'If he weren't an optimist, he wouldn't have asked for my help in the first place. This is going to be a great night!'

This time Boris only stared at her.

THE PERHAPS-LESS-THAN-OPTIMISTIC MAN in question was already in front of the Tweed Hall, his head bowed in conversation with a female druid whose swirling blue facial tattoos indicated she was highly placed within her community. Of course, not every guest attending the Imbolc party was a druid, and only one of the three women whom Mallory had selected was of druid origins. Unfortunately, the woman who was smiling at Alexander wasn't one of them.

Mallory waved off Boris and strolled up to them. She was still twenty feet away when Alexander's head jerked upwards and his nostrils flared as he scented her approach. She raised a hand, still feeling positive about the party. He was here, he was dressed to the nines in a sharp suit and he was making conversation with a woman. This was, Mallory decided, a very good start.

He smiled at her as she drew close and his already handsome face turned into a devastatingly attractive one. Mallory tightened her toes. 'Hello!' she exclaimed. 'You look fabulous!'

'Thank you,' he said. 'You look wonderful too, Mallory. That dress suits you.'

'It's a bit tight,' she confided. 'Boris kept telling me off for wiggling.'

Something flared in his amber eyes. 'If you want to wiggle, sweetheart, you wiggle.'

'Maybe later you can wiggle on the dancefloor,' the druid said. She smiled in greeting. 'I'm Alorine. Thank you for attending our little soirée. I hear you're responsible for dragging Mr MacTire here. It's a boon for us to have a werewolf of his standing in attendance.'

'It's a boon for me to attend,' Alexander said without missing a beat.

Mallory nodded approvingly. That was suave; more of that, and this evening would be a great success. 'Thank you for opening your doors to the likes of us.'

'Imbolc is an important time of year, a time of renewal and celebration.' Alorine held out a basket. 'Take a crocus flower. Not only is it a symbol of spring, it also represents love.'

Mallory couldn't help emitting a trill of delight. 'Absolutely perfect!' She reached into the basket and plucked out two flowers, tucking one behind her ear and handing the other to Alexander. 'You'll want this,' she said.

His fingers brushed against hers as he took the small purple crocus. He eyed it dubiously and pinched it between his thumb and forefinger. Mallory beamed. 'Put it in your buttonhole. It'll look great.'

Alorine nodded. 'It will. Enjoy your evening. Do come find me if you need anything.' She moved away, leaving Alexander still awkwardly holding the flower.

'Here.' He thrust it at Mallory. 'You do it. I'm too clumsy.'

'I'm sure you're perfectly capable of doing it yourself.'

He arched an eyebrow. 'Are you afraid to get too close to me?'

'Don't be silly,' she chided. She took the crocus and leaned towards his broad chest, fumbling until she found his buttonhole and threaded the stem through it.

'I think it's squint,' he said.

Mallory fiddled with it some more, her heels wobbling slightly on the uneven cobblestones. Alexander's hands reached for her waist. 'Steady,' he murmured. 'I've got you.'

She suddenly became very aware of him. His hands seemed to burn through the fabric of her tight dress and sear the skin beneath. He smelled of cinnamon and spice. She coughed awkwardly and stepped back, using the excuse of admiring the flower to compose herself. 'There,' she said. 'Now you'll blend right in.'

Alexander gazed at her. 'Just what I always wanted, to blend in and be like everyone else.'

She thumped him lightly on his arm. 'Don't be snarky.'

'Don't be violent.'

Mallory rolled her eyes. 'Yeah, yeah.' She gestured towards the door. 'Let's go inside, get a drink and then we can talk game plan.'

He bowed. 'As you command, my lady.'

When he held out his arm, Mallory shook her head. 'No, we

don't want anyone to get the wrong idea. A foot apart at all times. Nobody should think that we're a couple.'

'Heaven forbid. Very well.' But he drifted closer and by the time they entered the hall he was only a few inches from her side.

A tuxedoed waiter approached them holding aloft a silver tray of wine glasses. Alexander handed one to Mallory. She took a sip and immediately made a face.

'Not good?' he asked.

'It's a little … tart.'

He raised it to his lips, swallowed a mouthful – and choked. 'If the wine is anything to go by, this evening will be a bust.'

'It's a good thing the wine is terrible,' Mallory told him decisively. 'You need a clear head. I have high hopes for this party.'

He eyed her. 'I thought this was supposed to be a practice run.'

'That doesn't mean you won't meet Miss Right. And either way, practice makes perfect.'

As she put her wine glass down on a table and glanced around the room, her eyes immediately alighted on her first candidate. Excellent. 'You see the blonde woman over there in the long red dress?'

He followed her gaze. 'Yes.'

'That's Alicia Van Borgen. She's a witch – she leads a coven that's small but definitely up and coming. She's whip smart, adept at magic and she's not long out of a relationship.'

'You mean she's on the rebound.'

'I mean,' Mallory said patiently, 'that she's single.'

As if the witch had heard her, she lifted her head and looked in their direction. Her eyes slid over Mallory and settled on Alexander with a very direct, very approving stare. Mallory grinned.

'Too easy,' Alexander said as he watched her. 'She's already giving me come-hither eyes.'

'You're not looking for a one-night stand,' Mallory reminded him. 'If that were the case, I'm sure you'd have no difficulty.'

'Because I'm handsome and charming and, let's face it, sex on legs?'

Unbelievable. 'You are *not* looking for a one-night stand,' she repeated. 'You are looking for a life partner.'

'You didn't answer my question, Mallory.'

Exasperated, she muttered, 'Sure. Whatever. You're handsome, charming and sex on legs.' She nudged him. 'Now go and talk to Alicia.'

'No.' He raised his glass politely in the witch's direction and turned away. 'She's not the one.'

Mallory's mouth fell open. 'You've not even spoken to her!'

'I know her type and I know what she wants. If I speak to her now, the entire evening becomes a fait accompli and carnal knowledge is guaranteed.'

'How is that a bad thing?' she asked. Surely that was why they were here.

'I don't want sex, Mallory.'

She couldn't help herself. 'Ever?'

Now Alexander sounded exasperated. 'You're being deliberately obtuse. As you pointed out, I don't want a one-night stand. That woman, lovely as she may be, doesn't want a relationship. She wants a shag. There's nothing wrong with that, although it might irritate you.'

Mallory crossed her arms. 'The only thing that irritates me is that you've made up your mind about her before you've exchanged so much as a single word.'

'I'm an excellent judge of character.'

'We both know that's not true,' she retorted. 'When we first met, you were so suspicious of me that you kept growling.'

He quirked an eyebrow. 'You're complicated. Anyway, the jury is still out on you.'

This was ridiculous. 'I can leave now and we can call it quits for good,' Mallory said firmly. 'All you have to do is say the word and we can cancel our contract. Besides, *everyone* is complicated. You can't give someone a single look and decide you know exactly who they are and what they're like. Go and talk to Alicia.'

'Is that an order?'

'Yes.' She gave him her sternest look.

He chuckled. 'If you want me to do your bidding, Mallory, you'll have to look fiercer than that.'

She abandoned her attempt and smiled sunnily. 'Actually, I don't have to look fierce at all.'

'Why not?'

'Because Alicia is taking the initiative and coming over here.' And with that, Mallory reached for her glass of wine and spun away, leaving Alexander to meet the woman on his own.

She wove in and out of guests to the other side of the hall; the more space she could give him, the better. Other than her lack of werewolf heritage, on paper Alicia Van Borgen was an ideal candidate. All he had to do was give it a bit of time, talk to her properly and—

'I told you she was a no.'

Mallory's head jerked up. Alexander was beside her again. 'Seriously? You couldn't have spoken to her for more than thirty seconds.'

'It was more than enough.' He took a sip of his wine, grimaced and put the glass down. 'There must be something else here we can drink.'

'Don't change the subject.'

He gave her a long look. 'There's nothing more to say. She's a perfectly nice woman but she is not who I am looking for.'

Mallory winced internally. *Nice?* As compliments went, that was damning by faint praise. She shook her head, then a thought occurred to her and she glanced at him, assessing him with fresh eyes. 'You want a chase,' she said.

Alexander's brow furrowed in a brief scowl.

'You think that if it's too easy it's not worth having,' she said, warming to her topic. 'You want to be in control. It pissed you off that Alicia showed initiative and approached you. You have to be the alpha, not just in your own pack but in all things.'

'That's not true!'

She ignored him. 'So my second suggestion will be even better because you'll have to work for her. She's got far less confidence than Alicia, but what she lacks in that department, she makes up for in quiet strength and brutal intelligence.' Mallory nodded. 'Yes. This will be much better.'

Alexander didn't look convinced. 'Who?'

Mallory searched across the heads of the crowd. 'There,' she said. 'Lynnia McIntosh. She's a druid. She's standing by the bar ordering a drink.'

They watched as the tall woman handed over some money and received a balloon-shaped glass filled with a bright-green liquid, a puff of dry ice, a little parasol and sparks of orange flame.

'She's drinking some sort of hideous cocktail.' Alexander's lips were pursed with disapproval.

'So she doesn't like the wine either.' Mallory shrugged. 'You're allowed to have different tastes to your partner.'

'That particular cocktail is a Green Goblin. Having different tastes is one thing but enjoying the nastiest concoction in the world is something completely different.'

'You can teach her about wine,' Mallory said. 'You can

mansplain about corkage and vintage and different types of grape to your heart's content.' She nudged him. 'Go and chat her up.'

He huffed dubiously but thankfully he squared his shoulders and set off across the room to speak to the druid. This time Mallory watched; if he turned away after anything less than a full five minutes of conversation, she would have serious words with him.

Fortunately he finally appeared to be taking the venture seriously. He adjusted his cuffs, smoothed his hair and approached Lynnia McIntosh with a smile that suggested friendly, polite interest.

Alexander's lips moved and the druid nodded back. He spoke some more, angling his head towards her in a way that suggested enthusiastic engagement. She shook her head. He spoke again. She rolled her eyes, scowled, finally opened her mouth and spoke at some length. She didn't look pleased. Oh dear.

'Lynnia McIntosh is allergic to werewolves,' Alexander informed her, when he returned to her side looking sheepish.

'Don't be silly.'

'It's true! Well, she's allergic to alpha werewolves with over-the-top personalities who think they have the authority to tell her that she shouldn't drink acid-green cocktails that will burn her guts, because she'll drink whatever the fuck she wants to drink.'

Mallory considered; it was a fair and measured response from the druid. 'You're not very good at this, are you?'

Alexander drew himself up to his full height. 'What? I'm great. Just because she took offence when I suggested she was risking her health doesn't mean I'm not good at chatting up women.'

Mallory pretended not to hear him. 'Now it makes sense

why you came to me. You're successful in your professional life but you can't translate that to your personal life because you're intimidated by smart women. You fumble conversation with anyone who's not a werewolf in your own pack. You put on a brave front, but the thought of getting to know a *real* woman terrifies you.'

'That's not even remotely true!'

Excellent: he was taking the bait. 'Prove it, then. I have one final candidate for you. She's a werewolf. She's in a small pack, but she's just been promoted to beta. She has a degree in linguistics – and I know for a fact that she likes wine rather than neon-green cocktails. She came out of her last relationship more than a year ago so she's definitely not on the rebound or looking for a one-night stand.'

Alexander put his hands in his pockets. 'Go on,' he said. 'Who is she?'

Mallory pointed. 'Cathy West. Right over there.'

He followed her finger. 'She's brunette.'

'If the colour of her hair is the deal-breaker I'll void that blood contract and damn the consequences,' Mallory said cheerfully.

'Fine. I'll go and talk to her.'

'No, that's not enough. You will go and talk to her and prove to me that you are genuinely prepared to accept my help. You will get her to agree to go on a date with you.'

Alexander's eyes narrowed with suspicion. 'Cathy West was your plan all along, wasn't it?'

She looked at him serenely. 'If you can meet your future mate weeks before the Wolf Ball then we both win. Right?'

He sighed. 'Right.'

'Off you go, Alex.'

He muttered something under his breath – but he did as he was told.

Mallory had to admit that Alexander MacTire could do many things when he applied himself. She'd known from the start that Cathy West was the most likely candidate; lupine heritage notwithstanding, she was intelligent and capable.

From the other side of the room, Mallory watched Alexander chat to the woman. She saw Cathy start to relax and laugh at what he had to say. He was smart enough to snag a passing waiter and order a different bottle of wine. Cathy appeared pleased to accept and in fewer than fifteen minutes, the pair were absorbed in conversation to the exclusion of anyone else.

When Alexander gestured towards the dance floor, Mallory held her breath. Cathy nodded and within moments they were deftly navigating a waltz. Mallory hadn't realised that Alexander could dance; in truth, he was so good that it was difficult to drag her eyes away from him.

'So did you escape from your temporary prison?' a voice murmured in her ear. 'Or were you released?'

Mallory turned towards the twinkling eyes of Liam Ferguson. 'Shhh,' she said conspiratorially, placing a finger on her lips. 'Keep your voice down. I'm a fugitive on the run.'

'And you thought the perfect place to hide out was a busy Imbolc party? Makes sense. Don't worry. Your secret is safe with me.'

'I appreciate that.' She winked at him.

He smiled. 'So, assuming none of that is actually true, are you here for business or pleasure?'

'It's a party,' Mallory replied smoothly. 'What do you think?'

'Given that I know what your business is, it could be either.'

'What about you?' she asked. 'Are you here for fun?'

'I know a lot of druids and Imbolc is my favourite druidic celebration. There's something wonderful about the start of spring. My spirits always lighten when I see the first snowdrops on the ground. Winter is not my favourite season.'

'Every season has its benefits,' Mallory told him. 'Winter is cold and sometimes bleak, but you get to snuggle indoors with roaring fireplaces and mugs of hot chocolate and cosy blankets. It's not all bad.'

Liam smiled. 'I suspect that your hot chocolate mug is always half full.'

'I like to think so.'

He glanced away from her then rubbed his jaw, rasping his stubble. 'Well,' he said ruefully, 'I guess that answers one question.'

Confused, Mallory frowned. 'What do you mean?'

He shrugged. 'You're here for pleasure, not business. Alexander MacTire wouldn't be glaring at us so ferociously if you weren't with him on a date.'

Mallory turned to the dance floor. Alexander was still waltzing with Cathy but he was watching Mallory and Liam from over his partner's shoulder. And Liam was right; he looked absolutely furious.

'It's not what you think,' Mallory said, as the song ended and Alexander turned back to Cathy.

'It rarely is,' Liam murmured. 'Either way, I think I'll take my leave.' He stepped back. 'Enjoy your evening.'

'You too,' she said distractedly as Alexander bowed to Cathy.

She beamed at him as he returned. 'I knew you had it in you! What did you think of Cathy?'

'She's fine,' he snapped. 'Are you working for Liam Ferguson?'

Startled, Mallory blinked. 'What?'

'It's a simple enough question.'

'That I'm not going to answer! I don't talk about my other clients.'

He glared at her. 'So that's a yes, then.'

'It's a "mind your own business",' she said mildly, though she felt unusually rankled.

'You're here for me, Mallory. I need to know that you're not getting distracted by other work.' His jaw hardened. 'Or did you suggest we come to this party so you could double-dip?'

And just when she'd thought they were getting along. Mallory returned his angry stare with one of her own. 'Now you're being rude – and I am certainly not double-dipping, as you call it. Yes, I have other clients but tonight you are my focus.'

For some reason, Alexander appeared even angrier. 'So that was a social chat?'

Mallory hissed, 'It was nothing.' She tightened her toes and tried hard to compose herself. 'Tell me how it went with Cathy.'

'It went fine.'

'Alexander...'

He sighed. 'We're meeting for dinner next week after the next full moon.'

Thank goodness for that. Mallory managed to smile. 'Great!'

'Wonderful,' he said flatly. He sniffed. 'I think we've done all we need to do here. Let's go.'

She didn't move. 'No. You're my client, Alexander. I work for you, but I'm certainly not beholden to you and you can't talk to me like that. I understand you're annoyed because you thought I was being distracted but that doesn't give you an excuse to act so rudely.'

A muscle throbbed in his cheek and he looked away. 'I'm sorry,' he muttered. He drew a deep breath. 'I know I sometimes appear flippant but this is important to me. I really do need to find a mate.'

Mallory softened. 'It's alright,' she said gently. 'I get it. I'm on your side, you know, and we will find the right woman for you. If not Cathy, then someone else.'

As she started to turn away Alexander took her hand, an odd expression in his eyes, both troubled and thoughtful at the same time. 'I really am sorry, Mallory. I won't act like that again. I don't know what came over me.'

'You don't need to apologise twice. It's fine.'

He rubbed the back of her hand with the base of his thumb and they smiled at each other. The uncomfortable moment was over – but Mallory's stomach was flip-flopping all the same, and it didn't settle down until some time after Alexander MacTire had let go of her hand.

Objectively speaking – and romantically focused werewolves aside – Preternatural beings were fascinating to watch when they were angry. Veins bulged on the foreheads and necks of trolls; dryads and nymphs both flushed bright green. Furious magic often sparked at the tips of witches' forefingers, and vampires turned so pale that you'd be forgiven for thinking they were on the verge of passing out.

'It's completely unacceptable,' Chester Longchamps declared, his skin as white as parchment. 'This is Coldstream. There must be a usable bellarmine jug somewhere!'

'You're certain that there are no vampires who have a spare?' Mallory asked. After all, if the Clouded Map would help prevent future vampiric deaths they ought to be queueing up at Longchamps' door to hand over any number of jugs.

'If any of them do then they are selfish bastards who are refusing to give them to me.' He paced up and down the length of his drawing room, his sharp heels scuffing the floor. 'They don't get it. They're too complacent and they don't think that they're in danger. That's the trouble with longevity, you start to think that real death is something that happens to other creatures even when you're faced with the prospect yourself.'

Mallory sat on the long leather sofa, hoping that it would encourage Longchamps to stop pacing. 'This creature,' she said, 'the one that's killing vampires.'

He sent her a fearful look. 'What of it?'

'It truly terrifies you.' She gazed at him. 'Is it a threat to other Coldstream residents?'

'Are you worried about your own longevity, Ms Nash?'

Her expression cooled. 'I won't deign to answer that.'

Chester Longchamps grimaced. 'I apologise. That was uncouth.' He sighed. 'No, the only risk is to vampires. The creature is contained in an area that is safely away from anyone who doesn't possess a thirst for blood, pale skin and an inability to appear in mirrors.'

'Ah.' That made sense. 'It's somewhere in the Understream, then.'

He stared at her. 'How do you know about the Understream?' A flicker of rage passed across his face. 'Who told you?'

'I broker favours and secrets,' Mallory said patiently. 'Of course I know about the Understream.' The network of tunnels that sprawled beneath the city of Coldstream was a well-kept secret but she was good at her job and she'd known about it for years.

He wasn't mollified. 'Have you ever visited?'

'I know what would happen if I tried to enter the Understream without permission.' She tried to lighten the tone. 'Written permission in triplicate, rubber stamped and notarised by a solicitor.'

Her attempt at weak humour fell flat. 'You'd be lucky to escape with your life,' Chester said darkly.

This time Mallory responded seriously. 'I'm aware.'

The dangerous flash of white fangs showed that she hadn't

appeased him. Mallory knew that vampires took the Understream seriously but she hadn't appreciated quite how seriously. For the first time, she felt she was on shaky ground; Longchamps could easily swing into sudden violence despite their blood contract and him needing her services.

'Its existence is supposed to be a fucking secret.' There was an ugly twist to his mouth.

'It *is* a secret,' she soothed. 'Few people in Coldstream know about it.'

'It had better fucking remain that way.'

'You should know by now that I can be trusted.'

A muscle jerked in his cheek but then he relaxed slightly. 'Fine.' He paused for a long moment. 'Although I can't help wondering what other secrets are rattling around in that head of yours.'

This time, Mallory thought it would be prudent to stay quiet. Longchamps watched her for another moment or two then heaved in a breath and changed the subject. 'Regardless,' he said, 'I cannot find anyone who can give me a bellarmine jug, even on loan. You will have to find one.'

'I told you that I've already tried every witchery store I can think of, and I don't have any contacts who...'

Instantly his face filled with rage again. 'You will find me a bellarmine jug so I can take possession of the Clouded Map,' he spat. 'Or there will be consequences. Terrible consequences. You are supposed to be good at this, Ms Nash. That's why I hired you.'

Temperamental bastard. Mallory drew herself up. 'I *am* good at this. As per the terms of our contract, I will do my best to find a jug. However—'

He didn't allow her to finish her sentence. 'You'd better find one.' Chester Longchamps turned his back and made it very clear that their meeting was over.

'THIS IS why you shouldn't deal with vampires,' Boris told her. 'They're mercurial, dangerous and given to ripping out your throat at a moment's notice.'

'My throat is fine, thank you very much,' Mallory said, despite still feeling disturbed by her meeting with Longchamps. She'd dealt with scary clients before and she knew how to hold her own, but there had been a brief moment when she'd genuinely feared he would attack her.

She shivered. All she had to do was try her hardest to find a bellarmine jug and she'd have completed her side of the bargain. She'd performed plenty of difficult favours in the past and she wouldn't let a piece of damned earthenware thwart her. 'It will be fine,' she said aloud.

Boris shot her a dubious glance. 'Are you trying to persuade me or yourself?'

She ignored him. 'We can't get hold of a jug from a store but we're hardly out of options. Who else do we have from the witches who owes a favour?'

The spriggan pursed his lips. 'There's Alan North. He has a finger in lots of pies and he owes you two full favours.'

Mallory nodded. 'True. I heard some reliable whispers that his coven is considering putting in a rival bid for the tram network, which will certainly put the proverbial cat among the pigeons. But I doubt he has a bellarmine jug. He's new power, his family weren't original Coldstream settlers, he's not connected to the Council and he has several ancestors who were squibs. I doubt he has anything like a real bellarmine jug in his possession – but find out, just in case.'

'Freda Vargas, then?' Boris suggested. 'Her lineage is longer – she might have inherited a jug.'

Mallory nibbled her bottom lip. 'Try her. And I'll speak to

Salty Miller. The druids wouldn't typically have a use for one but there's a chance that he might have one lying around. He's that sort of person.'

'His slate is clean,' Boris reminded her. 'His contract was fulfilled on both sides last year.'

'That's okay. I reckon he'd be amenable to opening a new one, especially if it'll benefit him in the future.'

'You'll need to line your stomach before you go,' he warned.

Mallory pulled a face. 'Yeah,' she said. 'I've not forgotten what he's like.'

'Last time your hangover lasted four days.'

She shuddered at the memory 'Unfortunately, I haven't forgotten that either.'

MALLORY DIDN'T USUALLY venture out during a full-moon event. When she'd first moved to Coldstream and been far braver and more foolish, she'd wandered the streets during a full moon and ended up cornered by two young werewolves in full rampage mode. They'd trapped her down an alleyway and taken great delight in nipping her several times. Although they'd only caused a few bruises and had quickly grown bored with her, it had been a terrifying experience for a young human woman with little Preternatural understanding.

Although she'd been born in the English countryside, Mallory had moved to the city of Glasgow with her parents in her teens. As a sixteen year old in a large unfamiliar city, she had quickly learned how to hold her own and she had been used to dealing with raucous partygoers, but werewolves with huge paws, sharp teeth and moon-invoked bloodlust were a different matter. It had been a sobering night that she'd vowed never to repeat.

She was a very different person now, and Salty Miller was leaving for New Orleans at the weekend. If she didn't speak to him immediately it could be months before she saw him again. She was fortunate he'd managed to find any time for her at all.

She was carrying two vials of wolfsbane, one in each pocket, and was wearing plain dark clothing that was very different to her usual attire. Black would help camouflage her as she traversed the moonlit streets, and the tight-fitting leggings and top would make it easier if she needed to run. She'd tied her bouncy brown curls back and shoved them beneath a black cap. Under other circumstances, she'd have passed for a cat burglar or a ninja but all she really wanted to do was pass unnoticed.

She'd agreed to meet Salty at a druid bar on Hirsel Street. It wasn't a particularly friendly place unless you had blue tattoos, and its patrons would be even more on edge than usual given the time of the month, but there'd been no point trying to persuade him to meet elsewhere. If she wanted to talk to him, she had to agree to his terms.

At least Hirsel Street was less than a half a mile from her flat on Crackendon Square, and even allowing for packs of howling werewolves it was little more than a ten-minute walk. Slipping out at dusk also helped; although some werewolves would already be roaming the streets, it was early enough to avoid them. As long as she wasn't too late leaving Hirsel Street to return home everything would be fine. She hoped.

It was a few months since Mallory had frequented any of the boozy establishments along the busy street known throughout Coldstream for its nightlife and party atmosphere. When she'd started brokering secrets and favours, she'd spent countless hours haunting the bars and clubs. *In vino veritas* was as true now as it had been in Roman times, and she'd learned a great deal from alcohol-sodden tongues. She still kept many of the Hirsel bar staff sweet, and they were prepped to contact her if certain Preternatural bigwigs turned up. These days she didn't need to spend several nights a month trawling for secrets because more often than not people came to her, but part of her missed those frenetic days – even if her liver was grateful that it no longer had to work overtime.

As she'd expected at full moon, the small pub was quieter than usual although the usual diehards who would lock themselves inside and drink the night away were there. Although Mallory recognised almost every face, she knew better than to attempt small talk; she wasn't a druid and even her best chatter would not be welcome. Unfortunately, there was no sign of Salty Miller and she prayed silently that she hadn't missed him.

The barman eyed her coldly as he polished the glass in his hands in a manner that could only be described as menacing. She knew he wouldn't attack her but he wanted her to think that he could.

The only approach was to go into full sunshine mode, so she plastered on a brilliant smile. Twinkly eyes and shiny teeth, she told herself. You've done this a million times before. If she could deal with the likes of Chester Longchamps, she could certainly handle this guy.

'Good evening!'

The barman didn't react: he didn't blink, he didn't twitch and he certainly didn't smile. He simply continued polishing the pint glass and eyeballing her.

'Wow,' Mallory said. 'You really take your cleaning seriously. I'm impressed that standards haven't dropped since the last time I was in here – they were always high and now they're even better.' Her words served a dual purpose: she was complimenting the barman and, perhaps more importantly, she was telling him that she'd been here before. She understood the lay of the land: druid pub or not, she was *allowed* to be here.

The barman didn't noticeably crack but she was certain that

he'd paid attention to her words. 'What are you drinking?' he growled.

What she really wanted was a pot of coffee or, at a pinch, hot chocolate with marshmallows. A decent Merlot to sip and savour would be equally wonderful. However, none of those choices would ingratiate her with the barman and it was obvious that none of those delights were available. She sighed inwardly as she maintained her full wattage smile. 'It's been a long time since I had a decent pint. Nobody makes beer like the druids. You'll make my day if you have any Taliesin's Bitter on tap.'

Something shifted behind the barman's eyes and Mallory knew she'd said the right words. She'd revealed to a beer professional that she understood good beer; even better, she'd proved she was someone who understood good *druidic* beer.

In truth, she couldn't think of anything worse but it wouldn't be the first time she'd drunk a few pints for the sake of her work; neither would it be the last.

'Add a dram of the good stuff as a chaser for the lady, and I'll have the same again,' drawled a familiar voice in a heavy lowland accent.

'She's with you?' The barman stared at Salty Miller who'd appeared at Mallory's side.

'Aye.'

'You should have said,' he muttered accusingly to Mallory.

She shrugged and made a last-ditch effort to win him around. 'What can I say? I hate name dropping.'

For the first time, the barman's mouth tugged upwards. 'You're no druid,' he said, stating the obvious, 'but you're not so bad.'

Salty grinned. 'By Jove. I think he likes you.'

'Take a seat,' the barman told them. 'I'll bring your drinks over.'

'Table service, too?' Salty whistled. 'Wonders will never cease.'

Mallory nudged him sharply with her elbow before the barman changed his mind. 'Thank you,' she said. 'That's incredibly kind of you.' She turned away and headed for the table that Salty was pointing to. 'I didn't see you when I came in,' she said as they sat down.

Salty gave her an affable smile. 'I was taking a piss.' He held out his hands. 'Here,' he said, wiggling his fingers. 'I even washed my hands afterwards. You can smell them. That's actual soap.'

'Amazing.'

Her sarcasm delighted him. 'It's been too long, Mallory Nash. It's good to see you.'

'It's good to see you too, Salty Miller.' This time she meant it.

The barman appeared and placed their drinks on the table. Salty reached for his shot of whisky and downed it in one, gesturing to Mallory to do the same. She knew exactly what would happen if she didn't, so she lifted the heavy glass to her lips and swallowed the liquid. Its mellow warmth slipped down her throat. It was actually good stuff. 'Mmmm.'

Salty grinned and gestured to the hovering barman. 'Another two!'

He nodded and withdrew before Mallory had a chance to refuse another dram. 'I'm not here to drink, Salty,' she warned. 'This is business.'

'Och, you can have one or two, lass.'

She raised an eyebrow. 'It's never just one or two though, is it? Not with you.'

He laughed and thumped the table. 'You know me too well.'

More's the pity. 'The reason I'm here...' she began.

Salty was already shaking his head. 'Beer first,' he said. 'Business later.'

Mallory persisted. 'I have one quick question for you. That's all.'

'You know the rules.' His eyes danced. 'If you can't beat 'em, join 'em.'

There were no handy plant pots nearby into which she could surreptitiously pour her drinks, and in this magic-rich environment Mallory possessed no sleight of hand that would enable her to get rid of them. She could refuse, but the last time she'd tried that with Salty he'd shown her the door.

It was a different game with every client and this was Salty Miller's favoured play. He loved drinking but hated doing it alone; he'd happily use and abuse any opportunity he could get to drag others into his boozy orbit. Mallory steeled her stomach and crossed her fingers that she could steer him to the topic of bellarmine jugs by the time she'd finished her beer. She could at least hope.

It took two more beers and four shots of whisky before Salty was prepared to talk shop. Mallory had picked up her glass and was gazing at the amber liquid inside it when the druid cleared his throat and gave her a pointed look. She returned it with a burble of relief. She enjoyed his company and – if she were honest – the drinks, but at this rate she wouldn't be able to walk home in a straight line.

'I'm ready to talk business now,' he declared. 'What is it you want?'

Mallory lowered her glass to the table and focused her tipsy eyes on him. 'I need a bellarmine jug,' she said, glad that she wasn't slurring her words.

Salty's expression didn't change. 'I take it you mean a real bellarmine jug, not a knock-off version that we sell to tourists.'

'Naturally.'

'A real bellarmine jug designed to transport delicate materials that cannot be exposed to an unmagicked atmosphere for more than a few minutes at a time?'

'Yep.'

'An undamaged bellarmine jug?'

'Yep.'

'With a sealed, warded stopper?'

'Yep.'

'How long do you need it for? Is this a permanent acquisition?'

Mallory felt a surge of hope; by the sounds of it, Salty had one or he knew where she could get one. She shook her head. 'No. I only need it until the end of August then it will be returned in the same condition.'

'I see.' He tapped his mouth thoughtfully.

'Salty...'

He gave her a wry, almost sad smile. 'Sorry, Mal.'

Her heart dropped. 'Come on, Salty.'

'I really can't help you. I only know one person with a bellarmine jug and it's already in use. They won't be persuaded to hand it over even for a short period.'

She pushed away her glass, annoyed with herself as much as him. If she hadn't had so much to drink, she'd have realised he was stringing her along. This entire evening had been a waste of time.

Salty understood her expression. 'You must have known it was a long shot. Hardly anyone has an empty bellarmine jug these days – not ones that work. There's a chance that some of the renegade covens that choose to live away from Coldstream have one buried away, but they're unlikely to talk to either me or you. Unfortunately, there's nothing I can do and nobody I know who can help.'

'If you'd let me ask you when I first got here then...'

'Then I'd have been denied the pleasure of your company.' He grinned. 'C'mon. You've enjoyed yourself too.'

Mallory grumbled under her breath.

'How about another drink to soften the blow?'

'No. I'm going to head home.'

'It's the full moon, Mal. It's not safe.'

She glanced at her watch: a quarter to eleven. The streets would be cock-a-hoop with werewolves, but she had wolfsbane in her pockets and she'd be home in ten minutes if she hurried. She was dimly aware that the alcohol in her system was making her over-confident but she wasn't the innocent she'd been when she first arrived in Coldstream. She knew how to handle werewolves now. She was far, far more experienced. 'I can look after myself.'

'You're just a squib,' he said, as if telling her something she didn't know.

Mallory sniffed. 'I can still look after myself.'

'Stay,' he urged. 'I'll walk you home in the morning before I leave the city.'

'I am not staying out all night drinking, Salty. I've got things to do.' She wobbled to her feet, wove her way to the door and opened it wide just as three snarling werewolves bounded past.

Mallory watched them thunder towards the end of Hirsel Street while behind them several high-pitched howls filled the street. She closed the door and turned to Salty. 'Alright,' she said with heavy reluctance. 'Maybe I'll stay.'

He raised his glass. 'Wise choice.'

Mallory returned to the table and sat down. 'This was your plan all along, wasn't it?'

Salty grinned. 'Don't be cross. You know you'll have fun. I'll make it up to you at some point.'

'Unless you've got a bellarmine jug tucked away in your coat, that's not going to happen.'

There was a knowing glint in his eye. 'You know I don't.' He leaned forward. 'But let's get some more drinks in and if anything comes to mind, or I think of anyone who might help you find a bellarmine jug, I'll let you know.'

Mallory sighed. At this point, resistance was futile.

Dawn was less than thirty minutes away when Mallory finally stumbled out of Hirsel Street. Salty had stayed true to his word and declared that he would walk her to her flat but Mallory had declined forcefully and told him to get himself away. After all, he did have a long-haul flight from Glasgow to catch.

By this hour, most of the werewolves would have found their way back to their homes to sleep off the excesses of the full-moon furry extravaganza. Although some die-hards might still be enjoying the last hour before they returned to human form, even the most determined would be fading, and energy-sapped werewolves were both easier to avoid and easier to talk to. Their wilder inclinations would have subsided and their more rational sides would have returned. Which was just as well because Mallory's own rational side had all but vanished.

She skipped, swayed and sang, happily belting out several of the songs that the occupants of the druid pub – including the gruff barman – had been singing not too long ago. It might not have been the night she had planned or wanted, but she couldn't deny that she'd had a fabulous time.

'Sometimes,' she mumbled, 'it's definitely better to beat 'em when you can't join 'em.' She paused. 'No. That's not right. It's better to join 'em when you beat 'em.' She frowned. 'If you can't join 'em then...'

Her voice trailed off. Screw it; it didn't matter. She launched instead into a belting rendition of 'I Will Survive' but she'd barely managed the first few lines when a deep growl from the shadows to her right forced her to stop. 'Wolfie?' she asked.

There was another long growl.

'You should be home in bed by now,' she admonished. She stumbled slightly, only just managing to regain her balance before she collapsed in a heap on the cobbles. 'Then again, so should I.' She waved in the vague direction of the growl and spun around, ready to continue on her way.

Unfortunately it appeared that the wolf had other ideas. As it padded out of the shadows with its massive, furred body facing her head on, Mallory realised that she must be very drunk indeed.

She'd never seen such a huge werewolf before. Its dark fur was glossy and gold-tipped but that didn't disguise the powerful muscles that rippled beneath. Intelligence blazed at her from narrowed golden eyes and, for the briefest second, the wolf pulled back its lips and offered her a brief silent snarl.

'I've got wolfsbane,' she warned loudly, 'and I'm not afraid to use it.' The werewolf huffed. She squinted and put her hands on her hips. 'Did you just roll your eyes at me?'

It responded by drawing closer and a tingle of anxiety penetrated her drunken haze. The wolf had shown no signs of aggression except for the tiny snarl, but what if it wasn't alone?

She glanced upwards. The sky was already lightening so it wouldn't be long before whoever was locked inside those lupine eyes would be forced to become human again for another month. She wasn't naïve enough to think that only creatures on four legs could do her damage – two-legged beasts were often far more dangerous – but shapeshifting took energy. Even the most powerful werewolves would be tired and need time to recover, time she could use.

Mallory reached into her pocket; it wouldn't hurt to prove that she really was carrying wolfsbane. Before she could pull it out and wave it, however, the huge werewolf started to circle her. Uh-oh.

Unwilling to have a predator at her back, she spun with it, keeping its sharp teeth in sight. It wasn't moving quickly but, given her inebriation, that didn't matter. Before they'd both completed a single turn, she was feeling horrendously dizzy.

When they were only halfway through their second spin, she knew with absolute certainty that she was about to either throw up or collapse. 'Stop,' she pleaded.

The werewolf tilted its head. She fumbled with the wolfsbane in her pocket and this time managed to grab a handful and pull it out. 'I'll throw it,' she warned. She squared her shoulders and did her best to look threatening. 'I will. I'll throw it in your face and…'

The wolf lunged and for a heart-stopping moment, she was certain it would bite her – but all it did was brush the tip of its snout against her closed fist. It may not have been an attack but the surprise was enough to make her to drop the wolfsbane.

Mallory gasped and side-stepped. And the second she did, her foot slipped and she plummeted to the ground.

She braced for the impact but somehow it never happened. She found herself dangling face down, hovering an inch from the ground. For one stupid moment, she fancied that she was no longer a mere squib and, through dint of drinking whisky, had discovered magic residing with her that allowed her to fly. Then she felt the hot breath on the nape of her neck and realised that the werewolf had grabbed her and was holding the collar of her coat in its teeth.

As she twisted, the wolf released her onto the cobbles and she rolled onto her back. The damned werewolf was straddling her body. It – no, *he* – was staring at her with genuine fury. Her mouth dried. Then the werewolf's muzzle split and fur melted into skin. Suddenly she was no longer looking into golden eyes but amber ones.

'For fuck's sake, Mallory!' Alexander MacTire's handsome face was glaring at her. 'What the hell do you think you're doing?'

'Oh, it's you.' She blinked at him. 'I guess I won't be eaten after all.'

'Not for lack of trying! You reckless, foolhardy idiot! Not only is it still dark and still the full moon but you're completely wasted! How much have you had to drink?'

She smiled. 'Lots,' she said. 'Lots and lots of whisky. You know, sexy Lexy, your eyes are the exact shade of a good single malt.'

Alexander stared at her in astonishment. Then Mallory passed out completely.

THERE WERE headaches and then there were *headaches*. Mallory groaned and squeezed her eyes even more tightly shut but it didn't ease the pounding in her all-too fragile skull.

She knew she only had herself to blame; she also knew that she was far too old for hangovers of this magnitude. She ought to be counting her blessings that she'd made it home safely.

In fact, she couldn't even remember getting home. She groaned again. 'You're an idiot, Mallory,' she whispered.

'On that count, we are in perfect agreement,' Alexander MacTire's voice said.

Her eyes flew open and she shot upright, clutching the duvet. 'What are you doing here in my...' She stopped. Wait. This wasn't her duvet. It wasn't her bed. Neither was it her room.

'You're in my house,' he said. 'I brought you here after you passed out.'

Passed out? She didn't... Her shoulders sagged. Oh. She looked around. 'Is this your bedroom?' she whispered.

'Don't be silly. I've got plenty of guest rooms, Mallory. And if you think I'm the sort of man who would take advantage of a drunken woman then you've learned absolutely nothing about me.'

Actually, she didn't think he was like that at all but this was an unusual situation. She swallowed and peeked underneath the duvet.

'I took off your socks and shoes,' Alexander said, clearly exasperated. 'Otherwise you're still fully dressed.'

'Doesn't hurt to check,' she mumbled.

He folded his arms. 'What would you do if I did try something?'

Her eyes flew to his. Abruptly she had a vision of Alexander MacTire's mouth on hers, his hands on her breasts, his head then moving... *NO. Stop that, Mallory.* She coughed. 'Uh...'

'That's right,' he said, with more than an edge of disdain. 'You couldn't have done a damned thing. Do you do anything at all to look after yourself?'

She wished that her head didn't hurt so much and that he wasn't glaring at her with such ferocity. 'Can we talk about this later?'

He didn't appear to have heard her. 'The disregard you have for your own wellbeing makes me wonder if you have a death wish. Last night was the full moon! Any number of werewolves could have found you. You might be a squib, but you've lived in Coldstream long enough to know that not every wolf is experienced enough to control their beast side after they've shapeshifted. Smart people stay home! You could have been attacked, Mallory. You could have been *hurt.*'

'I had wolfsbane with me,' she told him, feeling uncharacteristically disgruntled.

'That you were too drunk to use properly! What the *fuck* were you thinking? You were so out of it that I've had to sit here for hours because I was afraid you'd choke on your own vomit.'

That last admission explained a lot, but before Mallory could respond appropriately the mention of vomit roiled her insides. She swallowed hard. It didn't do any good: nausea had completely overtaken her. 'Bathroom?' she managed.

Alexander took one look at her face and understood. 'Over there,' he pointed.

She heaved herself from the bed and ran. Her humiliation was now complete.

CHAPTER
TEN

There were two things to be thankful for: first, that Alexander had left her in peace to hug the porcelain with her clammy hands and retch up her guts and, second, that the act itself now meant she felt far better.

Mallory splashed her face with cold water, rinsed out her mouth and returned to the now-empty bedroom. In possession of greater control of her faculties than when she'd awoken, she realised that she was obviously in a guest room. Tidy, expensive and anonymous, it didn't even smell like him.

She found her shoes and socks and pulled them on then curled and uncurled her toes several times but her trick for relaxing didn't appear to be working. 'Fake it till you make it, Mal,' she muttered, then she went to look for Alexander.

Unlike the last time she'd been in the MacTire stronghold, there were people everywhere. Most of them also looked hungover, although their morning-afters were the result of post-shapeshifting shenanigans rather than whisky. She tried to recall if Alexander had looked bleary eyed but all she could remember was the fury in his amber gaze. Hey ho. She did her best to shake off her lingering embarrassment. What was done was done.

Most of the werewolves were too wrapped up in their own recoveries to pay her any attention, but some nodded at her with surprising respect. Nobody seemed shocked to see her padding around the hallways of the MacTire mansion. She started to greet everyone she saw, each greeting getting brighter as she moved further away from her hangover and shame, but when she saw the stern, leather-clad woman waiting for her at the foot of the main staircase she blanched. That was most definitely Samantha, beta of the MacTire pack and the scariest woman alive. Given the Preternaturals Mallory had got to know in recent years, that was a considerable claim.

Determined not to be intimidated and to retain her sunny sparkle, Mallory pushed away her anxiety and smiled. Although Samantha didn't smile in return, at least she didn't appear angry like Alexander had; if anything, she looked perplexed. And she certainly didn't appear to be suffering any ill-effects from the previous night. She was probably one of those were-wolves who, like Alexander, required zero recovery time.

Given that Mallory's head was still throbbing and the only thing furry about her was her tongue, she felt very jealous.

'Good morning, Ms Nash,' the woman said.

'Good morning.'

'I'm Samantha.' The ice-cool werewolf extended an elegant hand and for a moment Mallory wasn't sure whether to shake it or kiss it.

'I know who you are,' she said. 'Your reputation precedes you.'

Samantha quirked an eyebrow.

'Not from Alexander,' Mallory said hastily. 'You're well known in your own right.'

If Samantha was pleased or dismayed by that news, she

didn't show it. 'He asked you to call him Alexander,' she said thoughtfully. 'Interesting.'

Was it? 'He's pretty friendly for an alpha,' Mallory responded.

'Uh-huh.' Samantha suddenly looked amused. 'He likes you, you know.'

Mallory wasn't so sure about that, especially after the way he'd been glaring at her less than an hour ago, but she continued to smile. 'Most people do, once they get to know me.'

'I imagine likeability is important in your line of work.' Samantha's voice softened. 'What you're doing for him is incredibly important to all of us.'

Mallory eyed her dubiously. 'He's told you?'

Samantha laughed. 'Of course. Alex's choice of First Mate affects us all.'

True. Mallory relaxed slightly. 'So who do *you* think would suit him?' Samantha was his beta; she was bound to have an opinion.

'A woman who's not afraid of him would be a good start.'

'A werewolf?'

'To be honest, I'd prefer it if he chose someone who wasn't lupine.'

'Less competition?' Mallory asked.

There was a flash of surprise in Samantha's eyes but thankfully she didn't take offence. Quite the opposite. 'Other packs have had ... trouble when their alphas have taken on First Mates who are werewolves and who think they deserve a high rank simply because of who they're shagging. Not to mention that Alex doesn't always know what's best for him.'

'But you do?'

Samantha laughed again. 'I have no romantic designs on my own alpha, you can trust me on that score.' She paused. 'Regardless of my feelings about his choice of partner, he's been in an extraordinarily good mood since you arranged the date with Cathy West. Even though she's a wolf, she seems like a good fit.'

Mallory held up her hand and crossed her fingers. 'Here's hoping.'

'Whoever he chooses, she'd better make him happy.' There was a glint of furious loyalty in Samantha's green eyes. 'He deserves that much.'

Perhaps the MacTire beta wasn't so scary after all. 'He certainly does.'

They exchanged smiles. 'Come on,' Samantha said. 'I'll take you to his office.'

'Is that because you're afraid I'll slink out of here without thanking him if I don't have an escort?'

'He was worried about you.' Samantha hesitated and eyed Mallory with a brief return of her earlier perplexed expression. 'Really worried.'

Mallory felt her cheeks warm. 'I had too much to drink, that's all.'

'Mmmm.' Samantha continued to examine her, then eventually she shrugged. 'It happens to the best of us.'

They walked down the hallway towards Alexander's study. The door was already ajar. Although Samantha raised her fist to knock, he was clearly aware of their presence and he called out before her hand connected with the wood, 'Bring her in.'

Mallory grimaced. He still sounded annoyed.

She was expecting Samantha to walk in with her but instead she nudged Mallory inside and closed the door, leaving her alone with the MacTire alpha. It wasn't ideal; between scary Samantha and angry Alexander, the former definitely seemed the preferable choice. There was only so much disapproval Mallory could take.

He was sitting behind his massive desk. She walked to the

centre of the room and faced him, took a deep breath and then faltered; either she was in a different room to last time or he'd been doing some decorating.

The curtains had been changed; rather than an oppressive dark brocade, they were now a light-grey velvet which shimmered in the midday sun. The walls were no longer a murky green; they'd been given a lick of bright paint so they reflected light rather than absorbing it. At her feet was a fluffy orange rug. There were even four vases of flowers dotted around, their fragrant scent mingling with Alexander's cinnamon and spice aftershave.

'Oh.' Mallory blinked. 'You've redecorated.'

'I took your advice.'

'It looks good.'

He inclined his head. 'I'm glad you approve.' He gestured to a silver tray on the desk. 'Coffee? And a bacon roll? It'll help with your hangover.'

'You're amazing.'

'I know,' he replied dryly.

She helped herself. 'I was expecting another scolding.'

He growled, 'You need another scolding. But as it would be inappropriate for me to put you across my knee and spank you, I thought I'd take a different approach.' She stared at him in mid-bite. 'Have a seat, Mallory,' he went on. 'It makes me nervous watching you hover by my desk like that.'

She managed a grin. 'Because I intimidate you?'

'Because only a few hours ago you collapsed in front of me and I'd rather not repeat the experience.'

She considered his words and decided that a chair wouldn't be a bad thing. Mallory sat down, swallowed her mouthful and gave him a long look. 'First of all, while I appreciate your concern and I'm grateful for your help, I don't need to be scolded like a child. I'm an adult and last night I was actually being very sensible.'

'Really.' Alexander's voice was flat.

'It's true!' She gulped a mouthful of coffee. 'I don't have to explain myself to you but, for what it's worth, I had to go out for work. I ended up stuck inside a pub on Hirsel Street. Given the full moon, it wasn't wise to head home during the darkest hours so I waited until it was almost sunrise.'

'Dawn hadn't broken when I found you.'

'It wasn't far off. The likelihood of meeting any werewolves who couldn't control their basic instincts was practically nil. And,' she pointed out, 'I *did* have wolfsbane with me for emergencies.'

'Which you couldn't use,' he shot back. 'You were completely legless.'

'Not completely. I'd have reached home with no problems if I'd not bumped into you.'

'That's up for debate.' His eyes narrowed. 'Who were you drinking with? I know it wasn't Liam Ferguson because he'd have been furry and on all fours.'

'Liam Ferguson has nothing to do with this and it's none of your business who I was with. I don't go blabbing about you to other clients and I'm not going to start blabbing about them to you.' She sighed. 'I know that you mean well, but my wellbeing is not your responsibility. I would've been fine if you hadn't started spinning around me like a whirling dervish.'

'Hardly a dervish! Besides, it's in my interests to ensure your safety while you work for me.'

Mallory opened her mouth but he didn't give her time to speak.

'I'm an alpha, Mallory. It's in my nature. Telling me off for wanting to look after you is like telling off a scorpion for stinging.'

'That analogy is surprisingly apt.'

Alexander pulled a face. 'And what analogy would suit *you*?' He tapped his mouth as if seriously considering the question. 'Terrible diet, high maintenance...'

'I'm not high maintenance!'

He ignored her. 'And you have an absurd propensity to throw yourself into dangerous situations that you can't handle.'

'I didn't throw myself into a dangerous situation!'

Alexander waved a lazy hand around the room. 'You're here alone with me, aren't you?'

Mallory's mouth was suddenly dry. She swallowed then did her best to recover. 'Well, there's a simple solution to that, isn't there?'

'Tie you up so you never escape my clutches?'

She met his gaze head on. Screw it: Alexander MacTire was proving far more trouble than he was worth. She wouldn't break the contract between them – but he could. 'Declare our contract null and void, then I'll be out of your hair for good.'

'I'm certainly not going to do that,' he said silkily. 'Especially when we're finally making headway.'

'Huh?'

'My date with Cathy West is in three days' time,' he reminded her. 'But I've been thinking about what you said the other night and I believe I need some extra ... support.'

Mallory frowned. 'Support?'

'I think you were right. I'm intimidated by smart women and I don't know how to talk to them. I rely too heavily on my looks and my status, and I'm not particularly skilled at first dates.'

She gaped at him. Of all the turns she'd expected this conversation to take, an admission like that from Alexander MacTire was not one of them.

He regarded her seriously. 'It's clear that I need extra coaching.'

'Extra coaching?'

'Yep. The practice run at the Imbolc event was a good idea but I need more practice. I think we should spend the next couple of days together – high-intensity training.' His eyes gleamed. 'Make me Mr Right, Mallory Nash.'

'I'm going to need stronger coffee before I can even begin to think about this.'

'I'll make it worth your while.' He smiled but there was an edge to his expression that Mallory couldn't quite decipher. 'In return for your extra help, I will help you.'

She couldn't suppress a flicker of suspicion. 'How?'

'Self-defence training. You don't have magic to rely on but you do have a habit of getting yourself into trouble.'

'No, I don't!' she protested. 'I'm very careful.'

MacTire stood up, moved from behind his desk and stepped towards her. 'So if I came at you right now? If I grabbed hold of your arm,' he reached out and gripped her upper arm lightly in his right hand, 'and pulled you towards me,' he did just that, pulling her gently out of the chair until her body was pressed against his, 'and moved my teeth towards your exposed neck...'

Mallory could feel his hot breath against her skin. Her heart rate had ratcheted up and she was brutally aware of the feel of his body against hers. She licked her lips.

She twisted slightly. 'You seem to forget that I'm holding a cup of coffee,' she said. 'If you did that, I'd fling the contents in your face. The coffee is still hot. Would you like me to demonstrate?'

Alexander released her and stepped back. 'That won't be necessary.'

She snorted and tried to regulate her breathing. 'Sure?'

'Quite sure.' He adjusted his cuffs. 'But you won't always be holding a hot drink.'

She shrugged. 'I might be a squib, but I'm not a weak damsel in distress. I've managed perfectly well for more than thirty years.'

He held up his hands. 'It's your choice. I thought self-defence classes might be something you could benefit from, but I'm certainly not forcing them on you. It was actually Samantha who suggested them, and they seemed a fair trade-off for more help with my dating technique. But we can come to another arrangement, if you prefer.'

As much as Alexander's approach unbalanced her, self-defence coaching from a werewolf might be a good idea. Mallory pursed her lips. It would be a distraction from searching for a bellarmine jug; a few days' break might help her to look at Chester Longchamps' problem with fresh eyes and she could always instruct Boris to keep searching.

'No,' she said aloud. 'It's a good idea. I'll have to make arrangements for my other clients first, but I can come back this afternoon to make a start.'

Something akin to triumph flared in Alexander's expression. 'Fabulous,' he murmured. 'You can stay in the same guest room until the weekend. It'll save you time commuting. This is win-win for both of us.'

CHAPTER

ELEVEN

By the time Mallory had returned home, showered, packed a small bag with enough clothes to see her till the end of the week and spoken to a sniffy Boris, she felt like a new person.

'I'm never drinking again,' she declared.

'Uh-huh.'

'Okay,' she conceded, 'I'm never drinking *whisky* again. And I'm certainly never getting that drunk again.'

'Until the next time you need something from Salty Miller,' Boris scoffed. 'It's not even as if he was any help – meeting him was a total waste of time. And Alan North and Freda Vargas were no use. I've spoken to both of them and they can't help.'

Mallory wasn't deterred. 'There will be an empty bellarmine jug somewhere in Coldstream. Several, probably. It's simply a case of finding one.' She grinned.

'I'll do my best,' he said dubiously, though his expression suggested his best wouldn't be good enough.

'That's all I can ask.' Her grin widened. 'As long as we all do our best, there's no such thing as failure.'

'You sound like a motivational slogan hanging on the wall above the fireplace of a twee cottage in the Cotswolds.'

'Live, laugh, love, Boris.'

He rolled his eyes. 'There are two client contracts that have almost come to an end. What do you want to do about them while you're off playing with werewolves?'

'Oh. Uh…' Mallory tried to think of anything she needed other than the magical jug. 'Perhaps one of them could provide coffee? There's none left in the flat.'

'Coffee?'

She shrugged. 'It's what I need.'

The spriggan clicked his tongue. 'Anything else?'

'Nothing's coming to mind.'

'What about the Wolf Ball?'

Mallory gave him a blank look. 'What about it?'

He raised his eyebrows patiently. 'You've agreed to attend it with His Furry Highness. What are you planning to wear?'

She hadn't given it a moment's thought until now but she suddenly had an inkling as to what Boris meant. 'Does Gia Vanderlan happen to be one of those clients who is running out of time?'

He smiled approvingly. 'Yes. You helped her source black jade last year so she could complete a design for a Fae prince.'

'I remember. How long is left on her contract?'

'Twenty days.' Boris looked at her pointedly.

'Perfect. Ask her to conjure me up a dress for the Wolf Ball. It doesn't need to be fancy or anything. I don't want to draw too much attention to myself.' She patted his shoulder. 'Good thinking!'

He shook his head slowly. 'How did you ever manage before I came along?'

She beamed. 'It's a genuine mystery!'

He sighed. 'You will be careful with that damned wolf,

won't you? I swear he's up to something with the offer of these lessons.'

'Alexander MacTire can be a bit tetchy but he's a good guy.'

'If you say so, Mallory.'

'I do. Understanding people and their needs is what I do.'

'And what does Alexander MacTire need?'

'The love of a good woman. And in three days' time, when he has a date with Cathy West, he might achieve it.' There was an odd twinge in the centre of her chest as she said those words.

Boris tilted his head. 'Fingers crossed,' he muttered.

Mallory's smile was a fraction too bright. 'Indeed.'

MALLORY'S entire flat could have fitted inside the MacTire fitness suite three times over. There was a large area for sparring, several running machines, and complicated looking weights machines. A door to the right opened to a sauna while another led to a lap pool. There were two changing rooms. There was an array of small jars along one wall, each neatly labelled with the names of various magicked concoctions, and a special warded area for practising with them. Every single thing had been thought of; it was truly extraordinary.

Mallory whistled. 'Wow.'

Alexander, dressed in loose sweats and a tight T-shirt, was observing her. 'It's important to stay in shape and be prepared for anything. I like to work out for an hour or two before break-fast, and I encourage the other MacTire werewolves to maintain a healthy regime.'

She gave him a mock salute. 'Sir! Yessir!'

He rolled his eyes. 'You should tie back your hair or it'll get in the way.'

Mallory patted her springy curls. 'I'll try, but my hair doesn't tend to obey orders.'

Alexander flashed a grin. 'Par for the course considering you don't obey my orders.'

'I'm not yours to order,' she told him, but she found a scrunchie in the bottom of her bag and did her best to tame her curls into temporary submission. One could only try.

As she took up position at the side of a mat, Alexander wheeled over a dummy. 'We'll practise on this to begin with.'

Mallory eyed its blank face. 'What's his name?'

'He doesn't have a name. He's a dummy.'

She gasped and covered its non-existent ears. 'Shh. You'll hurt Kevin's feelings.'

'Kevin?'

'If you'd rather call him something else...'

Alexander was already shaking his head. 'Kevin is fine. Now,' he instructed, 'imagine that the dummy is threatening you.'

'Kevin, you mean.'

'Whatever. Kevin is threatening you.'

Mallory pouted. 'Kevin is mean.'

'Very.' He pointed at the dummy. 'He's coming at you and there's nobody around to help. What are you going to do?'

Mallory considered the matter. Then she shrugged, twisted her body to face Kevin and kicked him hard in his stuffed groin. 'Now Kevin is crying.'

Alexander blinked rapidly. 'I think I might be crying on his behalf, too. That was a good move, Mallory. Do you have anything else?'

She slammed the base of her palm into Kevin's head and the dummy fell backwards. 'Don't bother me again, Kevin!' she yelled. 'I'm friends with Alexander MacTire. I'll tell him about you and next time he'll bite you!'

She looked up at Alexander, who was gazing at her with an odd look on his face. 'We're friends now?' he asked.

Mallory shrugged and returned her attention to the dummy. 'I'm *not* friends with Alexander MacTire, but he'll still bite you because he's an over-protective alpha!'

Alexander hissed and she grinned. 'Alright,' she said. 'We're friends. But stop shouting at Kevin.'

'Okay.'

He picked up Kevin and returned him to his original position by the wall. Mallory shook her fist. 'Nobody puts Kevin in the corner!'

'Let's forget about Kevin,' Alexander said dryly. He moved to one of the doors and pulled it open. 'Out you come,' he said. A moment later his nephew Nick appeared.

The teenager grinned awkwardly. 'Hi, Mallory!'

'Hi, Nick.' She glanced questioningly at Alexander.

'You can beat up a dummy, but can you beat up a real person?' he asked.

'Nick?' Mallory squeaked. 'He's a kid! I'm not going to beat him up.'

'Nick is young but he's still a werewolf. Before I put you up against someone stronger, I thought it would be wise to try you against someone your own size.'

She looked at the boy dubiously; Nick might be young but he was at least a foot taller than Mallory.

'He's the best I could get on short notice,' Alexander continued as he pointed them to opposite sides of the room.

'I've been practising, Mallory,' Nick assured her. 'I won't hurt you much.'

'Much?'

'He knows what he's doing. Now concentrate. You're walking down the street. Nick is coming towards you and it's clear he's planning to attack.'

Nick pasted on a mock-angry expression and clenched his fists. 'What's your first thought, Mallory?'

'Avoid him.'

'Good instinct.'

She nodded and turned away to walk in the opposite direction.

'Nick is on a mission and you have no choice but to defend yourself,' Alexander went on. 'He's coming from behind. What's your plan now?'

Mallory paused. 'I can't get away?'

'No.'

'He's definitely going to attack me?'

'Yes.'

She thought about it, then turned and swung her fist at Nick's head. He dodged it easily – but what he didn't see was her right foot snaking out and connecting with his ankle. He yelled sharply and collapsed onto the mat with a thud.

Mallory winced. 'Oops. Sorry, Nick. I tried not to kick you too hard.' She held out a hand to help him up.

'I'm alright.' He glanced at his uncle. 'I don't think Mallory needs self-defence lessons.'

Alexander frowned. 'You can go, Nick. Thanks for your help.'

'Any time you need a punchbag, give me a shout,' he said.

Both Mallory and Alexander winced. 'Sorry, Nick,' she apologised again.

'I didn't mean for that to happen,' Alexander told him.

'You mean you wanted *me* to be the punchbag?' Mallory asked.

Alexander ground his teeth. 'Nobody is a punchbag!'

'Apart from Kevin,' she pointed out.

Nick's eyes widened. 'Who's Kevin?'

Alexander ran a hand through his hair. 'No one. Grab a shower, Nick. If you need a doctor...'

Nick made a show of limping badly and groaning, then laughed and straightened up. 'I'm not hurt, honest.'

Mallory breathed a sigh of relief that she'd not done the poor boy any real damage and watched him leave the room. As soon as he'd gone, Alexander turned to her. His expression didn't give much away but eventually he nodded and walked to the opposite side of the mat. He gestured to Mallory to return to her original position.

'Are you the bad guy now?' she asked.

'I am Kevin. I won't hold back.'

'Okay.'

'I mean it, Mallory. A real attacker wouldn't hold back and neither will I.'

'Okay,' she repeated, smiling brightly.

Alexander started to stalk towards her, his muscles tense, his eyes sharply focussed. She gave him a little wave and strolled forward to meet him. His arm snapped out and he grabbed her right wrist. Mallory thrust her left hand across her body and jabbed his eye with lightning speed.

He recoiled and released her. 'That was effective,' he grunted. 'But what if I do this?' He lunged for her again and twisted her around until he had her pinned in a bear hug, her spine pressed against his chest.

Mallory didn't hesitate. She dropped her weight and spread her legs wide before swinging her hips first left and then swiftly right. She hooked one leg around his ankle then crouched lower until she could free enough of her arms to grab his knees and yank them hard enough to shove him away.

He came at her again and reached for her hair, which was already escaping the scrunchie. Mallory ducked away in the nick of time. Alexander's eyes darkened.

'I did tell you I could look after myself. Although it helps that I'm sober,' she admitted ruefully.

'You've had training.'

She shrugged. 'I'm a squib in Coldstream – of course I've had training, though I'm not dippy enough to believe my skills are foolproof. You said you wouldn't hold back but you're obviously doing just that.'

Alexander growled, 'I don't want to hurt you.'

'I'm not made of glass.' Mallory pulled away the irritatingly loose scrunchie and shook out her curls. Alexander's nostrils flared and a split second later there was an explosion of colour as he leapt towards her, not as a man but as a wolf.

Mallory was so shocked that she froze. Before she could draw breath, his massive front paws landed on her shoulders and knocked her backwards. She fell onto the mat with the huge werewolf on top of her, his yellow eyes piercing into her soul while his hot breath scalded her cheek.

'I didn't know that was possible,' she whispered. 'I didn't know you could transform like that.' The full moon was only hours behind them, but she was still astonished. 'Okay, you've made your point. I can defend myself against someone on two legs but I don't know what to do when I'm faced with four.'

He didn't react even though his snout was barely an inch from her nose.

Mallory licked her lips. 'Uh, Alex?'

He blinked and sprang away. There was another colour explosion and she caught a brief glimpse of smooth human skin before he vanished through the door leading to the male changing room and she was left alone.

CHAPTER

TWELVE

After her second shower of the day, Mallory sat on the edge of the guest bed thinking about Alexander's astonishing transformation.

Samantha came to fetch her. 'The boss has asked you to join him for dinner. Apparently you're coaching him through it or something?' The beta werewolf shrugged. 'Last time I checked he could hold a knife and fork and maintain a sensible conversation, but it's not my place to question my betters.' From the look on her face, that's exactly what she was doing.

Deciding that it would be a good idea to have the scary beta on board, Mallory explained. 'He's too alpha.'

Samantha's eyebrows shot up. '*Too* alpha? Isn't that what women like?'

Mallory snorted. 'Is that what *you* like?'

'Well, no – but I can't speak for everyone.'

'A fantasy boyfriend can be deliciously alpha,' Mallory said. 'But a real boyfriend – a real-life partner – should be someone who is confident and sexy but who also treats you like an equal and is nurturing and kind.'

Samantha didn't blink. 'Alex is all of those things.'

125

'So why aren't *you* his girlfriend?'

'Ugh. It would be like dating my bossy older brother.'

Mallory snapped her fingers. '*Bossy*. There you go.'

'He has to be bossy – he's the damned boss.'

'I'm not trying to change his personality or his alpha position, I just want him to show more of his vulnerable side and to think carefully about what he really wants in a partner. Does he want someone to order around or does he want someone to share his life?' Mallory shrugged. 'If it's the former, then okay. I'll adjust my search parameters.'

'Alex doesn't want a doormat. He's not like that.' This time Mallory stayed quiet and Samantha filled in the silence. 'That's not what he needs. And certainly not what *we* need as First Mate.'

Mallory thought about what he'd told her earlier in the day. 'Is Alexander intimidated by smart women?'

Samantha gaped. 'Definitely not!'

'Does he know how to talk to women?'

'Yes! Believe me, Alex can charm the knickers off almost any woman he sets his sights on.'

'So why hasn't he settled down yet?'

'It's not a personality defect,' the werewolf said defensively. 'He's just not met the right woman.' Her eyes narrowed a fraction as she stared at Mallory.

'What is it?'

Samantha shook her head. 'Nothing.'

Mallory stood up. 'Well, I hope I can help him find who he's looking for.' She smiled. 'Are you escorting me again?'

'Just showing you the way. This is a big place. You might get lost.'

Mallory nibbled her bottom lip as they descended the grand staircase. She wasn't sure whether to broach the subject or not, but this was good intel and it would help her cause in the future if she knew the answer. 'Samantha,' she hedged.

'Yes?'

'Earlier today when we were in the gym, Alexander changed.'

'He doesn't work out in a suit, Mallory. Sometimes he wears sweats.'

'That's not what I mean. He *changed* – not his clothes but his skin. I know it was the full moon last night but I thought werewolves returned to human form once dawn broke. Alexander seemed to shapeshift at will.'

Even the most self-absorbed person would have noticed Samantha's sudden tension. 'What time did this happen?'

'Maybe around four?'

Samantha scowled.

'Can all werewolves do that?' Mallory persisted. 'Is it something you keep secret from the rest of the world?'

'Definitely not. Ninety-nine percent of werewolves can only shapeshift from dusk till dawn during the night of the full moon. Only a very few can shapeshift outside those hours.'

'Can you?'

'Not a chance. And that is one of the many reasons why Alex is so special,' she said softly. Then she clammed up and said nothing more.

SOME ENTERPRISING MACTIRE werewolf who was keen to suck up to the boss had arranged a table for two in the back garden next to a heat lamp that held the chilly evening air at bay. To be fair, Mallory reckoned calling the beautifully landscaped, perfectly pruned verdant vision a 'back garden' was a misnomer It deserved a grander moniker – 'botanical oasis', perhaps. Or 'estate park'.

Alexander caught her wide-eyed stare. 'Impressive, isn't it? A few older MacTire members are keen gardeners. There's a kitchen garden beyond the fountain that we use as well.'

Doubtless there were also plenty of magical plants dotted around. 'No silphium?' she asked archly, referencing the lost magical plant that had led her to Alexander at Vallese in the first place.

He barked a quick laugh. 'No, alas, no silphium. Although from what I hear, Kit McCafferty solved that particular problem all by herself and soon Coldstream will abound with the stuff. Of course, my lips remain sealed on the matter to anyone other than you and her.'

Mallory grinned. 'Of course.'

'Shall I pull out your chair for you?' he asked. 'Or is that being too overbearing?'

She gave him a mock-exasperated glare and he smirked. He pulled back one of the elegant chairs with a flourish and Mallory sat down, making a show of looking prim and proper.

'Wait.' Alexander frowned. 'We need to backtrack. Stand up.'

'Pardon?'

'Stand up. We need to take this back. I'm meeting Cathy at the restaurant. If I'm there before her and she walks in, how do I act?'

'You know what to do, Alexander. You've done it a million times before.'

'I want to get it right. I know to stand up when she comes towards me, to smile and tell her she looks wonderful. But do I take her coat? Kiss her hand? Kiss her cheek? Shake her hand?'

'You're over-thinking. Do what feels right in the moment.'

He shook his head. 'Let's practise. I want to get this right,' he repeated.

She looked at him suspiciously, certain that she was being played, but his expression appeared honest. She stood up and moved back several feet while he sat down in his chair again. 'Okay,' she said. 'I'm walking into the restaurant towards the table.'

On cue, he rose. 'You look beautiful.'

Mallory inclined her head. 'Thank you.'

He took her hand, raised it to his mouth and pressed his lips against her skin with a faint slurping sound. Mallory giggled. 'What?' he asked, sounding annoyed.

'Nothing!'

'Mallory...'

'It just feels a bit silly and over the top – but Cathy might like it.'

'You've researched her. You already know what she'll like.'

True. 'Okay. Don't kiss her hand. It's too old-fashioned and it won't put her at ease.'

'Fine,' Alexander said. 'Back up and let's try again.'

Mallory returned to her starting point then walked forward. Alexander stood up from his chair. 'You look wonderful,' he said.

'Thank you. You look good, too.'

They stood a foot apart, staring awkwardly at each other. After a moment or two, he cleared his throat. 'Please,' he said. 'Sit down.'

Mallory looked at him flatly. 'That was too weird.'

'Yes,' he agreed. 'Not that. Let's try another approach.'

She'd half-turned when she caught a glimmer of amusement in his eyes. 'I knew it! You're making fun of me. You're perfectly capable of playing the role of suave gentleman!'

'As you've been telling me, I shouldn't be playing any role. I should be trying to be myself, my vulnerable self.'

'Touché.' Mallory raised a finger. 'But you've still been playing me.'

The corners of his mouth curled upwards. 'A little. It was just too tempting.'

'Yeah, yeah.'

'Tell you what,' he said. 'Let's start again from the very beginning. I'll act as much like me as I can and try not to be too much of the alpha that annoys you so much. If I get anything wrong, you can point it out, otherwise we'll let the evening run its course. Good enough?'

Mallory released a breath. 'Perfect.'

She backed up. When she walked forward, Alexander's gaze was long and smouldering; it was so heated and held so much smoky promise that her breath caught in her throat.

'Mallory, I'm so glad you're here,' he said. 'I've been thinking about you all day. I'm not normally an impatient man but this evening and this meal couldn't come fast enough.'

She was certain that she should respond and that Cathy would have said something, but for some reason her mind was completely blank. 'Uh…'

Alexander smiled knowingly and dipped his head to brush his lips against her cheek. 'You know, I can recognise your scent from a thousand paces.'

She couldn't stop herself. 'What do I smell like?' she whispered.

'Honey,' he said. 'Sunshine.' He grinned. 'And magic.'

Mallory blinked rapidly. He wasn't talking to *her*, he was talking to Cathy. Mallory was a squib; if there was one thing she didn't smell like, it was magic. Focus, she told herself. This is business, not pleasure.

'You have a good nose.' Then, because she needed to put

some distance between them, she sat down quickly before he could pull out her chair. He continued to smile as he sat opposite her.

Nick appeared wearing jeans, a white T-shirt – and a bow-tie. 'Good evening, I will be your waiter this evening. Would you like to hear the specials?'

Alexander raised his eyebrows at her. 'Um, yes?' she said.

'Roasted tomato soup, beef wellington with dauphinoise potatoes and creamed spinach, and lemon tart to finish.'

'Seriously?'

Alexander leaned back in his chair. 'We like to eat well after the full moon, it's something of a tradition. And I dread to think how long it's been since you ate a proper meal.'

'I eat!'

'On the go and in a rush. Tonight you'll have the time to savour every mouthful. And we have a decent wine cellar. What would you like to drink?'

Mallory shuddered; the morning's hangover was still fresh in her memory. 'Water, please.'

'You can have whatever you desire.'

Her mouth was suddenly very dry. 'Definitely water.'

Nick nodded. 'I have arranged a special amuse bouche for you.' He opened a bag of salt-and-vinegar crisps and tipped one onto the plate in front of Mallory and one onto the plate in front of Alexander. They both stared at his offering. 'Too much?' he asked with an arch wink.

'Too much,' Alexander agreed. 'Off you go.' The teenager grinned and loped away.

'He's a good kid,' Mallory said.

'He is. He's been through a lot but he's coming out the other side. You know his parents died in an accident?' Mallory nodded. 'I was close to Nick's mum – my sister – when we were growing up. Have I mentioned my bastard of a father?'

'Yes,' she said softly.

'Partly because of him, Andrea and I stuck close to each other, for comfort as much as physical safety. As soon as she was old enough, Andrea couldn't wait to get out of Coldstream. She wasn't interested in being a werewolf – she'd have ripped that part out of her body if she could have done. For a long time we barely spoke, not because we'd argued but because we simply drifted apart. We were just starting to regain our old relationship when she died.'

As he drew in a breath and looked away, Mallory realised how difficult this was for him. He was trying to open up, to show his more vulnerable side; he really was much more than just his job title.

'I'm so sorry, Alexander.'

He smiled wanly. 'Thank you.'

'What was your sister like?'

'Nothing like me.' His smile grew warmer. 'She was fun loving and not afraid to say exactly what she thought. People always think I'm the strong one in the family but it was her. She wasn't afraid of anything.' He glanced at her. 'You remind me of her.'

'I always wanted a sister,' she said. 'I was an only child.'

'Are your parents still around?'

'No.' She sighed, though it wasn't an unhappy sound. 'They were lovely people and I had a really happy childhood. They never quite understood my fascination with Preternaturals and Coldstream, but they knew I wanted to live here and they were happy for me when I found my place here. They visited a few times before they passed, but I usually went to see them. They found Coldstream quite unnerving.'

Alexander examined her with frank curiosity. 'Do you wish you had magic?'

'Sometimes.' Mallory shrugged. 'In the same way that I

sometimes wish my hair was poker straight or I was good at maths or better at organising myself.'

'You shouldn't.' He cleared his throat. 'You're already perfect as you are.'

Mallory smiled. 'Thank you, Alex. So are you.' His eyes crinkled with pleasure. 'And you're already getting top marks for tonight, even though we've not even had the starters. Be this version of yourself with Cathy and she'll be completely charmed.'

A muscle jerked in his cheek. 'Have I charmed *you*?'

Far, far too much. Mallory continued to smile and answered lightly, 'Absolutely. You've rocketed to the top of the class.'

THE NEXT FEW days passed in a blur. Although she'd proved she was more capable than her squib status suggested, Mallory had several sessions with Samantha and some other MacTire werewolves to improve her self-defence techniques. It was good to brush up on old skills and she learned far more about what werewolves were capable of during the full moon. Each session confirmed that Alexander had been right; she should never have ventured out during those dark hours. She wouldn't tell him that, of course, and in any case he stayed away from the gym. She tried not to wonder why.

Mallory had dealt with numerous werewolf clients over the years and counted several of them as friends, but she'd never spent this much time in their company and she marvelled at the intricate relationships they formed as a result of being part of a pack.

There were forty-one members of the MacTire pack, including Alexander, although only a dozen or so of them lived in the main stronghold. They treated each other like siblings even though not all of them were blood relatives and there were vast differences in age. It was akin to being part of the Waltons if the fictional family had been larger in size, considerably more sweary and turned furry once a month.

'No, not the Waltons. Think of us as more like the Medicis,' said Hannah, one of the younger werewolves who'd joined the MacTires with her mother from a failing wolf pack almost a decade ago. 'Dynastical, powerful and,' she pulled a face, 'occasionally corrupt.'

Mallory blinked. 'Corrupt?'

'Not now Alex is in charge,' she said. 'But in the past...' Her voice trailed off. She was referring to Alexander's father and possibly others who were also long gone. Mallory nodded her understanding.

Hannah twisted her fingers. 'It was my mother who made the decision to join the MacTires. I didn't get a say in the matter.'

Mallory chose her next words carefully; she sensed that the younger woman needed someone to talk to who wouldn't judge her for her darker thoughts. If Hannah wanted to confide in someone, she was prepared to listen. 'Do you wish things had turned out differently?' she asked softly. 'Do you wish you weren't a MacTire wolf?'

Hannah took a long moment before answering. 'Not really, but sometimes I wonder about the road less travelled, about what some of the MacTires were doing before we joined up and if you can rub away the stains of what's gone before. I'm happy here but...' Her eyes were sad. 'What if everything changes again? Some of the things that happened here were truly despicable.'

'I've seen nothing about the MacTire pack that suggests anything other than deep-seated camaraderie.' Mallory hugged her briefly. 'You can't let the past steal your present, Hannah.'

The girl smiled faintly. 'That sounds like something Alex would say.'

Something twanged deep in Mallory's chest. 'The easiest way to make sure your mother made the right decision for both of you is to make sure your voice is always heard.'

Hannah chewed a fingernail. 'I thought about suggesting a monthly forum where the less powerful members of the pack could have their say.'

Mallory considered. 'No, not monthly. For it to have substance, you need to meet more often than that. Make it weekly and divide it into two sections. Meet on your own first so everyone can talk freely, then for the last fifteen minutes invite Alex or Samantha or whoever so you can tell them your concerns.'

Her eyes widened. 'That's a good idea. Do you think he'd go for it?'

'Why don't you ask him and find out?'

HANNAH HAD OBVIOUSLY TAKEN her advice. When Mallory met Alexander later for another prep session, he told her Hannah had come by earlier with an idea for a forum to give the weaker members of the pack a chance to say what they were really thinking.

'What do you think of it?' Mallory asked.

'It's a great idea. I've been trying to think of ways to allow everyone's voices to be heard and by coming to me with this proposal she's already achieved that. Thank you for encouraging her,' he said quietly.

It took some time before the glow inside her subsided, even when their conversation turned to the nitty-gritty of his forthcoming date. They discussed what topics of conversation should be avoided, namely any mention of werewolf politics or past relationships, and what he wanted to ask Cathy about. When he produced a list that included questions on her plans for the future, her strengths, weaknesses and how she would deal with pack conflict, Mallory had to persuade him that it wasn't a job interview. 'Keep it light-hearted and fun. It's a first date,' she told him firmly.

'These are things I need to know,' he argued. 'I'm not looking for a roll in the hay, I want a life partner. And how do I keep things light-hearted and fun whilst also showing her that I'm vulnerable?'

'Don't put on an alpha façade.'

'It's not a façade!'

Mallory sighed. 'This is making me want to gouge my eyes out with a spoon.'

Alexander raised his eyebrows. 'Don't do that. You'll need your sight later to critique my appearance.'

'I'm not the person to do that, Alexander.' She gestured to herself. 'I have frizzy hair and I wear patchwork clothes in bright colours while you...' Her voice trailed away.

His expression turned studiously blank. 'Me, what?'

'You're ... you.'

'What does that mean?'

She drew in a breath. 'You never have a hair out of place, your stubble is designer and your clothes are professionally tailored in shades that complement your skin tone.'

'You don't like the way I look?'

'I didn't say that.'

He reached up and mussed his hair. 'How about now?'

Mallory gave him an exasperated look, though his ruffled hair gave him a raffish air that only highlighted his handsome face.

When she saw him next, he was wearing a brightly coloured

T-shirt with a rainbow unicorn emblazoned on its front. 'Andrea bought it for me as a present a few years ago,' he said smugly.

'She bought it as a joke, right?'

'Or because sparkles suit me.'

Mallory smiled serenely. 'They do suit you. You should wear that on your date.'

His amber eyes danced. 'Do you want me to fail?'

She clicked her tongue and didn't let herself think about the question, not even for a moment.

Unsurprisingly, on the night of the date he dressed in a charcoal-grey suit and white shirt. 'Well?' he asked. 'Do I pass muster?'

'Absolutely. The colour suits you and a suit is an uncontroversial choice.'

'You mean boring.'

'I didn't *say* boring and I didn't *mean* boring. It's perfectly appropriate. You look great. Now, remember everything we've talked about. Don't be afraid to ask Cathy on a second date or to invite her to be your companion for the Wolf Ball. She could be the one for you. This could be the start of the rest of your life.'

Alexander gave her a sideways look. 'Too melodramatic?' she asked.

'Too cheesy.'

'I love cheesy!'

'I'm not even remotely surprised,' he said drily. 'Will you wait up so we can discuss how the date went when I get back?'

'Sorry, Alex, I can't stay any longer. Now that your date is actually happening, I'm going home. I've got work to do.' Work which she'd been ignoring for far too long.

He frowned.

'I have other clients.' Mallory wondered why she felt a tad guilty about not being there for him later; after all, she'd already spent far more time with Alexander MacTire than she'd intended to. 'The past few days have been great but I've been neglecting my business. Besides,' she added gently, 'if things go well tonight, you don't want me hanging around and cramping your style.' His frown deepened. 'Cathy might get the wrong idea about us.'

Alexander's eyes pierced her. 'Why would she get any idea at all about us? What could make her think there's something between me and you?'

'Nothing,' Mallory said. 'There's nothing. But all the same, it's better if I'm out of the way.'

'With your other clients.'

'Yes.'

'Do you stay at their houses, too?'

Mallory tightened her toes. 'No. Not usually.'

He gazed at her for a long moment then dipped his head towards hers. 'Mallory—'

'The car's here!' Nick called from the door. 'You look great, Uncle Sandy!'

Alexander stepped back. 'I have repeatedly told you not to call me that, Nicholas.'

'Yeah, yeah. Come on. If you don't go now, you'll be late.'

Alexander looked at Mallory. 'He's right,' she murmured. 'Have a great time. I'm keeping my fingers crossed for you. Cathy is an amazing woman – you'd be as lucky to have her as she'd be to have you.'

His eyes searched her face for another moment. 'Yeah,' he said finally. 'I'll come to your place tomorrow and let you know how it goes.'

She nodded. 'You'll have to tell me if my presence at the Wolf Ball is no longer required.' She kept her tone light, but Alexander nodded soberly in return.

Seconds later, he was gone.

CHAPTER

THIRTEEN

When she finally got home, the flat felt very quiet and very empty. Mallory might have only been at the MacTire stronghold for a few days but she'd grown used to the hustle and bustle of dozens of werewolves constantly coming and going.

'It's good to finally get some peace,' she said loudly. Her voice echoed around her empty living room. She wrinkled her nose and started flicking through the letters and notes that had been left at her door.

There were four letters from Chester Longchamps, which was quite a feat given that she'd only been away for three days. She sighed; no prizes for guessing what he wanted. She supposed she ought to show willing either way and read them. He was an important client and his favour was definitely a work in progress.

The first letter was a rolled-up scroll sealed with scarlet wax. Mallory thumbed it open to reveal headed notepaper with Longchamps' name and address. As she read the looping, handwritten script, she noted with grim amusement that he styled himself as 'lord'.

. . .

DEAREST MALLORY,

I trust this finds you in good health and warm spirits.

I assume that you are not at home as you are out seeking a bellarmine jug. I would very much appreciate it if you could keep me updated daily on the search. I have full faith in your capabilities and I expect you will locate a bellarmine jug for me by the end of the week.

Kindest regards,
Lord Chester Longchamps

MALLORY PURSED HER LIPS. Although the message was pointed, his language was polite and there was no indication of the rage he'd directed at her during their last meeting. She reached for the second letter, which was in a normal envelope albeit addressed in the same handwriting using the same ink.

DEAR MALLORY,

I am concerned that you have not been in touch with me as agreed. Update me ASAP on your search for a bellarmine jug.

Regards,
Chester Longchamps

MALLORY GLANCED at the date at the top of the page: he'd left it two days earlier. Uh-oh. With a sense of foreboding, she picked up the third note. It wasn't in an envelope; in fact, it was nothing more than a folded piece of paper. The ink was also different.

As she squinted at it, she realised he'd scrawled his words in blood. For goodness' sake. The idiot vampire was making a point – and it wasn't a particularly subtle one.

MALLORY,

 What is happening? Where is my jug?
 Chester

SHE ALREADY HAD an inkling what the fourth letter would say and the smart move would have been to discard it without reading it, but unfortunately Mallory wasn't always smart. She picked up the scrap of crumpled paper and tried to decipher the barely legible handwriting.

WHERE THE FUCK ARE YOU? And where the fuck is my fucking jug? If you don't come up with the goods as promised within the next twenty-four hours, I will gut you and feed your roasted entrails to my thralls.

HE HADN'T BOTHERED SIGNING his name at the bottom.

She stacked the four letters, put them on her coffee table and gazed at them for a long moment, then shook her head, got to her feet and started to prepare.

THE MAGICKED BLOOD on the stone steps leading to Longchamps' front door continued to glisten and sparkle in the moonlight. Mallory avoided it and marched down, raising her fist to knock loudly against the door.

It wasn't long before the iron grate in the door's centre rattled and the face of the same thrall as on her first visit peered out at her. Strange shadows covered his cheekbone and his frown was heavier than usual. 'It's you,' he muttered. 'He's not expecting you.'

She gave him her sunniest smile. 'Hi, Eric!' It wasn't his fault she was here; he wasn't the one who'd ruined her quiet night at home. 'I bet he'll see me if you tell him I'm here.' She made a point of adjusting her backpack; she'd ensured it was bulging and heavy before she'd left home.

Eric glanced at it and then at her. 'You've found one,' he breathed and his expression transformed. 'Thank goodness. Another day and I'm not sure we'd have made it.'

Mallory's brow creased with confusion, but when he opened the heavy door and she saw more of his face it was clear that the 'shadows' were actually purple bruises that curled around one eye and reached down his cheekbone.

'Wait in your usual spot,' he told her. 'I'll tell Lord Longchamps you're here.'

She had barely sat down on the uncomfortable wooden bench when the Cursed Portrait started its refrain. 'You're going to die.' She glowered at it. 'He hates you now and he'll make sure you suffer. You'll wish you'd never come here. You'll wish you were never born. You...'

'Shut up,' she said loudly and distinctly.

The Cursed Portrait cackled.

Mallory reached into her pocket and pulled out the Zippo lighter she'd picked up before leaving her flat. She flicked it open, thumbed it and gazed at the small flame. '"Though she be but little",' she whispered, '"she is fierce."'

The painting didn't say a word. Mallory raised her hand – and the burning flame –in its direction. 'What did you just say? I didn't quite catch it.'

From the confines of the frame, the painted figure blanched and started to cower. 'I didn't say anything.'

'You definitely did. Go on.' She smiled. 'What was it?'

'Sorry,' the Cursed Portrait mumbled. 'I said sorry.'

'That's what I thought you said. Thank you. Apology accepted.' The lighter clicked as she closed it.

'Lord Longchamps will see you now,' Eric declared.

Mallory rose smoothly to her feet. 'Great. No need for you to escort me.' She patted him on the shoulder. 'I know the way.'

A wide smile was plastered across Chester Longchamps' face when she walked into his drawing room. He extended his arms as if to embrace her but she was careful to maintain a distance between them.

'Mallory Nash! You came through! I had no doubt that you would succeed. You are truly fabulous! You are magnificent! I will sing your praises to anyone who wishes to hear them because, squib or not, you are truly magical!'

She didn't say a word, just swung the backpack off her shoulder and let it fall to the ground with a thud.

Longchamps winced dramatically. 'Don't break the damned thing! We need it!' He darted forward, picked up the bag and ripped open the zip. In a second his expression altered dramatically. 'What is this shit?' He turned the bag upside down and a large bottle of water, a wrapped sandwich, an apple and a large envelope fell onto the floor.

'I keep getting told off for not eating properly,' Mallory said cheerfully, 'I thought it would be wise to bring some snacks so if I get peckish I can nibble on some food and satisfy my hunger.'

Longchamps was growing paler; much more of this and he'd be whiter than the envelope lying at his feet. 'Where is my jug?' He stepped towards her. 'Where is my fucking bellarmine jug?'

'I haven't found one yet,' she said pleasantly. 'Have you?'

The vampire roared, 'No! That's your job! You *have* to find one!' He opened his mouth and displayed his sharp fangs. 'If you do not come up with the goods and fulfil the terms of our contract...'

Mallory cleared her throat. 'About that. You did read the contract before you placed your blood on the dotted line, didn't you?'

Longchamps faltered and stared at her.

She sighed. 'I told you to read it before signing – any sensible person would have read it. But my assistant, Boris, seems to think that you didn't and your attitude reinforces his suspicions.' She curled her toes together and held her breath.

'Of course I fucking read it!'

'Then what's the problem?' She bent down and picked up the envelope. 'You have your own copy but this one is mine – I brought it along just in case.' She drew out the single sheet of paper. It was short for a reason: the less complicated and lengthy a blood contract, the less chance there was for confusion and confrontations like this one.

'Clause three,' she said.

Longchamps snatched the paper out of her hands and his eyes widened as he scanned it: *Mallory Nash will make every attempt to locate the necessary equipment required to transport and use the Clouded Map so that it is not damaged. She will not be held liable if such equipment cannot be found. In such an eventuality, this contract will be rendered null and void.*

His face twisted into an ugly snarl. 'It doesn't say that in my version.'

'They are exact copies. I'm happy to wait while you check.'

He glared at her then marched stiffly to the door, yanked it open and shouted for the thrall.

'I would also like to draw your attention to clause six at the bottom of the page,' Mallory went on. 'It's a boiler-plate section that I include in every contract.'

Longchamps' hands tightened as he looked at the sheet of paper again then he read out loud, '"*Threats of violence from either party are not acceptable and are subject to penalties. Any violence incurred is subject to the mirrored enchantments bound up in this paper.*"'

'In other words,' Mallory said, as the thrall appeared with Longchamps' copy of the contract, 'anything you do to hurt me will be reflected back onto you.' Many years earlier it had cost her a great deal to invoke that particular contract witchery but this wasn't the first time she'd been glad she'd gone to such expense. Unfortunately, sometimes it was necessary.

She waited patiently as Chester compared his version of the contract with hers. 'You bitch,' he hissed. 'You tricked me from the beginning. This entire thing was a scam designed to take advantage of me while I was vulnerable.'

'I assure you that's not the case. As far as I am concerned, our contract remains in place and I will continue to search for a bellarmine jug. My intention is not to antagonise you but to clarify the situation – I still believe I can find a jug that will enable you to use the Clouded Map. I'm not giving up.'

She smiled at him to emphasise the truth of her words then hardened her voice. 'But I didn't trick you. The contract protects both of us and those clauses are there for a reason. They were not hidden from you.' She drew breath. 'If you are still unhappy, we can come to an agreement and end our business now without consequence.'

Chester Longchamps' cold eyes sparked with malevolence; this was a very different person to the one she'd met during their first meeting. Mallory wasn't surprised, but she hoped he'd see sense; despite his aggression he was her client and she would rather see the contract through to completion. She was, after all, a professional.

She waited; it took a moment a two but eventually he calmed down. 'There is no chance of obtaining the Clouded Map without a bellarmine jug?' he asked.

'None. Once the map leaves the controlled environment where it's currently stored, it won't survive without the jug's protection. Even the best preservation spell will only last a few minutes and the map is simply too delicate.'

His tone was cool but even as he asked, 'And you truly believe you can find a bellarmine jug?'

'I do. I'm aware that time is an issue and the Clouded Map must be returned to the Witches Council by August, and I am also aware that there are very few unused bellarmine jugs in existence. Even so, I think I can find one. I wouldn't have agreed to this contract if I hadn't believed it was possible.' She met his eyes. 'We can set a time limit, if you wish. Perhaps four weeks from today?'

It was Longchamps who looked away first. 'That is acceptable to me.'

'Good. I'm glad that we've ironed out our differences,' she said amiably. 'I can see that this was nothing more than a misunderstanding.'

He grunted, but he got it.

'All that remains are the threats of violence that you sent me,' she went on and Longchamps' head jerked up. 'I am willing to let them pass if there are no more and...'

'Done!' he barked.

She wasn't finished. 'And you give me your word that you will inflict no more violence on your staff. Especially Eric.'

Longchamps looked at her blankly; he clearly had no idea what she was referring to.

Mallory sighed and indicated the poor, bruised thrall who

was still hovering in the doorway. 'Him?' Longchamps appeared genuinely astonished. 'But he's just a thrall. Why would you care about him? He's nothing.'

Eric winced and dropped his head.

'He's a loyal servant who deserves your respect and your protection,' Mallory replied.

Baffled, Longchamps nodded. 'Fine,' he said. 'Whatever.'

'I need your spoken vow.'

'You ask a great deal for someone who's nothing more than a pathetic squib,' he snapped.

When Mallory didn't respond, he huffed and folded his arms. 'Fine. I give you my vow that I won't hurt any members of my own staff.'

'Great.' She scooped up the bag and started replacing the items inside it. 'I'll tell you as soon as I find a bellarmine jug, otherwise I'll provide a report every Friday morning so that you are apprised of my progress.' It was more than she was required to do but she understood that Longchamps was desperate and communication was essential.

'Good,' he said shortly. Mallory glanced at him. 'Thank you,' he added with considerable reluctance.

'You're welcome.' She smiled. 'Good night, Mr Longchamps. I'll see myself out.'

CHAPTER

FOURTEEN

Late the following morning, Mallory sat cross-legged on her sofa frowning and muttering as she flipped through the pages of her notebook for the umpteenth time, searching for someone who might own a bellarmine jug that they'd be willing to lend out.

It was starting to feel like a needle-in-a-haystack situation and she was very aware that she was fumbling. To be successful, she needed a more focussed approach: wandering around Coldstream asking random strangers if they could help was unlikely to produce results.

Distasteful as Chester Longchamps might be, she wasn't going to give up. Nothing was impossible as far as Mallory was concerned and she certainly wasn't about to admit defeat; such a scenario was a very long way off.

'Strategy,' she said aloud. 'It's all about strategy.'

None of the witchery stores had any bellarmine jugs in stock. Mallory had visited every single one of them, even the small outfits on the fringes of the city, and she had the blisters to prove it. Despite her lack of success with commercial stores, she reckoned that witches were still her best bet. They had invented the jugs and bound special magics into the pottery process; that might be a lost art form in these modern times, but it stood to reason that it was a witch who could help her now.

Over the years Mallory had dealt with many of Coldstream's covens. While the smart choice would definitely be one of the covens that had been around for generations, she didn't think that approaching a wealthy or large coven was a good idea. Wealthy covens rarely needed her services and probably kept their important and precious documents sealed up in bellarmine jugs, so they'd have none to spare. Large covens might have the odd empty jug but wouldn't necessarily know where they were kept and likely wouldn't care. A small, old, cash-poor coven was the way to go.

She scanned most of the handwritten entries in her book before finally dismissing them. It was only when she squinted at her scrawled, sparse entry for the Pitcairn coven that she felt a surge of optimism. They fit the bill perfectly.

Mallory reckoned that a visit to the Pitcairns wouldn't be a bad way to spend her day, and it might even lead to something useful. She stood up, collected her bag and headed for the door. Even if they didn't own any bellarmine jugs, they might point her in the right direction. And their street was smack-bang in the centre of a coven-heavy suburb, so if they couldn't help she could always drop in on a few of their neighbours. The Bigstones, perhaps, she mused as she pulled her front door open, or the Hammerwells or the—

At the sight of a figure standing on her narrow landing, Mallory gave a high-pitched yelp of surprise.

'I apologise,' Alexander MacTire said. 'I didn't mean to frighten you.'

She blinked at him. 'More surprised than frightened.' She'd not heard the stairs creak, the usual indication that she had a visitor. 'How long have you been standing there?'

To her astonishment, he flushed. 'Not long.'

She tilted her head, examining his expression. 'Alexander,' she asked, 'are you alright?'

'I am perfectly fine. However, you asked me to come and tell you how my date with Cathy went.' He spread his arms wide. 'So here I am.'

'I didn't ask you to come around,' Mallory said slowly.

'You did.'

She shook her head. 'No. You told me you'd come around with an update. I didn't *ask* you to.'

He shrugged as if to say it wasn't important. Mallory supposed he was probably right. 'Let's go for lunch,' he said instead. 'I'll fill you in on all the gory details.'

Lunch sounded great but she owed Chester Longchamps' business her full attention. 'I'm sorry, but I've got to work.'

'Have you eaten today?' he asked softly.

She tried to remember. 'Yes!' There was a note of misplaced triumph in her voice as she recalled the toast she'd hastily crammed into her mouth while she was working through the lists of witches in her notebook.

'Really?'

'I had toast.'

'With butter and jam?'

'Uh...' Actually, she'd eaten it dry; her cupboards were mostly bare.

His amber eyes darkened thoughtfully. 'No. Not jam. You had it with honey, right?' Alexander's tongue briefly dipped out to lick his lips. 'Sweet, golden honey drizzled from edge to edge, seeping into buttery crevices so that sweetness coats your lips with every bite and,' he dropped his voice and moved an inch closer, 'lingers like an intimate sensual kiss.'

He slowly licked his lips a second time and Mallory realised she was staring at his mouth, imagining it coated with honey. *Good grief.* 'Have you swallowed a book of poetry this morning?' she managed.

He flashed a grin. 'Perhaps I have. Come and have lunch with me and I'll tell you about last night. I'll release you to your other clients afterwards.'

Her stomach took that inopportune moment to growl. Loudly. Alexander's eyebrows rose and she yielded; after all, she did want to know how things had gone with Cathy.

'Alright, but only one hour. No longer. There's a café at the corner where the service is fast.'

'Perfect. I'll even set a timer,' he promised. 'Lead the way.'

He stepped back but the landing was so small that even with his body pressed against the wall it would have been difficult for her to squeeze past him. She considered it then shook her head.

'I don't bite,' he whispered.

Mallory lowered her voice to match his. 'But maybe I do.'

Alexander winked in delighted response.

THEY MANAGED to snag a table in the corner and ordered sandwiches from the smiling waitress. 'Please bring me the bill afterwards,' Alexander said firmly. 'I'll be paying. With money.'

Mallory snickered. 'You sound like a pompous dick.'

'I invited you here. I want to pay for the meal.' He wagged his finger. 'You have form in places like this.'

The waitress agreed. 'Yeah, Mal doesn't usually pay for her

food here. She's got some kind of arrangement with my boss.' She nodded and moved away to deal with another customer.

Alexander grinned knowingly. 'I rest my case. Although one must question why you eat so badly when you have so many restaurant owners keen to feed you.'

She sniffed, although in truth he had a point. 'You still sound like a pompous dick.'

He grimaced. 'Unfortunately that's what Cathy West thought.'

Abruptly Mallory realised that she wasn't dismayed in the slightest, though she did her best to look disappointed while mentally castigating herself. Cathy was a great fit for Alexander; she was everything he wanted. And if the date had gone well, Mallory would be freed from all future obligations. Damn it.

'What happened?'

'Honestly? I'm not entirely sure. I was the epitome of charm...'

'And modest with it,' Mallory muttered.

'If you'd prefer misplaced modesty, I'm sure I can conjure some up.'

She held up her hands. 'No, you're right. Stay as you are.'

He laughed. 'We chatted. We had lots in common, I made her laugh in the right places and I don't think I made any terrible faux pas. There was an awkward moment when I spilled some water but it landed on the tablecloth and not on her dress, so I think I got away with it.'

'And?' Mallory pressed.

'At the end of the evening,' he looked away as if embarrassed, 'Cathy thanked me for a lovely time and said she didn't think there was much point in a second date.'

Oh. That wasn't good. Mallory leaned back in her chair and considered as the waitress returned with their sandwiches. 'Okay,' she said finally. 'Cathy West isn't the one but it doesn't mean we can't learn from the experience. You didn't float her boat, but did she float yours? You're usually the one who's too picky, Alexander. How did you feel about her?'

He picked up his sandwich. 'I can't profess sudden undying love, though she seemed nice enough.'

'Nice enough?' Mallory whistled. 'No wonder she wasn't interested in a second date.'

'What's wrong with nice? Cathy was nice. I liked her and I enjoyed her company. She was definitely ... nice.'

Mallory took a bite of her sandwich, chewed it thoughtfully then swallowed. 'Were you attracted to her?'

'She's very pretty.'

'That's not what I asked.'

'Okay,' he said. 'Yeah. I guess I was attracted to her a bit.'

'Uh-huh.' Mallory nodded. 'What was she wearing?'

Alexander stared at her. 'Is this a test?'

'Answer the question.'

'A dress,' he said. 'She was wearing a dress.'

'Long? Short?'

'Medium.'

'What colour was it?'

'Her dress? Does it matter?'

'Humour me, Alexander.'

He hesitated. 'I think it was red.'

'You think?'

'It was definitely red.' He still sounded unsure.

'Was her hair up or down?'

'Up?'

'Are you asking me or telling me?' Mallory asked.

'It was up. What does it matter?'

'Was she wearing perfume?'

He wrinkled his nose. 'Mallory...'

'You're a werewolf. Perfume is something a werewolf would notice.'

'In that case, no,' he replied. 'She wasn't.'

'Definitely?'

'Probably. I'm not sure.'

Mallory exhaled. 'You weren't attracted to her at all.'

'I'm a man! I don't notice things like clothes or hair or perfume.'

'Alexander,' she said, trying to hold on to her patience, 'you dress impeccably. How much did that suit cost?'

'This old thing?'

She gave him a long-suffering look. 'Even if you weren't the type of man who cared about clothing, if you'd fancied Cathy you would have paid attention. At the very least you'd be able to conjure up an image of what she looked like last night.' She nodded decisively. 'But that's okay. This is something we can work with.'

He raised an eyebrow. 'It is?'

'Absolutely. There's a week until the Wolf Ball so that gives us plenty of time.' She pursed her lips and tried to estimate when she could spare a few hours away from Chester Longchamps' problem. 'Tonight,' she said eventually. 'Hirsel Street. Let's meet at eight o'clock by the fountain in the centre.'

'Hirsel Street? I assumed you'd had enough of alcohol and partying after the full moon.'

'There will be no alcohol whatsoever, not for me or for you.'

'Why do I have to suffer?' he asked, with a glint of amusement.

'You need a clear head and alcohol will impair your judgement. And this certainly isn't about partying, this is business.'

'Whatever you say, Mallory.' He finished his sandwich without further argument and smiled at her. 'You know,' he said, 'that colour suits you.'

'Huh?'

'That top, the blue and green suit you. I liked the patchwork dress you had on last week that had similar colours. They match your eyes.'

Mallory stared but before she could gather her thoughts the waitress returned with the bill. 'I'll get this,' Alexander said. 'You can head off to your other clients.'

Mallory scratched her neck. Then, because she wasn't sure what else to say or do, she did as he suggested.

FIFTEEN

No matter how much Mallory tried to push him out of her thoughts, Alexander MacTire kept sneaking back into her head as she turned onto the street where the Pitcairn coven's house was located. She was starting to get irritated with her inability to put him into a compartment and shut its proverbial door. She hit the side of her head with the palm of her hand as if self-inflicted violence would drive him away, then squared her shoulders and marched up to the Pitcairn front door. Its glossy paintwork reminded her of the sheen of Alexander's hair. *Goddamnit.* She gritted her teeth and tried to focus.

She was well aware that cold-calling rarely got results; she'd tried it during the fledgling days of her brokering business when seven full days of knocking on doors had yielded a grand total of three rather dubious clients. Trying such an approach on the Pitcairns without good reason would only lead to abject failure but fortunately her scribbled notes had already offered her a way in.

The Pitcairns had spent several months complaining to anyone who would listen about a long-standing restrictive covenant that their ancestors had foolishly agreed to during the early nineteenth century. According to the terms of the covenant, which was held by the Association of Ogres who owned premises on the street behind the Pitcairns' house, the coven members were not allowed to grow any magical herbs in their back garden without incurring harsh penalties. It was the sort of odd rule that had made sense a couple of hundred years ago when there was considerable worry about magic leakage and cross-contamination across residential properties but, during the last fifty years, magic wards had become more sophisticated and such covenants had usually been allowed to lapse. The Association of Ogres, however, was not willing to budge on this one. Not yet, anyway.

Mallory smoothed down her hair and checked her clothes. Did these shades of blue green really match her eyes? She muttered under her breath then she reached forward and rang the doorbell.

The male witch who answered looked friendly enough. He was tall and lanky and his stained apron suggested that she'd interrupted him in the middle of something. Nevertheless, he smiled at her. 'Can I help you?'

'Actually, I think I can help you,' Mallory said. 'My name is Mallory Nash and I'm here to talk to you about the ogres and the restrictive covenant on your property.'

The witch's expression froze. He wiped his hands on his apron and gazed at her for a long moment before nodding slowly. 'In that case, you'd better come in.'

She followed him into a long hallway lined with shoes then into a side room that appeared to be a study area. Two walls were lined from ceiling to floor with crammed bookshelves and there were four separate desks, each laden with papers and office detritus.

Only one of the desks was occupied. Mallory knew instantly

who the older woman leaning across the old oak desk with a fountain pen in her hand was because her black robes with their violet trim were a dead giveaway. This was Vanessa Pitcairn, High Priestess of the coven.

The witch cleared his throat. 'We have a visitor,' he said.

Vanessa Pitcairn looked up. She had a round face with laughter lines around her eyes and an upturned nose covered in freckles, all of which suggested she was a warm, friendly woman who would bake you a pile of chocolate-chip cookies at a moment's notice. Mallory knew not to underestimate her, however, or to mistake her kindly demeanour for weakness. A small, poor coven this might be but Vanessa was High Priestess for a reason and her grey eyes reflected a fierce intelligence.

The witch shuffled his feet. 'Her name is Mallory and she says she's here about the ogres.'

Vanessa's mouth tightened a fraction, although that was the only indication that she had heard him or that she cared.

'Mallory Nash.' She offered her full name. 'I live locally but I'm just a squib.'

'You're not *just* anything, Ms Nash,' Vanessa said. 'I know of you. I heard what you did for the Sunbake coven a few years ago.'

Mallory was genuinely startled and Vanessa Pitcairn went up another inch in her estimation. Mallory's work for the Sunbakes had been secret and it had required a light touch and finesse that had taken months to achieve. That Vanessa Pitcairn knew of it was nothing short of extraordinary.

'I'm on very good terms with their High Priest,' Vanessa added. There was a teasing glint in her eyes that went a long way towards explaining what those very good terms involved. Suddenly everything made a lot more sense.

'In that case this will be an easier conversation than I expected,' Mallory offered.

'I'll be the judge of that,' Vanessa snorted. She waved at the male witch, who quickly withdrew, then leaned back in her chair.

Mallory knew she was still on shaky ground. She couldn't relax until she'd been invited to sit down. 'I'll get straight to the point. You have an issue with the Association of Ogres and I may be in a position to help you with that.'

Vanessa nodded slowly. 'I appreciate someone who doesn't waste my time beating around the bush, but you're not here out of the goodness of your heart, Ms Nash. You want something from us first.'

There was little point in denying it or in prevaricating. 'I need to find a useable bellarmine jug. I only require it for a period of a few months but it's proving incredibly difficult to find one.'

Vanessa Pitcairn was giving very little away. 'And you think that we could help you?'

'Let's say that I *hope* you can help me,' Mallory replied carefully. 'Nothing is definite.'

'Indeed.' The High Priestess tapped the end of her pen on her desk. 'What do you know about our issue with the Association of Ogres?'

No offer of a chair yet, but this was progress. 'They have a restrictive covenant in place on this property that forbids you to grow magical plants or herbs of any sort.'

'Yes.' Vanessa sniffed derisively. 'They have resisted all our efforts to void the covenant, even though it's completely redundant. We have a vast garden at the back of the house that we could use for all manner of things, but we're being held to ransom by market forces because we have to buy in all our supplies. Have you seen the price of vervain lately?'

Mallory opted for honesty. 'I can't say I have, but I can

imagine. Why is the Association so determined to uphold the covenant?'

'Spite. There can be no other reason.'

Mallory wondered if that was true; it seemed possible, but she'd reserve judgement until she knew for sure. 'Well, I think I can help you. All I ask for in return is the temporary use of a bellarmine jug.'

Vanessa was already shaking her head. 'We don't have one.'

Mallory's heart sank to the soles of her shoes. It had always been a long shot and on this occasion her optimism had definitely gotten the better of her.

'However,' Vanessa said, 'I may be able to procure one. I have connections with many of the covens in the area and I believe I know of someone who may have a bellarmine jug stored away that they could lend you.'

'Which coven?'

The High Priestess gave a tinkling laugh. 'I'm not telling you that! You'll simply cut out the middle man and I'll be hung out to dry with those damned ogres.' She paused. 'Tell you what, let's have a chat about how this might work. I believe there's a good chance we can do business together. Have a seat.'

Mallory smiled.

THE OGRES WERE one of the smaller Preternatural communities in Coldstream and Mallory had never had any of them as clients, but that didn't mean she didn't know anything about them. She was certain there were a few entries in her notebook, although she didn't think there was any detail about their association. She couldn't check because her notebook was currently lying on her coffee table at home; it was far too precious to bring out with her.

It would be foolish to go back and read what was written there when she was a mere hop, skip and a jump from the association's building. There was a chance that Mallory could solve her entire bellarmine jug conundrum within the next hour – a tiny chance, to be sure, but she crossed her fingers.

Although the Pitcairn coven maintained their house and clearly looked after it, they hadn't been able to disguise its somewhat shabby and dilapidated air. The Pitcairns were feeling the pinch, which went a long way to explaining why they were so desperate to get rid of the restrictive covenant and start growing their own magical supplies.

The building that belonged to the Association of Ogres was an entirely different affair. Although it wasn't especially large, it was certainly grand; looking at the pristine sandstone, perfect paintwork and immaculate planting around the building's perimeter, Mallory didn't doubt that these ogres were doing very well for themselves. Vanessa Pitcairn had mentioned that the coven had offered £20,000 to void the covenant and that the association had turned them down flat. The ogres obviously weren't short of a bob or two and certainly had no need for the witches' pennies.

Mallory eyed the tall irises on either side of the front door; they were truly stunning. Several of them were almost the same shade of amber as Alexander's eyes. Her steps faltered briefly and she gritted her teeth. '*Enough*, Mallory,' she hissed. This was getting beyond ridiculous.

She stepped up to door and knocked. By the time it opened, she'd plastered on her most professional smile, and she maintained it even when the person in front of her obviously wasn't an ogre. She hadn't expected to find a nymph here, let alone a water nymph with delicate blue skin.

'Good afternoon!' she said brightly. 'My name is Mallory Nash and I'd like to make an appointment to speak to Richard

Stone-arm. I believe he's the head of the Association of Ogres. It's vitally important I talk to him as soon as possible.'

The nymph blinked at her with wide, limpid eyes. 'He ain't here.' She started to close the door.

'Somebody else then,' Mallory said quickly. 'Another ogre.'

The nymph sighed. 'Ain't no ogres here at all.'

'This is the Association of Ogres, right?'

The nymph shrugged. Mallory continued to smile. 'I'll take that as a yes. Where are they if they're not here?'

'AGM.'

'Uh...'

The nymph rolled her eyes. 'Annual General Meeting, innit? Ogres love a damned meeting.'

'Of course!' Mallory exclaimed, as if she'd known that already. 'Remind me – where is it taking place?'

'Not telling.'

Okay. 'How long will it last?'

'Not telling.'

Mallory inhaled. 'Is there anything you *can* tell me?'

The nymph considered. 'Sure.'

Mallory waited; when nothing more was forthcoming, she prompted, 'What, then?'

'I can tell you that there ain't no ogres here.' For the first time, the nymph flashed a smile, then started to close the door again.

Mallory wedged her foot between the door and the frame, forcing the nymph to keep it open. Although she preferred carrots to sticks, she'd play hardball if she had to. 'I'm not done yet.'

'Move your foot,' the nymph muttered.

'No.'

'Move your foot!'

'No.' Mallory steeled herself and went for it. 'I know you're a water nymph,' she called through the gap.

'Wow,' came the sarcastic rejoinder. 'Ain't you the clever one?'

'I also know that water nymphs are forbidden from working for other Preternaturals until the vernal equinox – you're all supposed to be focused on Jacob's Well. Unless the ogres also have a vested interest in that particular patch of water, then...'

She didn't have to finish her sentence. The nymph opened the door wide and glowered. 'I'm broke, alright? I need the money. That's not a crime. It's only a few bloody hours here and there. We can't all afford to sit and stare at a damned ancient water spring for weeks on end because of some daft ancient tradition.'

'I'm not judging you.'

The nymph's lip curled. 'But you *are* blackmailing me.'

'Yeah.' Mallory nodded sadly. 'I am. I'm sorry. It makes me feel very grubby and I'm not trying to make your life difficult, but I need you to answer a few simple questions. That's all.'

'For fuck's sake.' The nymph crossed her arms. 'Alright, already. The AGM is taking place at the Belladonna Hotel. It's on until next Wednesday.'

That was a long AGM: the ogres really did love a meeting. 'Thank you.'

The nymph huffed.

'One more thing...'

The blue-skinned woman bared her teeth. 'What?'

'What's the deal with the Association of Ogres and the Pitcairn coven?'

'That's why you're here? Those bloody witches?'

Mallory waited. The nymph laughed. 'They want their silly covenant rescinded but the ogres here won't do that.'

'Why not?'

'Because of Old Man Stone-Arm.' She paused. 'Not the current boss but his father. He hates people and he's a petty wanker who takes pride in making life as difficult as possible because he's a grumpy old bastard. His son humours him because it's easier that way. No-one really cares about those witches or that covenant, they just want to keep Old Man Stone-Arm happy.'

Mallory beamed. Fabulous: ornery, petty bastards were her speciality. 'Thank you,' she said.

'That's it?' The nymph glared at her as if she'd been blackmailed into giving away her firstborn.

'That's it. Have a good—' Mallory didn't get to finish the sentence because the nymph had already slammed the door in her face.

SIXTEEN

Rushing to the Belladonna Hotel to speak to Stone-Arm – either Junior or Senior – wouldn't be a smart move. Mallory reckoned she'd only get one shot at persuading them to release the restrictive covenant and that shot had to hit its target, which meant taking her time and being careful. For the first time in days she felt like she was making progress, and she was humming happily as she bounced into Hirsel Street towards the fountain where she was due to meet Alexander.

'Well, well, well, Ms Nash,' drawled a familiar voice. 'You look very happy today.'

Mallory glanced to her left and smiled when she saw Liam Ferguson. 'I'm almost always happy,' she said in a mock whisper as if it were a secret.

'I can believe that.'

'You're looking remarkably louche,' she commented. It was true; the beta werewolf was the image of rakish decadence.

'Louche?' He touched his chest. 'It's the blue-velvet jacket, right?'

'That and the gold medallion, the snakeskin boots and the rumpled linen shirt.'

Ferguson gave her an arch look. 'I can't tell if you approve or you think I look like a complete wanker.'

Mallory grinned. Anyone who knew her well would have said that Liam Ferguson's fashion choices were right up her street; all that was missing was a battered straw hat. 'Definitely the former.'

'No,' another deep voice broke in. 'Definitely the latter. You look like a complete wanker.'

Alexander MacTire did not look louche; even his sister's sparkly unicorn T-shirt hadn't been able to give him that particular edge – not that he was wearing it now, of course. He was dressed in an impeccable smoke-grey suit with a crisp white shirt that didn't have a single crease or wrinkle. He looked like a millionaire estate agent, or perhaps a London-based stockbroker. Or, Mallory reflected, an alpha werewolf; in other words, about as far from her preferred type as was possible. So why the hell did her heart skip a beat when she saw him?

Fortunately Liam Ferguson wasn't offended. He touched his forelock. 'I'm going to go out on a limb, Mr MacTire, and suggest that you don't own any blue-velvet jackets with brass buttons.'

'You're right.' Alexander wasn't rude but his tone was definitely cool. 'In my experience wolf fur and velvet don't go together. There's only so much time I'm willing to yield to a lint roller.'

Ferguson tapped the side of his nose. 'Ah, there's a secret to that which I'm willing to reveal to you because you're the MacTire alpha and my superior.'

Alexander eyed him.

Ferguson continued undeterred. 'I don't wear velvet when

I'm in wolf form.' He winked at Mallory. 'I don't wear anything when I'm in wolf form.'

Mallory couldn't help herself; she burst out laughing, which only made Alexander's expression darken.

'Well,' Ferguson continued, 'I should go. I have a date waiting for me in the whisky bar who's been wanting to stroke my velvet for some time. I shouldn't keep her waiting.' He dipped his head to Mallory then deepened the movement towards Alexander, indicating that despite his jocular attitude he respected the alpha a great deal. Then he loped off without a backward glance.

Alexander huffed beneath his breath and Mallory flicked him a look. 'I was under the impression,' she said mildly, 'that it's important to maintain good relations with other werewolves.'

'It's important when they're werewolf alphas. That boy is a mere beta.'

Liam Ferguson certainly wasn't a boy, and Alexander wasn't usually a snob. 'A mere beta who is going places,' Mallory commented. 'He clearly likes you. It would be a good relationship to cultivate.'

'If he'd stopped flirting with you, perhaps I might have spoken to him sensibly,' Alexander growled.

She raised her eyebrows. 'Are you alright? You seem very grumpy this evening. If you're not in the right headspace we can postpone this for another night. Everyone has off days.'

'*I* don't.'

His face suggested otherwise but Mallory decided to take him at his word. 'Okay.' She pointed. 'I thought the Irish bar would be a good spot. It has a great view of the street.'

'People don't usually come to Hirsel Street for the view.'

Mallory grinned. 'Perhaps not, but it's why we're here tonight. Come on.'

They snagged two seats by the window. Mallory ordered two lime sodas at the bar then hopped onto the stool next to Alexander.

'So I take it that you have a plan for this evening,' he said.

'I do. Tonight we will focus solely on sexual attraction.'

Alexander gazed at her. 'Will we?'

'Yes.' She nodded in her most businesslike and professional manner. 'It's not the be all and end all of a successful relationship but it's definitely important, wouldn't you say?'

He didn't take his eyes off her. 'Absolutely.'

'And we already know from your date with Cathy that it's important for you be attracted to someone. You told me that you prefer sleek blondes...'

'No.'

Slightly confused, Mallory squinted at him. 'You're not attracted to blondes?'

'It was Nicholas who said I preferred blondes, not me.' Alexander's tone was a tad smug. His eyes roved across her face. 'Truthfully, my preferences are more ... eclectic.'

'That's not very helpful.'

He shrugged. 'What's your type, Mallory?' he enquired. 'Who are you attracted to?'

'This isn't about me. I'm not looking for a mate.'

'Humour me. Would you be interested in a relationship with a werewolf?'

Exasperated, she sighed. 'If this is another dig at Liam Ferguson—'

A deep growl rumbled from Alexander's chest. 'I'm not talking about Liam bloody Ferguson. I want to know about you. Are you attracted to werewolves?'

Mallory felt inexplicably flustered. 'Stop putting me under a microscope. This is nothing to do with me!'

'It's everything to do with you.'

'What does that mean?'

Something passed across his face that Mallory was still trying to decipher when he replied. 'This is your operation. You're in charge. That's all.'

She nodded vigorously, still confused. 'Yes, I'm in charge – and I'm not talking about myself. We're looking for a partner for you, not me.' She looked at the street. 'We both need to know what sort of woman really floats your boat, Alexander. There's a blonde druid to your left. What about her?'

'Are you going to make me talk to her?'

'No, this is purely window shopping.'

'Alright.' He moved his head and glanced at the druid. 'She's beautiful.' Mallory released a breath. 'But I'm not attracted to her.'

'Is there a reason why?'

'Not that I can put into words.'

Fair enough. Sensing she wouldn't get any more detail, Mallory looked past the blonde. 'How about the raven-haired witch passing the karaoke bar? The one who's laughing?'

Alexander followed her gaze. 'She looks like a lot of fun. But no.'

'Not at all?'

He shrugged.

'Redhead,' Mallory said. 'Twelve o'clock. She's a werewolf, right?'

Alexander looked. 'Annie Slade. I know her father.'

'I'm not asking if you're attracted to her father, I'm asking if you're attracted to *her*.'

'I suppose.'

She checked his face. 'So no, then. Good.'

He turned to her. 'Good?' Light flickered in his eyes.

'Yep. It's not looks that attract you, it's personality.' She patted his arm. 'You're a real man, after all.'

'Is that helpful?'

'Very.' Mallory pointed at his glass. 'Drink up. We have another place to visit.'

'What sort of venue?' Alexander asked suspiciously.

'It's not far. You'll enjoy this.'

ALEXANDER FROWNED at the neatly arranged tables lined up with two chairs on either side of each one. 'I don't understand. What is this?'

'Speed dating.' He stared at her. 'It's a straightforward concept. Twenty women. Twenty men. You spend three minutes with each woman then you move on.'

'I'm aware of what speed dating is, Mallory. What I don't understand is why I'm here.'

He knew exactly why she'd brought him here, he only wanted to hear her say it. 'I think your problem is that you don't know who you want or who truly attracts you. This will help you work it out.'

'I can assure you that I know what I want and I know who I'm attracted to.'

'Who?'

He didn't answer, just looked at her as a muscle jerked in his cheek.

'Well,' Mallory said. 'That settles it.' She checked her watch. 'You ought to get ready. It's about to start.'

'Mallory...'

'Don't be nervous! You'll be great!' She walked away before he could protest and hoped that this wouldn't turn into a car crash of an evening.

'Are you taking part?' the barman asked as she sat on a bar stool that had a clear view of all the tables.

'No. I'm here purely as a chaperone.'

'Sounds kinky.'

She shook her head. 'Not at all.'

She checked on Alexander who was glowering at her from the other side of the room. When a bell sounded, he was ushered to a chair; the fact that he wasn't walking out of the room in a huff was something, Mallory decided, though it was a shame that his first 'date' was staring at him with wide-eyed, fan-girl astonishment. Still, he might enjoy a bit of that.

Mallory checked his body language: crossed arms, tight shoulders. Maybe not.

It was a long three minutes. Alexander spoke a few times but the woman was painfully nervous and scarcely opened her mouth. Mallory couldn't blame her. The vibes emanating off Alexander were neither warm nor friendly; he looked like a man who'd been dragged here against his will. Although that wasn't totally inaccurate, it wasn't very helpful.

As soon as the bell rang to indicate the end of the first round, Mallory went over to him. Alexander was already on his feet. 'Get me out of here.'

'Absolutely not.'

'This is a nightmare. I'm in hell. I've not always been an angelic soul but surely I've not been bad enough to deserve this! Save me, Mallory. Please.'

'Hush. And loosen up, for goodness' sake. You looked as if you were about to bite that poor woman's head off. Smile. Act as if you want to be here.'

'But I *don't* want to be here.'

'Pretend.' She gave him a tiny shove. 'Next date. Go.'

He sat on the next chair and Mallory returned to the bar. 'I see what's going on here,' the barman said. 'You're not his chaperone, you're his trainer.' He held up a beer-damp bar towel. 'Want this to dab off his sweat?'

Mallory smirked. 'Maybe later.'

Alexander's second date was only marginally better than the first; within sixty seconds, the witch opposite him appeared to have launched into a full-blown argument over something he'd said.

Mallory passed a hand over her face. Maybe this wasn't such a good idea after all.

She checked out date number three: a troll. An extraordinarily beautiful troll, in fact, with a perfectly tailored suit that was as out of place here as Alexander's. She was observing her current date with faint disgust. Mallory reckoned this would either be another abject failure or an absolute triumph; there would be no in-between.

'Here.' The barman placed an electric-blue cocktail in front of her.

Mallory stared at it. 'I didn't order this.'

The barman nodded to his right. 'It's from the gentleman in the corner.'

She glanced over and noted the good-looking witch who was raising his glass in her direction. Mallory smiled politely.

'I can't accept it,' she told the barman. 'I'm not drinking alcohol tonight and,' she gestured to Alexander, 'I'm working.' She mouthed a quick thank you and an even quicker sorry to the witch then the bell rang again and her attention was diverted as Alexander moved to the table where the troll was sitting.

Alexander smiled; the troll smiled. She said something and Mallory caught a flash of genuine surprise cross his face, followed by amusement. He laughed, and for the first time looked as if he might be enjoying himself.

Mallory's stomach dipped with dismay. Damn it: this was

what she wanted, right? It was what Alexander wanted – and from the look on the troll's face it was what she wanted, too. There was no reason for Mallory to feel anything other than delight but deep down she recognised that the sensation uncurling in her belly was absolute, total desolation.

She swallowed hard. Oh God. She'd fallen for Alexander MacTire and there was absolutely nothing she could do about it.

A voice broke into her thoughts. 'My drink isn't good enough for you?'

She stiffened. The witch from the other end of the bar had sidled up to her and was towering over her looking annoyed. 'It was very kind of you to send it over.' She smiled. 'But I'm not drinking tonight.'

The troll leaned towards Alexander then reached up and touched her hair in a time-worn gesture that suggested she liked him. Alexander dipped his head closer to hers.

'I paid good money for that drink,' the witch snapped.

'Please, take it,' Mallory said. 'You can drink it, then it won't go to waste.'

'I bought it for you.'

'And I don't want it,' she said, without missing a beat.

As Alexander murmured something in the troll's ear, her lips parted with delight.

'It's not the cocktail that's not good enough for you, is it? You think you're too good for the likes of me.'

The barman was right there, shoulders pulled back. 'Sir,' he said. 'It's time for you to leave.'

'Fuck off!'

The troll's hand was now on Alexander's arm and he was smiling at her, his amber eyes twinkling.

'I've got this,' Mallory told the barman. She looked directly at the witch. 'I already said no. That's your cue to walk away. I strongly suggest you do so.'

The witch spat then raised his hand threateningly, magical sparks dancing at his fingertips. The barman stiffened but Mallory had already reached for the blue cocktail so she could toss it in the witch's face and onto his hands and douse whatever nasty magic he was planning to fling in her direction.

Her fingertips had barely scraped the glass when two hands appeared out of nowhere, grabbed the witch by the shoulders and slammed him to the floor.

Alexander's face was a blank mask, but his eyes promised fire and brimstone. 'The lady said no,' he hissed. 'She didn't want your drink the first time and she doesn't want it now.'

Mallory slid off her stool. 'I had it handled.'

'I know you're more capable than you look, but it doesn't hurt to double down. It doesn't hurt,' Alexander said with a quiet snarl in the direction of the motionless witch, 'to make it very clear in every way possible that you should take no for an answer.'

The witch made a last-ditch effort to rally. 'That bitch was eyeing me up. She knew what she was doing. She was leading me on and then—'

Alexander punched him in the face; there was the sickening crack of breaking bone, and blood spurted out in several directions.

The barman motioned him away. 'I've got this now. I'll call the MET and make sure he's dealt with.'

'Good,' Alexander turned to Mallory. 'Are you alright?'

'I'm fine.' She realised she was trembling. She swallowed and drew a deep breath. 'Your intervention was unnecessary.'

'It was very necessary. I knew from the moment he clocked you that there'd be a problem. I hoped he'd walk away when you turned down the drink, but he was too stupid for that.' An angry expletive coloured the air.

Mallory stared at him. 'You were talking to the troll and you looked like you were getting on with her. I didn't think you'd noticed what was happening.'

Alexander reached for her hand and entwined his fingers with hers 'Believe me, Mal, I noticed. Of course I noticed.'

CHAPTER

SEVENTEEN

Boris was gazing at her with a strange expression on his face. 'So he walked you home after that?'

Mallory nodded. 'Yes. Sticking around for more speed dates didn't seem appropriate.'

'What about the troll?'

She shrugged helplessly. 'I told Alexander he should get her number and arrange a proper date. He declined.'

'Did he, indeed?' Boris murmured.

'What's that tone of voice for?'

He sighed patiently. 'Has it occurred to you that perhaps the reason he's proving so obstinate when it comes to finding a woman he likes is because he's decided he likes you?'

Heat rose in Mallory's cheeks. Obviously she'd wondered about that – how could she not? – but she knew it wasn't true. 'I am one hundred percent not who Alexander MacTire wants,' she protested.

'Really.'

'Really! The reason he intervened last night is because he's an alpha and it's in his nature to protect and defend. Right now

176

he sees me as part of his pack because I work for him, and as I'm a squib and not a werewolf I need extra attention, which he's only too happy to give. That's as far as it goes.'

'Mmm.'

'I'm not sleek nor polished nor Preternaturally powerful, and the MacTire First Mate has to be all of those things. You're jumping to conclusions.'

There was a knock on the door. Mallory untangled her legs and went to answer it. The bespectacled man on her doorstep was wearing the livery of the Coldstream Delivery Services and holding a woven basket. 'Mallory Nash?' he asked.

'Yes.'

He thrust the basket at her. 'This is for you. Enjoy.' He turned and thumped down the stairs.

Mallory gazed at the basket and its contents before she closed the door and carried it inside. 'Problem?' Boris asked.

She shook her head. 'No.' She put the basket on her coffee table and pulled off the card that was tied to the handle. There was only one word scrawled on it: *Alex XXX*

Boris reached inside. 'Crusty sourdough bread. Salted butter. Apples. Grapes. Cured meats. Coffee. Chocolate.' He pulled out a box and frowned. 'These appear to be home-made pancakes.'

Mallory felt a burst of warmth and ran her fingertip across the three kisses on the card.

'That's weird,' Boris said.

'What?'

'There are four different types of honey.' He pointed to the small glass jars. 'Runny honey, lavender honey, set honey and honeycomb.' He picked up the jar of lavender honey. 'This one has been laced with magicked tribulus. You know that's an aphrodisiac?'

Alexander's voice echoed in Mallory's head. *Sweet, golden honey drizzled from edge to edge, seeping into buttery crevices so that sweetness coats your lips with every bite and lingers, like an intimate sensual kiss.* Her mouth dried.

'He keeps complaining that I don't eat properly,' she said. 'That's all this is.'

'Sure.'

'My job is to help him find a mate, Boris.'

'Yep.'

'He doesn't want me.'

'Uh-huh.'

'He's only being kind.'

'Absolutely.'

She gave him a long look. 'If Alexander MacTire had any romantic designs on me, he would state them directly. He's not someone who plays games, he's very direct and truthful. If he felt anything for me, he'd tell me.'

As soon as she spoke, Mallory knew the words were true; just because she'd developed a painful crush on Alexander didn't mean that he felt the same way. Far from it. He was her client: this was *business* and she couldn't allow her feelings to get in the way. 'He sees me as a valued employee. Nothing more. Nothing less.'

Boris grinned. 'If you say so. You're better at understanding people than I am. Can we have some pancakes and honey now?'

It took longer than Mallory would have liked to arrange access to the exclusive Belladonna Hotel, although the distraction was helpful; it was good to focus on something other than the deepening ache in her heart.

While Boris researched Richard Stone-arm, she was forced to fill her hours with investigating various promising women who would be at the Wolf Ball. She made copious notes, checked backgrounds and even, on occasion, followed some of the more likely candidates for Alexander's hand as they went about their daily business. None of it was enjoyable and she was relieved when her contact at the Belladonna finally said that the arrangements were in place.

She was struggling to find a woman who seemed good enough for Alexander MacTire; he deserved someone truly amazing and so far Mallory hadn't found her. She needed to get a move on because time was running out; by the time she set off for the Belladonna Hotel on the last day of the Association of Ogres' AGM, the ball was only two days away. It felt less like the countdown to a posh party and more like a ticking time bomb.

The hotel's concierge, a whip-smart basilisk whose massive girth and height were matched only by his willingness to help, met her a few streets away from the rear entrance in a deserted alleyway that they both knew well.

'I'm sorry it took so long to sort this out,' he said. 'It was a lot harder than eavesdropping on a few secrets – I needed time to arrange the work shifts. Some of the other hotel staff won't pay you any attention because their heads are in the clouds or they simply don't care, but there are a few jobsworths that I needed to get out of the way.'

Mallory beamed at him. 'George, there's no reason for you to apologise. You've come through for me on this.' She pulled a sealed glass bottle out of her bag. 'Here, as payment. It's fresh.'

'Druid saliva?' George asked hopefully.

She shook her head. 'I've gone one better. This is vampire drool.' Despite his disgust at her request, Chester Longchamps had managed to produce a half-pint of the stuff when she'd told him it would help her find a bellarmine jug. He hadn't asked for details; it was probably better that he didn't know.

'Mallory Nash, you are amazing,' George breathed. He secreted the bottle in the folds of his overcoat then passed her a bag.

Mallory peered inside at the neatly folded uniform. 'House-keeping?' she asked.

He nodded. 'That gives you access to all areas.'

Mallory pushed herself on tiptoe and planted a kiss on his cheek. He blushed. 'Any new guests or surprising secrets I should hear about?' she asked while he turned his back as she hastily pulled on the uniform.

'It's been a quiet month.' He paused. 'Apart from a surprise advance booking for Samhain.'

Mallory adjusted her skirt and straightened her name badge. 'I'm ready,' she said.

George turned around and gave her an approving nod.

'I can try and tie up my hair to make it look neater?' she offered.

'I've got that covered.' He passed her a scarf. 'It's a shame to hide those curls but they're memorable and they don't meet the Belladonna's exacting dress code.' His expression curdled; it was obvious what he thought of such rules.

Mallory smiled: she understood that certain organisations did things in particular ways and it always reminded her that she was lucky to work for herself. She secured the scarf, managing to keep most of her springy curls in place. 'Who's the surprise guest?' she asked.

'We don't know yet, but the deposit came for our finest suite of rooms from the bank account reserved for the Winter Court.'

Mallory gaped. 'The Winter Court? The Fae Winter Court?'

He nodded. 'Yep.'

She whistled: this was thrilling news in more ways than one. 'How long has it been since a member of the Winter Court came to Coldstream?'

'Thirteen years. I checked.'

That was before Mallory had moved here. Even the lowest of Winter Court courtiers would be exciting to behold. 'You'll let me know when you find out who's coming?' There was a lot she could do with a secret of this magnitude.

'Of course.' He brushed some invisible dust off her shoulders. 'Ready?'

Mallory took a long, slow breath, slowly released it, tightened her toes and briefly closed her eyes. The successful completion of her deal with Chester Longchamps might well rest on the next sixty minutes. A fizz of adrenaline burst through her veins and she nodded.

'Ready,' she said. 'Bring on the ogres.'

It would have drawn attention to her presence if she'd strolled through the staff entrance with George, so Mallory waited five minutes after he'd gone back inside before she followed.

Although she'd never stayed at the Belladonna as a guest she knew the hotel layout, even if she was a little hazy on some of the finer details. That was good: she didn't have to waste time getting her bearings. The less time she spent skulking around the hotel's plush corridors the better.

She bypassed the kitchen, staffroom and several storage rooms. A white-coated waiter passed her heading in the opposite direction and she half-expected a challenge from him, but he barely glanced at her. Housekeeping was way below dining-room staff in the hotel's pecking order; her dull-green uniform ensured that she was beneath notice.

Her confidence grew. By the time she was in the employees' lift heading up to the conference room floor, she felt certain this venture would work.

When the lift door opened, Mallory was at the end of a dingy corridor lined with health and safety notices and warnings about performing unnecessary magic whilst on duty. No fear on that score, she thought.

She pushed open a door at the far end and was immediately greeted by a cacophony of sound, colour – and dozens upon dozens of broad-shouldered ogres.

The Association of Ogres didn't include every ogre in Coldstream; it was a relatively small organisation considering the number of them who lived in the city. Even so, Mallory was surprised by how many were there. The house behind the Pitcairn coven wasn't big enough for more than a dozen or so ogres to live in comfortably, and there were more than three hundred ogres in the Belladonna conference room. Luckily she'd found photos of the association's bigwigs in an old version of the *Coldstream Courier* and she'd studied them closely, so she knew who she was looking for.

Hotel staff were circulating with dainty canapés and scooping up empty cups, glasses and plates. Mallory scooted around the edge of the room and avoided them as best as she could as she kept an eye out for Richard Stone-arm, the current head of the association. She was interrupted on several occasions by ogres, most of whom pressed their dirty plates on her, albeit with polite smiles and murmurs of thanks.

One particularly gruff ogre wanted to complain about the lack of authenticity with the traditional troll-flesh vol-au-vents. Given that troll meat had been illegal for more than two hundred years and goat was used instead, there was no chance the small pastries could ever be described as authentic no matter who cooked them. Mallory knew better than to argue and simply murmured that she'd pass on the comment to the kitchen.

While that was a lie she didn't feel ashamed of, she did feel a trace of guilt when another ogre, who was crossing his legs and grimacing, asked for directions to the restroom. She made an educated guess as to where the toilets were and sent him to the right, hoping for his sake that she was correct.

After two full circuits of the room and no sign of any Stone-arms, let alone Richard himself, Mallory decided to abandon the conference area in favour of the guest rooms upstairs. George had told her which room Richard was staying in and it would be easier to get him to listen to her away from the crowds.

She was making a beeline for the exit, carrying a towering stack of plates, when she spotted him – and she immediately realised why she'd not noticed him before.

Ogres were typically tall creatures but that wasn't the case with Richard Stone-arm. He looked to be under six foot, which was extremely short for an ogre, and he'd been hidden by the rest of the crowd. Mallory wondered if his height was a genetic quirk; if it were and he'd spent his life compensating for his size, it might explain why he was so keen to assert his superiority in other matters, including pointless covenants.

Mallory spotted an empty tray and dropped the plates onto it, then pushed through the crowd towards Richard Stone-Arm. Unfortunately, she was not the only person who wanted to talk to him and a long queue of people were waiting their turn.

She'd have to be canny about this. She paused and considered, then instead of pressing forward she spun around.

Several doors opened out of the large room and Mallory checked them all, peering inside and taking an inventory before moving on; next she scanned the room for anyone on the periphery who wasn't eating, drinking or schmoozing.

There was a gruff-looking older woman wearing a suit who was leaning against the wall with her arms folded; it was possible she was a bodyguard or bouncer, though it was equally possible that she was merely bored out of her mind. Either way, she'd do.

Mallory approached her. 'Excuse me?' she squeaked.

The ogre glanced at her and clocked her staff uniform. 'What's housekeeping doing here?'

Ah: the woman was definitely some sort of security ogre; few other guests would have noted the difference in employee uniforms. Mallory dropped her eyes and shuffled her feet. 'Uh, downstairs asked me to drop by. There's an urgent phone call for Mr Stone-arm – it's come through on the switchboard but I don't know who Mr Stone-arm is and...'

The ogre sighed. 'Don't worry. I'll tell him.'

Whoop-whoop. Mallory pointed at one of the closed doors. 'There's a phone in the Glasgow Room. He can take it in there.'

'Thank you.' The woman pushed away from the wall and plunged into the crowd.

Mallory grinned then darted around the room and swiftly went through the same door. There was indeed a phone on the long sideboard and she picked up the receiver.

She didn't have to wait for long. The gruff security ogre walked in first and swung her head around to check for lurking intruders. Her eyes slid over Mallory, who was standing with the phone in her hand and a bright smile on her face. She was a squib and not a threat to anyone.

'Clear,' the ogre grunted and a second later, Richard Stone-arm walked in, a frown etched onto his forehead.

'You can leave,' he told the woman and moved towards Mallory.

She waited until the other ogre had closed the door before replacing the receiver and taking a step back. She folded her arms so he didn't think this was some strange, premeditated attack.

His eyes darkened in suspicion and he stopped moving. 'What is this?'

'I apologise, Mr Stone-arm.' Mallory knew that she had to explain quickly before he turned and left the room. 'There is no urgent phone call but I need to speak to you alone. My name is Mallory Nash. I can assure you I am no threat, but I desperately need to talk to you about the Pitcairn coven.'

His bushy eyebrows rose upwards. 'Those witches? This is about the stupid covenant? For fuck's sake.' He turned away.

'Mr Stone-arm, please.' Mallory kept her voice soft; he wouldn't respond well to even a hint of aggression. 'Yes, it's about the covenant and, yes, it's stupid. You know it's stupid. You're the head of the Association and you have the power to release the covenant. There's no reason for you not to do so.'

'Make an appointment with my secretary and we can discuss it later. Right now I'm busy.' He continued towards the door and reached for the handle.

'You're being a dick,' Mallory said in the same soft voice.

Stone-arm's back stiffened and his hand dropped as he turned to face her. 'Pardon?'

'You heard me. You're being a dick. You have no real reason to keep the covenant in place other than to exert your authority, to prove that you have power.' She invoked what she'd learned from watching Alexander. 'A real leader doesn't maintain power or gain respect by being mean. A real leader shows humility and kindness, whether towards their own kind or to their neighbours.'

His face spasmed into an ugly snarl. 'You've got some nerve coming here and talking me to like this!'

'It's the only way to talk to bullies. It seems to be the only language your kind understand.'

Mallory could almost taste his rage and she felt a tremor of fear. Had she gone too far? But by this point there was no choice but to stand her ground.

'You know nothing about the situation!'

'Then why don't you explain it to me?'

'I don't have to explain myself to the likes of you!' He was growing redder by the second. 'I don't even know who the fuck you are!'

Mallory persisted. 'Why do you hate the witches?'

'I don't hate them!'

It was the answer she'd been hoping for. 'Then why won't you let them buy themselves out of the covenant?' This time, Stone-arm didn't answer. She lowered her voice a notch. 'Is it because it's not you who refuses to break the covenant but your father? Is it because your father is the bully and he's bullying you, the Association of Ogres and the Pitcairn coven?'

The ogre's expression was pained. 'It's complicated.'

Mallory knew she had him. 'If I can uncomplicate matters and get your father to change his mind about the covenant, will you agree to let it go?'

'You're not going to do that. Nobody can.'

Mallory waited.

'For fuck's sake,' he muttered. 'Yes! I don't give a shit about that stupid covenant. I like the Pitcairns and I'd help them if I could – but you don't understand what my father is like. The witches can do away with the damned covenant for free if my father agrees, but he won't. I guarantee he won't.'

'Can I have your word on that?'

Stone-arm laughed coldly. 'It won't do you any good.'

Mallory shrugged. 'All the same.'

He rolled his eyes. 'Fine. You have my word.' Then he stiffened; although his relationship with his father was strained, he clearly didn't want anything bad to happen to him. 'If you try to hurt him in any way...'

'Please. I'm a squib,' she reassured him. 'I can no more hurt an ogre than I can fly.'

She curtsied and grinned. One down, one to go. That had been easier than she'd expected.

CHAPTER

EIGHTEEN

Mallory smoothed down the front of her uniform and knocked on Old Man Stone-arm's hotel-room door. 'Housekeeping!' she trilled.

The response from beyond the closed door was unequivocal. 'Piss off!'

She winced then used the skeleton key George had given her to unlock the door and walked in, whistling.

Old Man Stone-arm and his son had the same dark eyes, the same arching, bushy eyebrows and the same overhanging forehead that was so typical of ogres. Although he was sitting down in a chair by the window with a copy of the *Coldstream Courier* in his hands, Mallory could tell that he was also vertically-challenged. That must have been difficult for the Stone-arms, but it hadn't stopped them from achieving success. Far from it.

'What are you doing in here? I didn't say you could come in!' the old man spat.

'You don't want fresh towels?'

'No!'

'Would you like me to empty your bins?'

'No! Fuck off!'

'Do you need the fridge replenished?'

'How many times do I need to tell you to leave?'

She smiled professionally. 'How about your bed, sir?' She glanced at the perfectly smooth bedsheets and plumped-up pillows. 'Shall I make it up for you?'

'It's made up, you stupid girl! Housekeeping has already been here today so I don't know why…' His voice faltered and he stared at her. 'Who are you?' he whispered. 'You're not housekeeping, are you?'

'Nope,' Mallory said cheerfully.

His skin paled as he put down the newspaper and rose from the chair. He might be elderly but the muscles on his arms and neck, not to mention the fire in his eyes, suggested he was still a long way from his grave. 'You're from EEL,' he breathed.

It was interesting that his first assumption was that she was an assassin. 'No,' she said. 'I'm not here to hurt you, Mr Stone-arm.'

He clearly didn't believe her – and that was good. If he thought she was a highly trained killer, he might be less likely to attack her. Unfortunately, no sooner had that thought occurred to her than he lunged, grabbed her upper arms and squeezed hard.

'Then why the fuck are you here?' he snarled, releasing a cloud of stale coffee breath. 'What do you want?'

Mallory winced; he really was hurting her. 'I'm here on business, on behalf of a coven of local witches.'

Old Man Stone-arm immediately released her, threw back his head and cackled. 'The Pitcairns, I presume?'

Mallory did her best to look shocked. 'Oh no, definitely not them.'

He gazed at her; he was interested now, though but he was trying hard not to show it.

'The witches I represent have a far grander lineage than the

Pitcairns – more money, better connections and far greater magic.'

'Who?'

'I'm not at liberty to say.'

This time Old Man Stone-arm reached for her throat though he didn't squeeze it. His touch was feather light but his intention was very clear. 'I could *make* you tell me.'

Mallory tightened her toes. 'You could try, but I did tell you that my clients are powerful.'

'They've put a gagging spell on you?' His eyes widened.

Mallory neither confirmed nor denied it. That was the thing about gagging spells: if one was placed on you, you couldn't talk about it. She continued gazing at the ogre and waited for him to remove his hand from around her neck.

Thankfully, he did. 'Very well,' he sniffed. 'What do this coven want?'

'It's quite simple. They want you to keep the restrictive covenant in place to prevent the Pitcairns from growing their own magical plants and herbs – and they're prepared to pay you for doing so.'

Suddenly the old ogre laughed. 'Ha! There's no honour amongst witches! This coven of yours doesn't want any competition, does it? They want all the power for themselves.'

'I'm not a witch, and I can't speak for their motives.' Mostly because they don't exist, she added silently to herself.

Old Man Stone-arm barely heard her. 'Witches are all the same – grubby, money-grabbing bastards who only care about themselves. The Witches Council likes to pretend otherwise but I know the truth.' He paused. 'Is it the *Council* that you represent?' He licked his lips. 'That would be quite the thing,' he breathed.

Mallory stayed silent.

'How much?' he demanded. 'How much are they willing to pay for me to maintain the Pitcairn covenant?'

'They'll give the money to your son since he is head of the Association, not to you.'

The ogre grinned maliciously. 'There's a reason why you're here talking to me and not my little Dickie. He *pretends* he's in charge but everyone knows I'm still holding the reins. The money will come to me in the end.'

No wonder Richard Stone-arm had reacted so strongly when Mallory had called him a dick; it was the same word his father used against him. She felt a sudden sympathy for the younger ogre – then she pursed her lips and shrugged. 'That's not for me to say. I'm simply doing as I'm told.'

'You're the errand girl,' he sneered. 'Very well. Tell me, little girl, how much will they pay?'

Vanessa Pitcairn had already offered him twenty grand so Mallory doubled it. 'Forty thousand pounds,' she said. 'Forty thousand pounds to do absolutely nothing at all. It's the easiest pay cheque you'll ever get.'

Old Man Stone-arm's eyes gleamed. 'That's a lot of money.' He stroked his chin. 'The Witches Council is definitely behind this. They don't want any of the covens to succeed, especially the older ones like the Pitcairns.' He met Mallory's eyes. 'No deal.'

She flinched slightly. 'Fifty thousand.'

He leered at her. 'No.'

'How much then, Mr Stone-arm? What will it take?'

'There is no amount of money in the world that will tempt me to deal with the Witches Council! You can scurry back and tell them that I'll call the Pitcairn coven. As of this moment, the restrictive covenant on them is null and void.'

And with that, the old ogre laughed and laughed and laughed.

MANIPULATING people wasn't Mallory's preferred way of doing business; experience had taught her that being upfront and honest was by far the best way to proceed. However, sometimes it was important to adapt to particular clients and she didn't feel bad about twisting Old Man Stone-arm into doing what she wanted. Quite the opposite. And it was clear from High Priestess Vanessa Pitcairn's face when she opened her front door that the witch felt the same.

'I don't know what you did or how you did it, but you've worked a miracle.' Unexpectedly the witch drew her into a hug. 'A bloody amazing miracle,' she whispered. She pulled back. 'Richard Stone-arm phoned me less than an hour ago. The Association's solicitor is already preparing the paperwork and the restrictive covenant will be removed by the weekend.'

Mallory smiled happily. 'I'm pleased to hear it.'

'How did you do it? We've tried everything over the years – everything – and yet it's only taken you a few days. Are you sure you're just a squib?'

'You don't need magic to be powerful.'

'Clearly.' Vanessa gazed at her, still baffled as to how Mallory had achieved the seemingly impossible outcome the Pitcairn witches had always wanted.

Mallory took pity on her. 'It was quite straightforward. The problem wasn't Richard Stone-arm – in fact I suspect that he's very happy at the final outcome because it'll make his life easier. He told me that he likes you. It was his father, Old Man Stone-arm, who was causing the problems. Unfortunately he doesn't like witches very much, *any* witches, although the Witches Council is at the top of his list. Neither does he like being told what to do. Or rather,' she amended, 'what not to do. I simply played on those aspects of his personality.'

'I can't say I understand, but I'm definitely grateful,' Vanessa told her. 'This will change everything for us. It's only a few plants and herbs to you, but to us it's our entire livelihood. I can't thank you enough.'

'All I need is what we agreed upon.'

Vanessa nodded. 'The bellarmine jug is on its way. Give me your address and I'll come by your place with it on Sunday morning.'

Mallory held her breath. 'Really? An original jug?'

'Yes.'

'Without anything inside it?'

'Yes.'

Mallory wanted to be absolutely sure. 'That I can borrow until after August?'

Vanessa smiled. 'That you can keep. It's the very least I can do. I've pulled a few favours – something *you* will approve of. You will own the jug forever.'

Mallory exhaled; this was more than she'd expected. Given how difficult it had been to get hold of the darned jug, it would be good to keep hold of it once Chester Longchamps had finished with it. It might well come in handy in the future. 'Thank you,' she said whole-heartedly.

The High Priestess shook her head. 'No. Thank *you*. You are truly a wonderful woman.'

'Alexander MacTire deserves a wonderful woman, or so you keep telling me.' Boris jabbed at the first picture he'd pinned up on the wall. 'She,' he declared, 'is wonderful *and* almost perfect for him.'

Mallory frowned at the photograph. 'I'm not so sure.'

'She's his type physically.'

She was already shaking her head. 'I've established that looks aren't what turns Alexander on.'

'Bullshit. If he says that, he's lying.'

'It might be what draws his attention to someone but looks won't keep his attention. Remember, we're looking for someone who will be with him for life. He wants a mate, someone who'll be by his side as he leads the MacTires into the future. This has to be about more than looks.'

'Mallory,' the spriggan said patiently, 'we've been through the guest list several times and we've researched every available woman. These are the top five and you know it.' He pointed again at the first photograph. 'Isadora Jones has to be number one. She's intelligent, ambitious, kind and beautiful.'

Mallory picked up the first page of guest names; there was a star next to Isadora's. 'Alexander has dated her before.'

Suddenly Boris looked smug. 'I looked into that. They dated for a couple of weeks more than ten years ago. They're different people now, more mature. They know what they want whereas before they were young, naïve and easily confused.'

As Mallory stared at the picture of the stunning blonde werewolf, she had to admit that she'd be a good match for Alexander. On paper, anyway. She sighed. 'Fine.'

'Fine? Is that all you can say?' He eyed her suspiciously. 'Don't you want him to succeed?'

'Of course I do.'

Boris raised an eyebrow.

'I do!' Mallory protested. 'It's just that this isn't like navigating grumpy old ogres or managing angry vampires. It's not locating an object or finding out a scrap of information. It's somebody's *life* – two lives, in fact. I want to get it right, Boris.'

A tiny insistent voice piped up in the back of her mind: *You're lying. You want Alexander MacTire for yourself.*

'Okay. I didn't mean to suggest anything untoward. I know how seriously you take your contracts.'

'I've thrown my heart and soul into this business,' Mallory murmured, as much to herself as to Boris. 'I won't ever knowingly let a client down, blood contract or not.'

She had to do her best for Alexander MacTire; he wanted to find a woman to be his First Mate and she had to do everything in her power to achieve that – whether it made her heart ache or not. If she could find a damned bellarmine jug for Chester Longchamps, she could find the perfect partner for Alexander.

'You're right,' she said finally, looking again at the five photos pinned on the wall. 'Isadora Jones could be the one. I'll do some more research into her.'

'Great.' Boris sounded enthusiastic. 'By Sunday morning the Wolf Ball will be over and your role will be complete, regardless of the outcome.'

Mallory bit her lip. 'Great,' she said, echoing the spriggan. 'Wonderful.' She pasted on a bright smile. 'Absolutely fabulous.'

CHAPTER

NINETEEN

The last time Mallory had seen Gia Vanderlan, the fashion designer had been dressed in a bright-pink suit with cheeks to match; on this occasion her flush of excitement was the same but her clothes were lime green. You would certainly pick her out of a crowd.

Mallory hoped that the dress Gia had brought would be less showy. Alexander was due to pick her up for the Wolf Ball and there wouldn't be time to find an alternative.

'Thankfully Boris sent through your measurements.' Gia bustled around Mallory's small flat extracting various bits of kit. 'But I would have preferred at least one fitting beforehand.'

'I've been busy,' Mallory said. 'I meant to come by but...' Her voice trailed off and she felt the heat rise in her cheeks.

'She forgot that she had to wear a real dress,' Boris interjected unhelpfully.

Gia gasped in horror. 'But this is the Wolf Ball! It's one of the most important events of the season, Mallory. The fact that you have an invitation – and with Alexander MacTire of all people—'

'It's not a date,' Mallory said briskly. 'It's business.'

Curiosity lit up Gia's face. 'He's a client? What are you helping him with?'

She knew better than to ask that question and when it became clear that Mallory wasn't going to answer, she smiled. 'Well, whatever it is I know he's lucky to have you. I still haven't forgotten how you came through for me. I've worked really hard on this dress – it's the least I can do, favour or no. You deserve the very best.'

Over the years Mallory had learned to accept compliments, but for some reason accepting this one was difficult and she had to quash the rising sense of imposter syndrome. If tonight went as planned then she deserved those kind words, she told herself. And it *would* go as planned. Alexander *would* find success tonight. She couldn't entertain any other outcome. She muttered her thanks and Gia beamed.

'So,' the flamboyant witch said, 'although there wasn't a lot of time, I wanted to be sure you had something spectacular to wear.'

Uh-oh. Mallory tried to ignore the sinking feeling in her stomach.

'It's important that you feel sexy...'

Mallory gritted her teeth.

'...but I also wanted to make sure you were comfortable.'

She felt a sudden spasm of hope.

Gia recognised what her expression meant. 'Oh, Mallory! I saw enough of you last year to get a sense of your style. I'm good at what I do and I wouldn't put you in something you didn't like.'

'I'm holding out for lime green,' Boris said. 'With plenty of cleavage.' Both women frowned at him. 'Actually,' he added hastily, 'I'm clocking off for the night.' He bowed to Gia. 'Lovely to see you again, Miss Vanderlan. Mallory, good luck tonight.

I'm quite sure that Mr MacTire will walk away very satisfied with the outcome.'

Mallory swallowed as he waved and left. Gia had already turned away and was unzipping a garment bag. 'Ta-da!' She held up the dress in front of her.

Mallory stared. She didn't know what she'd been expecting but it certainly wasn't this. If she were honest, it was something of a disappointment. A modest empire design, the material appeared to be expensive black velvet. There wasn't a flash of lime green, hot pink or even a saucy thigh-baring slit in sight.

'Oh.' She smiled politely. To be fair, the dress, was ideal because it would help her stay in the background and that was her role. Gia had done exactly what was required of her. 'It's very pretty.'

Gia laughed aloud. 'Now tell me what you really think.'

'I'm not lying! It's very pretty! Thank you very much, Gia. It's exactly what I hoped for.'

'Just wait. Put it on and then we'll see.' There was something in her voice – merriment, perhaps. Or delighted anticipation.

Mallory looked at her warily as she took the dress and moved towards her bedroom. 'I'll only be a minute.'

'Take your time.'

Peeling off her dungarees and oversized shirt, Mallory clambered into the dress and fastened it. It fit perfectly, clinging to her every curve in all the right places and draping over the spots that she preferred not to highlight.

As she smoothed it down, she realised the fabric wasn't velvet; in fact, she couldn't tell what it was. It was soft but it had an unusual shimmer. She nibbled on her bottom lip. There was magic bound into this dress, she'd put money on it. Still, Gia had been right about one thing – it was definitely comfortable. She could wear this outfit all night and there would be no wriggling or twitching.

Padding into the living room, Mallory smiled. 'I take it back,' she said. 'It's not pretty, it's beautiful.'

Gia sprang up. 'It's not finished yet.' She looked her up and down with a critical eye. 'More boob,' she said, brandishing a pair of scissors.

Mallory's eyes widened in alarm. 'Uh...'

'Don't worry, this will only take a jiffy.' The witch stayed where she was, her fingers sparking with light, and the scissors started to glow. Mallory felt an odd tugging around her chest and glanced down. An inch of fabric peeled away, re-forming almost immediately into a perfectly stitched edge.

She gaped. 'That's some spell.'

Gia winked. 'You ain't seen nothing yet.' She reached for one of the many tools she'd unpacked earlier, a strange metallic curled stick. 'Close your eyes.'

'Um, Gia, I don't...'

'Trust me.'

Mallory drew in a breath and did as she was told. There was a hiss of air, followed by a strange crackle as the material of the dress stretched and altered.

'Oh yes,' Gia breathed. 'It's exactly as I imagined.'

Mallory opened first one eye and then the other. When she saw how the simple dress had been transformed, her mouth dropped open.

'I would never dress you in black, Mal. That's not your colour. You're sunshine sparkles, not a night-time diamond.'

Still unable to summon up words, Mallory continued to gape. The dress was definitely no longer black and it definitely wasn't shimmering velvet; in fact, the fabric seemed to have vanished and in its place were hundreds upon hundreds of glittering, golden butterflies. When she reached out tentatively and brushed one of them, its wings fluttered gently. 'Gia...'

'They're not real,' the designer reassured her. 'No butterflies were harmed in the making of this dress. Think of them of as a glamoured illusion.'

'I've never seen anything like it in my life.'

Gia smacked her lips in satisfaction. 'That's exactly what I wanted to achieve.' She turned away and picked up a small mirror. Muttering a few words under her breath and holding it carefully to one side so it was away from her body, she used a blast of controlled magic to enlarge the reflective surface.

Suddenly Mallory could see her full-length reflection. The golden hue did something to her skin, making it glow as if she were shimmering in the same way as the magicked butterflies. Her face was lit up and the overall effect was beautifully dramatic. 'It's amazing,' she whispered.

'I know.' Gia jerked her hand and the mirror returned to its original size. 'It's not perfect – there wasn't enough time for that, I'm afraid. If you make a lot of swift movements, the butterflies will struggle to keep up and there'll be, uh, flashes of skin.'

Mallory blinked. 'Pardon?'

'Try a few kicks,' Gia advised.

She did as she was told. Each time she moved her leg, the butterflies parted across her thigh to reveal her legs. 'Oh,' she said faintly. 'I see.'

'As long as you wear underwear, you'll be fine.'

'Uh-huh.'

'It lasts for a split second. Nothing more.'

Mallory made a mental note to make as few sudden movements as possible. 'Okay, I'll be careful.'

Gia smiled happily then her face fell abruptly. 'Oh no.' She shook her head. 'Oh no.'

'What?' Mallory asked. 'What is it?'

'Your arms! Those bruises!'

Mallory frowned and glanced at her upper arms: there were blue and purple marks encircling them where Old Man Stone-arm had grabbed her. 'They look worse than they are,' she said weakly.

'They look like somebody has held you down. Those are clearly handprints.' Gia put her hands on her hips and a surprisingly protective glint came into her eyes. 'Who did this to you? Are you alright?'

'I'm fine, I promise. It was a one-off thing with an old guy who I doubt I'll ever see again. I dealt with it. He didn't hurt me.'

'That's not what those bruises are saying.' Gia reached for another box. 'It's lucky I came prepared with some concealment spells so I can cover them up temporarily.' She wagged a finger. 'But you need to take care of yourself, Mallory.'

'I will.' She cleared her throat. 'I do.'

'Hmmm.' Gia looked only half-convinced but at least she changed the subject. 'I assume you've not given much thought to hair and make-up?' Mallory looked at her blankly. 'Any thought at all?'

Mallory pulled a face.

Gia gave a mock sigh. 'Sit yourself down. When I'm done with you, you'll be fit to party the entire night away with any werewolf who crosses your path. Bring on the glamour!'

IT TOOK MORE time than Mallory had anticipated for Gia to tame her hair into submission and endow her with a full face of dramatic make-up; in fact, it wasn't long after the witch had finished and left when there was a sharp knock on the door.

All of a sudden it wasn't only her dress that was an expanse of fluttering butterflies; now her stomach was full of them as well. She admonished herself. This was business and Alexander was a client. After tonight she'd never have to see him again because, if she did her job properly, he'd be far too busy wooing his future life partner to bother her again. She heaved in a breath and opened the door.

Alexander was standing on her narrow landing holding a corsage. Mallory stared at him: she'd been expecting him to wear a suit as he usually did, but he'd chosen a more traditional approach and was wearing a kilt, of all things. Her gaze travelled from his smart jacket, crisp shirt, to his belted waist, the blue-and-grey tartan complete with sporran, and then to his calf-high socks and the small skean dhu dagger that was nestling inside the right one.

She couldn't help herself. 'Wow.'

Alexander didn't say anything as he gazed at her, his expression inscrutable.

Mallory swallowed awkwardly. 'A kilt is a great choice. There's a romance about a kilt that any woman will approve of – it's rugged and masculine but it also suggests tradition and strength.' She was aware that she was babbling but she couldn't stop herself. 'And, of course, it helps that you have great legs.'

Alexander remained mute.

She raised her head and met his eyes. 'Uh, is everything alright?'

He cleared his throat and finally spoke. 'Mallory.' His voice sounded unusually hoarse. 'You're breathtaking.'

She'd hoped he'd appreciate her efforts but she hadn't expected that reaction. Her toes curled in her totteringly high shoes. 'Um, thank you.'

His smile was so tight and controlled that she wondered for

a moment if she'd somehow offended him. 'This evening is about you, not me,' she said. 'If the dress is too showy—'

A growl rumbled in his chest. 'It's perfect.'

She gazed at him then shrugged. 'Okay.' She gestured to the stairs. 'Shall we?'

He leaned towards her and seemed to inhale deeply. 'Yes,' he said eventually. 'Let's.'

~

Preoccupied by other matters, Mallory hadn't given much thought as to how they would travel to the Wolf Ball, which was being held in the heartbreakingly beautiful Grand Hotel eight miles outside Coldstream.

If she'd considered it, she'd have assumed they would take the tram to the outskirts and then clamber onto buses specially hired from outside the magical city for the event. The Coldstream streets were too narrow for large vehicles to navigate comfortably, and cars were rare – unless you were the likes of Alexander MacTire, and even then magic and technology didn't mix particularly well.

What Mallory hadn't expected was a carriage drawn by two gleaming black horses. 'We're travelling in *that*?'

'The first night we met you didn't appear impressed by the fact that I owned a car,' Alexander said. 'This seemed more appropriate. Besides, this is a ball. Horse and carriage is surely the best way to travel.'

'I'm Goldilocks, remember? Not Cinderella.'

A small smile curled his mouth. 'But I'm trying to be Prince Charming.' He opened the carriage door. 'Here, I'll help you up. I can assure you that it's quite spacious and comfortable.'

She allowed him to take her hand and she clambered inside. He was right: the carriage interior was large, with a padded seat along one side and – of course – a small bar along the other. Two chilled champagne flutes were waiting.

'A wee aperitif?' Alexander asked, once he'd settled beside her. 'I can promise you it's a good vintage.'

Feeling squirmingly awkward, Mallory nodded. 'Sure. Yes. Thank you. That would be lovely. Very nice.' She pulled a face.

Alexander turned his amber eyes on her. 'You're nervous?'

'Of course. I'm not used to this sort of thing and I want to make sure that we find you the right person. This is important.'

'It is.' He continued to watch her. 'I'm nervous, too.'

He didn't look nervous. Not now. She wetted her lips. 'A drink would be great.'

He retrieved a bottle of champagne from an ice bucket, poured two glasses and handed her one as the carriage rolled forward. The clip-clop of the horses' hooves on the cobbles was charmingly audible without being loud enough to intrude on their conversation.

'Neither of us should be nervous,' Alexander said. 'It's quite illogical to feel that way.'

Mallory raised her eyebrows and took a small sip from her glass. 'Go on.'

He grinned. 'You've already told me I look like a romantic hero in this kilt.'

'I didn't quite say that.'

'You said I had great legs.'

'I'll give you that,' she replied grudgingly.

'As I've told you before,' Alexander murmured. 'I'm hand-some, charming and sex on legs – sex on great legs, in fact. Can there possibly be a woman attending the Wolf Ball who won't think that?'

'I can't imagine so,' Mallory responded drily. 'And the best part is that you're so very modest.'

He laughed. 'Oh, I'm not reserving the compliments for myself. You will be a great success, too.'

She snorted.

'You're Mallory Nash,' he continued softly. 'Of course you'll be successful.' He raised his glass. 'To us.'

She swallowed. 'To us.'

He took a sip but he didn't stop looking at her. 'Mallory,' he began. 'I...'

'You'll find her tonight, Alexander,' she reassured him quickly. 'I'm sure of it.'

He blinked and looked away. 'Yes.'

She took another gulp of champagne. 'Do you remember Isadora Jones?'

His brow furrowed slightly. 'Yes.'

'You dated her ten years or so ago.'

Alexander pulled away another inch. 'You've been doing your research.'

'That's what you're paying me for.'

His expression closed and she felt a twitch. What did that mean? He didn't like Isadora? He hated the idea of approaching her again? Or did he actually think this was a relationship that could work? She pressed ahead; it was all she could do. It was why she was there. 'Have you spoken to her recently?'

Alexander put down his glass. 'Our paths rarely cross.'

He didn't seem to want to talk about Isadora but Mallory plunged ahead. 'You didn't date for long. Why didn't the relationship continue?'

A muscle throbbed in his jaw. 'It was a long time ago.' Mallory waited. Eventually he sighed. 'We were both too busy. I was having problems with my father and she had her own stuff going on.'

'So it was a timing issue.' Mallory's tone held a note of triumph that she didn't really feel. He didn't respond. 'She'll be there tonight,' she went on. 'You put a star next to her name to say that you'd already been in a relationship so I didn't look into her to begin with, but Boris has highlighted her many attributes and I think he's right.'

'Mm.'

She persisted. 'She's very intelligent. Her wolf pack is strong, so she's unlikely to rise much higher in the ranks, not because she isn't capable but because there are too many other good candidates for positions of power. In fact, she's supporting her cousin's bid for beta wolf, which proves she's more interested in helping others rather than in furthering her own cause. Isadora Jones has a genuine knack for getting on with people, and that will really help her if she marries into another pack.'

'Yes.'

'And the Jones' wolves would be great pack to form a strong alliance with. You should seek her out, have a chat with her. She's single at the moment but I doubt she will be for long. She's dating, but she's not settled on anyone.'

He drained his glass. 'I'll talk to her.'

'On paper she's the perfect woman for you.'

'On paper,' he conceded. He sighed. 'I will make sure I talk to her.'

Mallory would have liked a touch more enthusiasm but she was prepared to accept his answer for now. 'This is going to be a wonderful night.'

Alexander's hand covered hers and his heat seared her skin. 'Yes,' he said, sounding far warmer. 'It is.'

CHAPTER

TWENTY

Mallory had been to many fascinating places since she'd moved to Coldstream. Some had been grand and gorgeous, some had been grubby and dilapidated, plenty had been magical – but she'd never been anywhere quite like the Grand Hotel.

The building was the size of Crackendon Square and it put her less in mind of a swanky hotel than an ancient fortress built to withstand invaders. An army of dragons could attack the place with all the powers invested in them and the walls of the Grand Hotel would suffer nothing more than a few scorch marks.

For the purposes of the Wolf Ball, the grandest affair in every werewolf's calendar, it had been decked out. Its exterior was illuminated with witchlight, and bright colours in every shade of the rainbow were lighting every rugged crook and dramatic cranny. A long red carpet led up to the hotel's main entrance flanked on either side by a six-metre-high wall of blue fire.

A traditional pipe band, doubtless brought in from one of the larger non-magical cities in Scotland, was standing to one side. Mallory surreptitiously checked out the kilted pipers and drummers but none of them looked as good in a kilt as Alexander. She indulged herself for one pleasurable moment and allowed him to draw ahead so she could enjoy the swaying motion of the heavy fabric as he walked.

When he realised she wasn't by his side he paused, glanced over his shoulder then grinned at her expression. She felt a flush of embarrassment at being caught out.

'It's quite something, isn't it?' he asked.

'Uh...' Mallory floundered helplessly.

'The Grand Hotel was built in the eighteenth century. I've been here for the Wolf Ball every year for the past twenty-odd years and it still takes my breath away.'

'Yes.' She nodded vigorously. 'Yes, it's truly amazing.' She beamed at him, aware that her smile was overly wide, then caught up and they moved onto the red carpet behind the other guests.

The Wolf Ball was extraordinarily exclusive if you were not a werewolf or not invited by one, and also extraordinarily inclusive in that every single werewolf in Coldstream was invited regardless of their pack, standing or power. Few wolves missed it and few non-wolves attended. Mallory would have laid a decent bet that she was the first squib to be admitted. Despite the pressure of the evening, and the presence of her companion, she was genuinely awed – and they'd not even walked through the front door.

Two liveried footmen bowed as they passed beneath the arched entrance where a tall witch with a clipboard was marking off names. Security was unobtrusive, but Mallory had no doubt that it would prove impregnable if it were tested.

'Don't worry,' Alexander murmured. 'There'll be many others here who aren't werewolves. You won't be the only one.'

He paused. 'But you'll be the only one who looks so spectacularly beautiful.'

Mallory plucked self-consciously at her dress and the magicked butterflies fluttered at her touch. She was aware that she was already drawing curious glances from other guests, though she was certain that was more because of who she was with rather than what she was wearing.

Reminding herself of the reason she was there, and unwilling to appear romantically involved with Alexander, she stepped slightly away to put some air between them. He immediately stiffened but before she could explain herself, a tuxedoed werewolf approached them. 'Alexander MacTire! This is the first time I've seen you wearing a kilt at one of these shindigs!'

Alexander responded with an easy grin. 'I thought I'd make an effort.' He waved at the other man's outfit. 'After all, I'd hate to be mistaken for a waiter.'

The werewolf roared with laughter and turned to Mallory. 'And who is your glorious date?'

'A curious companion rather than a date,' Mallory replied swiftly. 'I'm Mallory.'

The wolf bowed. 'Alisdair Bartonwich, at your service.' He smiled. 'You're not a wolf.'

Alexander snorted. 'Well spotted.'

'My old friend here is terribly rude,' Alisdair said. 'I'm going to ignore him and focus on you because you are far more beautiful and considerably more interesting. So you're not a wolf, you're not a witch and you're not a druid. That much is obvious.' He sniffed the air. 'I can't smell any magic.'

Mallory curtsied and the hundreds of butterflies flapped and shimmered. 'That's because I don't have any.'

He stared at her. 'You're a squib?' He turned to Alexander. 'I knew you were a maverick, but this is definitely new. No wonder we've never met before tonight.'

'Now who sounds rude?' Alexander asked.

Alisdair bowed again. 'Forgive me. You usually have more powerful women on your arm.'

Mallory felt a stab of pain. She didn't need another reminder that she would never be right for Alexander MacTire, but here it was all the same.

Alexander only barked out a laugh. 'Oh, Alisdair, you truly have no idea of what real power is. Mallory may not be forced to turn furry once a month by the whims of the moon but she has far more power at her fingertips than you could ever imagine.'

'Interesting,' Alisdair mused. 'Very interesting.'

'It's quite true. Just ask my friend Kevin.'

Mallory blinked as Alisdair frowned. 'Kevin? Kevin who?' he asked.

Alexander laughed again. 'Never mind. Come on, Mallory, let's find our table.'

They moved away. 'Alisdair isn't a bad sort,' he told her, once they were out of earshot. 'But he enjoys hiding his aggression behind a polite veneer that only thinly veils his intentions. We are not exactly friends, regardless of what he might suggest.'

Mallory glanced first at him and then at the werewolves around them who were shaking hands, patting backs, dipping heads and murmuring to each other. 'This is much more than a posh party, isn't it?'

'Oh yes. The three Ps of the Wolf Ball: posturing, politics, and pretence.'

'What about the one R?' she asked. 'Romance?'

He looked into her eyes. 'That still remains to be seen,' he said softly. 'But I am very optimistic.'

THE VAST BALLROOM had a large stage and area for dancing as well as numerous tables, each one with plates, glasses, shining silver cutlery and small white cards with names written in exquisite calligraphy.

'Hold on a moment,' Alexander said. 'I'll find out where we're sitting. There ought to be a seating chart somewhere. The alphas are usually together.'

'There's no need,' Mallory said cheerfully. 'I know where we're sitting – and I'm afraid it's not at an alphas-only table.'

He frowned. 'How do you know?'

She didn't reply but moved to the right and made a beeline for one of the quieter spots to the side of the stage. 'It's this way.' Finally she paused and picked up a name card. 'We're right here.'

Alexander leaned over her shoulder. 'So we are.' He glanced at the name card to his left. 'There's you.' He turned and checked the name card on his right. 'Ah. Isadora Jones. How … fortuitous.'

'Indeed.'

'And how exactly did you manage that? The Wolf Ball planners don't take bribes – they're a law unto themselves and don't allow their vision to be swayed by anyone. Plenty of people in the past have tried to arrange the seating chart to their benefit and failed miserably.'

Mallory held up her hands and wiggled her fingers. 'More power than you could ever imagine,' she whispered.

'I deserved that.'

She smiled. 'You did.'

As he bowed towards her, she tightened her toes and took a deep breath, then she sat down and pretended that everything was absolutely wonderful.

It wasn't long before all the other guests had located their tables and taken their seats. Mallory spotted Isadora Jones long before the wolf found their table. Her date was a male werewolf called Sean, a blandly handsome member of the Jones wolf pack. Nothing Mallory had found out suggested he was anything more than arm candy; watching them stroll up, she could tell that although they were chatting easily there weren't any lusty undercurrents between them.

'I hope you know what you're doing,' Alexander muttered to her as they stood up to welcome the new arrivals.

'You're the one on show here, not me,' she retorted.

At least Isadora looked pleasantly surprised to see him. She kissed him on the cheek and smiled. 'It's been too long, Lexy!'

'I wish you wouldn't call me that, Dora.'

'As long as you don't call me *that*,' she returned with an easy wink.

Alexander introduced Mallory, then Isadora introduced Sean and the other guests at their table, a smattering of were-wolves from the Brady and the Callaghan packs.

'I saw you when you came in,' Isadora said to Mallory. 'That dress is exquisite. I've never seen anything like it in my life. Where did you get it?'

Mallory was only too happy to answer. 'Gia Vanderlan designed it for me.'

Isadora's mouth dropped. 'That's a *Vanderlan*? Now I'm even more impressed. I've been trying to get an appointment with her for months but she's always booked up.'

'I'll put in a good word for you if you like,' Mallory offered. 'But your dress is stunning, too.' It was true: Isadora was wearing a floor-length sheath spotted artfully with glittering diamante. She looked lithe, strong and very attractive. Isadora Jones was Gia's version of a night diamond, for sure.

'That would be amazing! Thank you!'

Mallory nodded, smiled and turned away to engage the surprised werewolf on her left in conversation, freeing Alexander to talk to Isadora. She was well aware that he could turn on full-wattage charm when the situation called for it, and he deserved the space to let himself shine.

Isadora and Alexander were well-suited, she told herself firmly. This could work, and when it did and there was some space and time between herself and Alexander, her uncomfortable feelings for him would fade away. It was all but certain.

ALTHOUGH THE CONVERSATION at their table was initially stilted, by the time the starters were served everyone had relaxed. On the one hand that was great: relaxed people were happy people, and the happier Isadora and Alexander were, the more chance there was of them connecting on a deeper level. On the other hand, as Colin Brady regaled them with tales of his recent exploits, it also meant that there was less opportunity for them to enjoy a quiet tête-à-tête.

When dessert was finished and coffee had arrived, the conversation turned to more serious matters. 'I've heard that the Worthington pack are having serious financial difficulties,' Sean Jones said.

Colin Brady's partner, a bearded werewolf with astonishingly dark twinkling eyes, nodded. 'There's a lot of that around at the moment. I noticed that only half of them are here tonight. It's the same for the Thomsons – not every pack can afford for all their members to attend the Wolf Ball, not in the current climate.'

'You know,' Colin grumbled, 'that instances of wolfsbane are on the rise again. It's supposed to be illegal but it's being sprinkled all over the place. I picked up a trace of it even here.'

Everyone at the table pulled faces. 'It will pass,' Alexander said. 'A few packs have been exerting their authority in unnecessary ways and this is how non-werewolves react as a result. Things will settle down before too long.'

Sean Jones gave him a knowing look. 'A little birdie told me that you've been buying up wolfsbane stock.'

Alexander grinned. 'If there's no wolfsbane on the market, then there's less opportunity for its misuse.'

Or, Mallory reflected, for instances of deepening aggression. Alexander was very quietly and very cleverly defusing any future problems that might result from increased wolfsbane usage. Smart.

'Speaking of packs who often misbehave badly and absent guests,' Isadora piped up, 'There's no sign of the Barrow pack tonight. I've not even seen Ashina, the Barrow alpha.'

Alexander looked surprised. 'Really?'

She glanced at him. 'You've not noticed? That's the sort of detail you used to be all over.'

'I guess I'm somewhat distracted this evening,' he murmured. 'I have other things on my mind.'

Isadora's eyebrows rose. 'Do tell.'

Alexander chuckled awkwardly but he was prevented from elaborating by the band appearing on the stage. 'Good evening to all my furry friends!' the lead singer bellowed into the microphone. 'And welcome to the eighty-seventh Annual Wolf Ball! I hope you're having a great time and you've enjoyed your meal. Let's work off some of that food and have a dance. I want to see everybody – and I mean *everybody* – on the dance floor!'

As he finished his words there was a tremendous clash of cymbals, then the guitarist immediately launched into the first chords of the opening song.

Mallory gently elbowed Alexander – this was his opportunity to leap in and ask Isadora to dance – but it was already too late. Isadora was on her feet with Sean by her side and the Callaghans and Bradys were up, too. It appeared that every single werewolf was following the singer's instructions and heading for the dance floor.

Alexander pushed back his chair, stood up and held out his hand to Mallory. 'Will you do me the honour of this dance?'

'You should be dancing with Isadora,' she protested.

'She's already spoken for. I'll ask her later. Right now, I'd like to dance with you.' He sounded as if he meant it.

She swallowed and nodded; it would look strange if she didn't dance with him. She gave him her hand and felt the gentle pressure of his fingers. A moment later, she was in his arms.

It was an upbeat, big-band number. Mallory couldn't profess to being particularly nimble and her sense of rhythm wasn't quite as developed as it could have been: more like she had two left feet and tended to spin left when she was supposed to go right. But now, with Alexander holding her, she felt as if she were floating on air. She didn't worry about getting the steps wrong or stumbling and falling over; she didn't really think about anything other than how good it felt to be dancing with him.

She ought to ask him how he felt things were going and if there was a spark with Isadora, but she was enjoying the moment too much. She could allow herself this, she decided. It was only five minutes.

His hand slid comfortably around her waist while her fingers lingered on his broad, muscled back. He lowered his head towards hers until she could feel his breath on her cheek as he guided her confidently to the left, then the right and then into a spin, stretching out the space between them as he twirled her with one hand.

Slightly breathless, she moved away and back towards him.

She smiled up at him – but his expression had frozen. 'What?' she asked. 'What's wrong?'

Wordlessly, he gestured towards her. Baffled, she gazed at him as couples danced around them. 'Alex?'

'Your dress,' he muttered. 'The butterflies. When you spin, they move and…' His voice faltered.

'Oh.' Mallory grinned to mask her embarrassment. 'Flashing too much skin?'

His cheeks were suddenly flushed. 'I wouldn't say too much. It took me by surprise, that's all.' His amber eyes darkened. 'In fact, I'd like to see—' He halted in mid-sentence. 'Never mind.'

She stared at him. The song ended and the other couples returned to their seats, but they continued to stare at each other. 'We should go back to the table,' he said gruffly after a moment or two then turned and stalked away, leaving her on the dance floor wondering if she'd offended him with her golden butterflies and bare skin – or if there was something else going on.

CHAPTER

TWENTY-ONE

It didn't take long after the first dance for the true politics of the Wolf Ball to kick in. Mallory had barely picked up her glass of wine for a quick sip when the first werewolf alpha appeared, head bowed in obvious supplication. 'Mr MacTire. You cut a fine figure in that kilt. Absolutely tremendous. Is that a family tartan?'

'It was specially commissioned for the MacTires several decades ago.' Alexander rose to shake hands.

'Well, I'm very envious.' Without missing a beat, the alpha started work. 'Now, tell me, have you had a chance to read my proposal concerning the full-moon bylaws?'

'Make an appointment with Samantha next week and we can discuss it,' Alexander replied.

'But...'

'Bryan,' he said, clapping the man on the back, 'this is a party. Let's enjoy it.'

The werewolf slunk away disappointed, but it wasn't long before he was replaced by another, then another and another. There was a steady stream of werewolves, each keen to press hands with Alexander MacTire and get into his good books.

Mallory entertained herself by considering how differently she would manage each situation if they were her clients. None of them managed to engage Alexander in conversation for more than a minute and none held his attention.

'I've never seen this before,' Isadora commented, leaning across the table to Mallory while Alexander greeted wolf after wolf.

'Isn't Alexander usually this popular?' Mallory asked, surprised.

'Oh, he definitely is, but I've never seen him blow off so many werewolves in such a short space of time. He usually spends the whole ball wheeling and dealing.' She waved a hand at some of the tables nearby where heads were bowed deep in conversation. 'Most alphas do.'

Mallory sat up straighter. Isadora had given away far more information than she realised. 'You've followed him over the years, then? Alexander? You ... pay attention to him and how he acts?'

Isadora's eyes widened a fraction. 'Oh.' She put an embarrassed hand over her mouth. 'I used to, but please don't think I have designs on him now. I can see he's smitten with you.'

Mallory tripped over her words in her haste to respond. 'No, no, no. That's not – I mean, he's not – er – we're not together. It's a business thing. Kind of. Alexander is single. But he's looking for a romantic partner,' she added.

'I did hear that,' Isadora admitted. She gave Mallory a side-long look. 'You and he really do seem as if...'

'We're not,' she replied firmly.

'Oh. Okay.' Isadora smiled ruefully. 'In answer to your original question then, yeah, I'll admit I've spent quite a lot of time watching what he does. We dated briefly ten years ago but it didn't work out, not for want of wishing otherwise on my part.

For several years afterwards I wondered if he was the one who got away and if I should have tried harder to make things work.'

Mallory held her breath. 'And now?'

Isadora laughed. 'Now I realise I was young and foolish and we were never meant to be.'

Ignoring the stab in her heart, Mallory dragged out the next words. 'Are you sure about that? You seem to have a good relationship. There was definitely banter between you, and you seem to get on.'

But Isadora was already shaking her head. 'No, it's water under the bridge. I don't think he's the one for me. Or vice-versa.' She eyed Mallory speculatively.

'Ask him to dance,' Mallory said. 'Talk to him. You might surprise yourself.' Then, because pressing the point would seem like overkill, she stood up. 'Where are the restrooms?'

When Isadora pointed them out, she murmured her thanks and beat a hasty retreat.

THE TOILETS WERE as opulent as the rest of the Grand Hotel but Mallory paid them little attention. 'Get with the programme,' she whispered to herself. 'Remember why you're here.'

She splashed cold water on her face, rubbed her eyes then braced her hands against the cool marble basin and stared into the mirror – before wincing. Oh. That had been stupid.

The bruises on her arms might be concealed by magical make-up but the cosmetics on her face were as unmagical as any product you'd find anywhere in the world and they didn't react well to either water or smearing. In the space of a few seconds Mallory had gone from looking like a sultry temptress with smoky eyes and a perfect lipsticked pout to an angry punk desperate to fight the establishment. Hey-ho. It had been good while it lasted.

As she dampened some tissues and started to wipe away the mess, figuring that by this point her face was beyond repair, there was a flushing sound from one of the cubicles behind her. A moment later, Samantha appeared. 'Mallory?' She looked surprised. 'Are you alright?'

'All good. Just a minor make-up disaster.'

Samantha, who looked as immaculate and intimidating as ever, clucked in sympathy. 'I have some spare powder and mascara, and I'm fairly certain Hannah has lipstick, eyeshadow and contouring powder. I'm not even sure what contouring powder is but I bet she's got some. I can go and borrow it.'

Mallory shook her head. 'No, it's easier to go bare faced. I'll only end up making a mess of myself again.' She managed a grin. 'I can't be trusted not to.'

'Are you sure?'

'Absolutely.' Mallory continued wiping away the smears. 'Are you having a good evening?'

'It's fantastic!' Samantha sounded genuinely enthusiastic. 'I had a good meal, I'm enjoying the wine and so far I've taken out three werewolves from other packs who decided that they wanted to pick a fight.'

Mallory stopped in mid-wipe and turned to her. 'Seriously?'

'No.' Samantha grinned and Mallory had the sudden sense that she was being very serious indeed. 'How's your night going?'

Mallory breathed in deeply. 'Make-up mishaps aside, so far so good.'

'Uh-huh.' Samantha gave her a long look.

'What is it?'

Myriad expressions crossed the wolf's face. It was obvious there was something burning inside her that she wanted to say but for some reason she didn't feel she could. After several long seconds, she grimaced. 'You're a people person, Mallory.'

'Yeah,' Mallory said, unsure where Samantha was going with this.

'You seem to have excellent insights into people and their motivations. You understand emotions and secret desires.'

'I'm not infallible,' Mallory said slowly.

'I'm aware of that. And you're particularly ... fallible when it comes to yourself.'

Mallory stilled. 'What do you mean?'

Samantha appeared to be searching for the right words. 'You can decipher thoughts and feelings and understand people – but not yourself.' She held up her hands. 'I'm not criticising. Please don't think that. I wish I was more like you.' She sighed. 'But if I could offer some unsolicited advice...'

Twitching warily, Mallory said, 'Go on.'

'Maybe you should apply some of those skills to someone a bit closer to home,' Samantha said gently. 'That's all.'

Mallory stared at her. So it was obvious then: everyone knew that she had a massive, painful and wholly inappropriate crush on Alexander. Her cheeks flushed. 'Uh-huh.'

Samantha nodded, apparently relieved to have said what was on her mind. 'I'll see you out there?'

'Sure,' Mallory answered brightly.

'Great!'

As soon as Samantha had gone, her shoulders slumped. She'd likely never get any werewolf clients ever again after this, and deservedly so. Then she wondered if Alexander had asked Samantha to talk to her. Maybe he wanted to make it clear that he would never think of her as anything other than a slightly odd, wholly unmagical, temporary employee. Fuck.

She splashed more water on her face and straightened up.

'Man or mouse?' she asked herself. 'You've still got a damned job to do, Mallory. Get out there and fucking do it properly.'

She lifted her chin and returned to the ballroom as if nothing were wrong with the world whatsoever.

Only Sean Jones and Colin Brady remained at the table, deep in conversation. Mallory paused, her hand on her chair, and glanced around; it didn't take long to spot Alexander and Isadora on the dance floor. Good. Fantastic. Absolutely wonderful. Everything would work out. She watched them, Alexander's arm around Isadora's waist, her head back as she laughed. They were enjoying themselves.

'Perfect,' she whispered, then reached for her glass of wine and downed it in one without tasting it.

'Feeling thirsty, Miss Nash?'

She looked up and her eyes met those of Liam Ferguson's. 'Parched.'

'I don't blame you. The Wolf Ball is hard work, especially on the uninitiated. Perhaps I can ease the pressure and ask you to dance?'

Mallory's immediate instinct was to decline: she wasn't here to dance or party, and she ought to focus her attention on Alexander. But standing here and staring at her client dancing with another woman while her own body screamed with jealousy wasn't very healthy. What the hell. Liam was a sweet guy and dancing with someone might be the distraction she needed to drag her libido back into line. 'Okay.' She nodded. 'Okay.'

Liam wasn't quite as accomplished a dancer as Alexander and she stepped on his foot almost as soon as they started. 'Shit. Sorry.'

'My toes can take the bruising. It's fine.' He twirled her around.

'How did things go the other night on Hirsel Street?' she asked.

He grinned cheekily. 'Fabulous. It was a very, very good night.'

'Good for you.'

'I might even meet her next week for a second round.'

'You say that as if it's a rare occurrence, Liam.'

'I'm a long way off settling down,' he told her. 'Unlike your date over there.'

Mallory swallowed. 'He's not my date.'

The werewolf raised an eyebrow, though he didn't say anything.

The bouncing beat faded away to be replaced by a slow number. 'And this is for all you lovers out there,' the singer crooned into his microphone.

'That's what I want right now.' Liam pulled her in closer.

For a horrifying moment, despite his delight in telling her about his Hirsel Road antics, she thought he'd discovered she was matchmaking for Alexander and was asking her to match-make for him. 'A lover?' she asked, unable to keep the dismay out of her voice.

'What? No!' He laughed. 'I can find any number of lovers, thank you very much. What I mean is I want to be like that singer – I want to play music and be in a band, to hold the attention of a ballroom full of people and get them dancing.'

Relaxing, Mallory looked at him with genuine interest. 'Are you in a band?'

'I mess around with a few friends from time to time and I think I've got a good voice.' He pulled a face. 'But I'm a beta werewolf. I'm supposed to be responsible, not to run away to pursue my dreams. Especially silly dreams.'

With a thud of empathy, Mallory recognised the desperate hope in his expression. 'Liam, it's not silly at all. You should keep playing, especially if it makes you happy.'

His face was transformed by a wide smile. 'Really?'

'Really.'

'And what makes *you* happy?' he asked.

Alexander. Alexander MacTire makes me happy. She sucked in a breath. Bloody hell. 'Coffee,' she said. 'Wine.' She paused. 'And honey.'

'Honey?'

'Mmm.'

'Too sweet for me.' He dipped his head and lowered his voice. 'I prefer spice – the hotter, the better.'

'I'm not surprised by that in the slightest!' Mallory laughed.

There was a sudden loud cough beside them. 'Allow me to cut in,' Alexander said, and Liam moved back before Mallory could say or do anything. Alexander stepped into his place.

'What the hell are you doing?' she spluttered.

'Dancing.'

'But...'

'I was polite to Ferguson,' he said. 'And I didn't even growl – and that's after he pawed at you.'

'He didn't paw at me!'

'He put his arms around you.'

'We were dancing! Just as you should still be dancing with Isadora! What happened?'

'Nothing, except that I don't want to dance with her any more. Especially not to this song.'

'Alex, you need to give it more time. I understand how you feel but...'

'No, you don't understand how I feel at all. But after watching you and Liam fucking Ferguson, I've decided it's time you learned.' His eyes were dark and intense, his voice low and rough. 'I've had enough of pretending – I should have done this a long time ago. I want to dance with you, Mallory. Only you.'

'P-pardon?'

'You heard.' He was looking at her as if she were the only

person in the room and all she could do was stare back at him. He reached for her, slid his hands to her hips and gently tugged her body against his. 'If you don't want this, Mallory,' he murmured, so close that it felt as if each word was scalding her skin, 'say the word and I'll walk away. Otherwise, let's stop talking and dance.'

She didn't speak; she wasn't sure that she could. Her throat was tight, her mouth was painfully dry and her heart rate had ratcheted up alarmingly. Everything inside her was spinning in exhilarated confusion.

Then something inside her gave way. Hands trembling, she reached for him and turned her head to rest it against his chest, and they stayed like that until the very last beat faded away.

Alexander pulled back an inch then dropped his forehead onto hers, his nose and lips a whisper from her own. 'Will you come outside with me for some fresh air?'

When she nodded mutely he took her hand, tugged gently and they walked out of the ballroom.

TWENTY-TWO

The cool air was something of a shock after the warm interior of the hotel. Mallory pulled her hand away from Alexander's and rubbed her arms vigorously, partly because of the change in temperature and partly because of her nervousness. She tightened her toes several times but, for once, her calming technique didn't appear to be working.

'You're cold?' Alexander asked. He'd taken off his jacket when they'd first sat at the table and it was still on the back of his chair. 'I can go back and get my jacket for you.'

'No, I'm fine,' Mallory replied quickly. 'I just need to acclimatise.'

He nodded. 'Okay. There's an impressive rose garden round the back of the hotel. It's more sheltered from the breeze. Why don't we take a wander through it?'

She swallowed. 'Sure,' she said shakily. Her stomach was doing somersaults. She cleared her throat. 'Sounds good.'

They strolled around the huge building, leaving the bright lights and glowing corridor of fire behind them. The rose garden wasn't pitch dark as Mallory had expected; instead it was illuminated by tiny dancing lights. She couldn't prevent a gasp from escaping.

Alexander smiled. 'Magicked fireflies,' he explained. 'They're brought into existence whenever there's an event, even though few of the guests will bother to come here and see them.' He tapped the side of his nose. 'You have to be in the know.'

Mallory licked her lips. 'And why are you in the know?'

'Because I'm Alexander MacTire,' he said simply. He took her hand again. 'Do you want to get closer?'

Mallory nodded. The effect of the small lights on the flowers had been extraordinary from a distance; close-up they were equally impressive, except now Mallory could smell the heady scent from the roses, too.

'It's early in the season and these are the last of winter roses. In summer, when the bushes are in full bloom, it's something else. We'll have to come back again in August and you can see for yourself.'

She turned to him. 'In August?' she asked faintly.

He reached out and cupped her face. 'If everything goes to plan.' He drew a single ragged breath. 'Mallory,' he said hoarsely, 'I...'

Fuck it. Maybe it was the wine. Maybe it was the scent of the roses. Maybe it was the aching longing in the centre of her chest every time she saw him and knew he would never be hers. Either way, *fuck it.*

Mallory grabbed the front of his shirt, pulled him towards her and kissed him.

His mouth was surprisingly warm and soft to begin with, as if he were unsure of himself, then he let out a low groan and pressed against her with greater urgency. His hands threaded through her hair, loosening the curls that Gia Vanderlan had tamed so carefully, as she moved her fingers to his cheek and brushed against the soft stubble that was already appearing across his jaw.

Desire kicked through Mallory's veins and tightened her belly. Alexander's hunger seared her and she could feel his heart thudding against hers. For this one perfect moment, nothing else mattered. There was only Alexander MacTire. There was only this.

But not even this could last forever.

When they finally broke apart, Mallory wasn't the only one trembling. 'You're shivering,' she whispered, gazing into his eyes.

'So are you.' He touched his mouth, then hers. 'You taste of sunshine and magic and honey. Exactly as I imagined.'

Mallory's breath caught: fifteen minutes earlier he'd been dancing with Isadora Jones. How had it come to this? She shook her head. 'What's happening, Alex?'

He swallowed and took a step back, his amber eyes sweeping across her. 'Well, it's obvious that—' He stopped mid-sentence and his gaze darkened.

'What?' she asked. 'What's obvious?'

Alexander had gone very still. His nostrils flared and Mallory sensed a deepening, ferocious anger. 'Your arms,' he bit out.

She blinked. 'Pardon?' She glanced down and realised that the glamour spell Gia had placed on her earlier had worn off. Perhaps she'd rubbed her skin or it was merely the passage of time, but either way there was no denying the blue-and-purple splodges circling her biceps.

'Who did this?' he growled. 'Who dared to put their hands on you in this way?'

'It's nothing,' she said, dismissively. 'It looks worse than it is.'

'Tell me who did this, Mallory.' Every word vibrated with fury.

She released an exasperated sigh. 'Just an old man with a bee in his bonnet. It's been dealt with.'

Alexander shook his head. 'I won't allow this.'

Whoa. 'Back up,' she said sternly. Whatever lusty, romantic atmosphere had existed between them had evaporated. She had no idea what was happening now but she knew she didn't like it. 'It's nothing to do with you.'

He glared. 'It's everything to do with me!'

'No, it's not. And I told you it's been dealt with so put a stop to all this alpha growliness.'

'No. Somebody hurt you. Now I'm going to hurt them.'

Mallory rolled her eyes. 'For fuck's sake, Alex. We've been through this already. I can look after myself.'

'You might know a few self-defence moves, Mallory, but you're still just a squib.'

She folded her arms and stepped back. 'Just a squib?' she asked icily.

'I didn't mean it like that,' he snapped. 'What I meant was that you don't have magic and...'

'I know exactly what you meant.'

She'd been weak. Maybe he fancied her a bit – she knew he enjoyed a chase and maybe he'd decided to chase her – but Alexander MacTire didn't want *just a squib*. Not really.

'Mallory.' He ground out her name but she was already walking away.

'I'm going back inside,' she said. 'There are plenty more blonde werewolves with power and strength and magic in there for you to speak to.'

'Wait!'

She didn't stop and she didn't turn around.

THE REMAINING hour or so of the Wolf Ball was very uncomfortable. Mallory had felt the sting of failure before, especially in her early years as a broker, but it had never been so closely coupled with the pain of humiliation. She'd failed to find Alexander MacTire a First Mate and she could hardly sidle up to him and suggest that he should chat up another woman, not after she'd kissed him like that.

She squirmed and twitched and castigated herself over and over again. Every time she glanced in Alexander's direction, her cheeks burned. Eventually she couldn't take it anymore. When a tuxedoed werewolf alpha from yet another pack appeared in front of Alexander for a power chat, Mallory leaned in to Isadora. 'I'm not feeling very well,' she said. 'I'm going to head home. Can you tell Alexander that I've left?'

Isadora took one look at her face, frowned, gave a long sniff and stood up. 'I can do better than that,' she said. 'Sean,' she told her companion, 'tell Alex that I'm taking Mallory home.'

The younger werewolf looked suddenly terrified. 'What?'

'Just do it. He won't hurt you.' She paused. 'He *probably* won't hurt you.' She glanced at Mallory then returned her attention to her date. 'Don't tell him until we've left the room.'

'You don't need to help me,' Mallory began.

'Do you have transport?' Isadora asked.

'No, but...'

'Well then.'

Mallory pulled back her shoulders. 'Just because I'm a squib doesn't mean I can't get myself home.'

'It's not because you're a squib, it's because you're a person.' Isadora put her arm around Mallory's shoulders. 'I'm sorry,' she said more quietly. 'I can see he's broken your heart just like he broke mine.'

They were almost at the door when Alexander caught up with them. Isadora scowled. 'I told Sean to wait until we'd left before he spoke to you.'

'He didn't say a word – I saw you walking out.' Alexander turned to Mallory. 'Can we talk before you run away? Please?'

'No,' Isadora told him. 'We're leaving.'

'This is not the time, Dora!' he snapped.

'It's okay,' Mallory said to her quietly. 'I'll only be a couple of minutes.'

'You're sure?'

Mallory nodded.

'I'll wait right outside the door.'

'Thank you.' Mallory turned to Alexander; he didn't look angry any more; if anything, he looked defeated.

He ran a hand through his hair. 'You don't have to run away without saying goodbye. You don't have to be scared of me.'

'I'm not scared of you.' That wasn't what was happening, not even close. 'I just need to get out of here. I'm sorry I've not found you a First Mate. I'll make sure Boris voids our contract tomorrow. You'll receive adequate compensation.'

'I don't care about the fucking contract!' He grimaced and several heads turned towards them, curious eyes wide. Alexander hissed and turned his back on them. 'I said the wrong thing and I'm sorry – but I'm not sorry that we kissed. I'm not sorry that you came here with me. Let me come to see you tomorrow and explain when it's just the two of us. I want,' he drew in a breath, 'no, I *need* to explain.'

Mallory's heart contracted painfully; the last thing she wanted was to draw out this unmitigated disaster for longer than necessary, but neither could she deny him. She'd brought this on herself. 'Okay,' she whispered.

He smiled shakily. 'Thank you. Around eleven? At your place?'

'Okay,' she said again. She managed a tremulous smile then glanced at Isadora who was hovering by the door and caught her eye. It was time to go home.

CHAPTER

TWENTY-THREE

Thump. Mallory groaned and put her head underneath her pillow.

Thump. Thump.

The best way forward would be to hide in her bed until the apocalypse happened.

Thump. Thump. Thump.

Surely there were only so many times you could replay the same event in your own head?

Thump. Thump. Thump. Thump.

It appeared that she wouldn't be allowed to bury her head after all; whoever was at her front door clearly wasn't going away. She crawled out of bed, staggered out and flung it open.

From the tiny landing, Boris gave her an arch grin. 'Good morning, Mallory. I'll assume by your delayed appearance that you got lucky last night and there's a delectable werewolf snoozing in your bed.'

Her only response was a grunt. She turned away and stomped into her kitchen to put the kettle on.

'Ah. You didn't get lucky then?' the spriggan asked.

Lucky was not a word she would use to describe herself, not right now. 'No,' she muttered.

'Do you have another hangover?'

'No.'

'Ohhhh.' Boris nodded wisely. 'I see what happened. It worked, didn't it? Alexander MacTire fell for Isadora Jones and they're tripping off together hand in hand into the sunset. You succeeded and now you feel like shit.'

'If I succeeded, why would I feel like shit?'

'Duh. Because you're head over heels in love with him and the only person you want him to have a happy ending with is you. But he's an alpha werewolf and you're a...'

'...squib,' she muttered. 'Just a squib.' Her shoulders slumped.

'Oh, Mallory.' Boris reached for her and, with uncharacteristic kindness, pulled her into a hug. 'I'm so sorry.'

'He didn't fall for Isadora Jones,' she mumbled into his shoulder. 'He didn't fall for anyone.'

Boris stepped back and squinted at her. 'Is that good news? Or bad news?'

There wasn't any answer to that so Mallory changed the subject. 'What are you doing here on a Sunday morning?'

'Vanessa Pitcairn, of course.'

She stared at him.

'The bellarmine jug? She's dropping it off. I took the liberty of contacting Mr Longchamps to tell him that you've been successful. He asked – surprisingly politely – if you'd take the jug to his house as soon as you can. He'll wait up for you instead of going to bed for the day as usual.' Boris beamed. 'And Nicola Sturgess is ready to meet him tonight to hand over the Clouded Map. This entire sorry saga is almost at an end.'

'Oh.' *Shit.* With all that had happened with Alexander,

Mallory had entirely forgotten about Longchamps and the damned bellarmine jug.

'I can take the jug, if you like,' Boris offered. 'The faster it's in that fangy bastard's bony hands, the faster we'll never have to think about him again.'

'You hate vampires.'

'Yeah, I do. But I can do this part.'

She shook her head. 'No. It's better if I deal with him.' She checked the time; it was only just gone eight o'clock and Vanessa was due at nine. Hmm. 'Mr MacTire is coming here at eleven. I'll deal with Vanessa then take the jug to Chester Longchamps. If I'm not back by eleven, let Mr MacTire in. He can wait until I get back.'

'Mr MacTire? What happened to Alexander?'

'It's not appropriate to call him that. He's a client, not a friend.'

'Uh-huh.'

Mallory sighed. 'I don't want to talk about it.' She glanced at the kitchen wall and the display of potential First Mate werewolf pictures and notes. 'Let's get this down before he arrives.'

Boris looked worried. 'Are you alright, Mallory? You don't seem yourself.'

'I'm fine.'

He wasn't appeased. 'I'll make the coffee and take these down. You have a shower and sort yourself out.'

Tears pricked the back of her eyes for no good reason whatsoever.

'Go,' he said gently. 'I've got this.'

BY THE TIME that Vanessa Pitcairn arrived Mallory was feeling, if not better, slightly more like herself and she managed to smile at the High Priestess. She even remembered to offer her a cup of coffee.

'No.' Vanessa shook her head. 'I'm on my way to brunch so I'll decline. I simply wanted to thank you again for how wonderful you've been.'

She'd not been wonderful last night.

'I know I've said it before,' Vanessa continued, oblivious to Mallory's inner turmoil, 'but you're a true miracle worker.'

Nope.

'I don't believe there's anything you can't be successful with.'

Not even remotely true.

'You're kind, helpful and truly amazing. And to think you're a squib! It's extraordinary.'

Mallory smiled so brilliantly she thought her face might crack. 'Extraordinary. Thank you, Vanessa.'

'Here.' Vanessa handed over the box. 'The bellarmine jug is inside, carefully wrapped. I didn't want to drop it on the way here so I might have gone overboard with the packing. This might be the last unused bellarmine jug in Coldstream – there's a chance one or two of the renegade covens who live up north might have a spare jug, but I'm not sure. Either way, you should take good care of this one.'

Mallory didn't need to be told twice. She opened the box and undid a portion of the packing material; it was most definitely a bellarmine jug, original and intact. At least something had gone right, but that didn't ease the aching hole in the centre of her chest. 'Great.' She forced far too sunny a smile.

'You're the best, Mallory,' Vanessa said as she headed for the door.

The best at screwing everything up. Mallory smiled even more brightly. 'You too, Vanessa! Good luck with the garden!'

From the look in Boris's pale eyes, her forced good humour was worrying him. 'Mallory…'

She dropped the act. 'It's fine, Boris,' she said tiredly. 'I'm fine.' She held up the box. 'At least we can draw a line under this business. I'll go straight to Chester Longchamps.'

'Okay. Are you sure I should let MacTire in? I'll happily tell him to fuck off if you want me to. In fact, I'd enjoy doing just that.'

He likely would. 'No,' she replied. 'I need to sit down and have a proper chat with him.' Her stomach twisted at the thought but she reminded herself she was a grown woman. She could do this. 'I'll be back here by quarter-past eleven at the latest. If I'm late, tell Mr MacTire to wait and that I apologise for my tardiness.'

'Take your time,' the spriggan told her with a snort. 'And don't apologise. The longer he cools his heels, the more fun I'll have.'

Mallory sighed. She had no idea what she would say to Alexander – Mr MacTire – but she had a couple of hours to come up with something. It would be alright, she told herself firmly. In the end, everything would be alright. It had to be.

IT WAS the first time Mallory had been to the Longchamps' residence in daylight and it looked far shabbier than it did in the dark. She supposed that Chester didn't care: he wouldn't notice the patchy paintwork or register the way the magicked puddles of eternal blood on the stone steps looked fake when sunlight hit them. Even so, she avoided the sticky red patches as she descended.

She gingerly lowered the precious box containing the bellarmine jug to the ground and knocked loudly. Nobody answered, not even Eric, the grumpy and often abused thrall. Mallory heard no footsteps and didn't feel any discomfiting prickle suggesting that she was being watched. She knocked harder. Still nothing.

She nibbled on her bottom lip. She wanted to hand over the bellarmine jug as quickly as possible; it would be incredibly vexing to lug it all the way back home again.

After another few moments, she raised her fist and knocked again. Third time lucky, but if nobody answered this time she'd give up and leave a message. She waited, but it was only as she was reaching into her bag to scrabble around for a notepad and pen that she finally heard some signs of life from beyond the heavy front door.

She didn't recognise the face that peered blearily through the grate. The woman with the unkempt hair and smudged eye make-up was definitely a thrall, but Mallory had never seen here before. She smiled politely. 'Good morning. My name is Mallory Nash and—'

'I know who you are.'

Considering that Mallory was bringing an item that Chester Longchamps had needed for several weeks, she'd anticipated a warmer welcome, but she wouldn't be the only person in Coldstream who was having a shitty weekend and she would do well to remember that.

She didn't smile sunnily or present this new thrall with a business-like façade; she no longer had the energy to pretend to be other than what she was. 'Good,' she said. 'Then you can tell Chester that I'm here and I've brought his jug.'

'It's Lord Longchamps to you,' the thrall replied shortly.

Mallory raised an eyebrow; even with her distracted state of mind, she could tell that something was wrong. 'What's the problem?'

'There's no problem.'

'Is *Lord* Longchamps here?'

'Yes.'

Mallory sighed. 'Then let me in so we can get this business over and done with.' The irritation in her voice would have shocked most people who knew her, but the thrall didn't bat an eyelid.

'You can leave the jug on the doorstep and I'll take care of it,' the woman said.

Not a chance. 'Let me in, or I'm leaving and taking the jug with me,' Mallory told her. The thrall rolled her eyes but at least she opened the door.

Nothing about the hallway appeared different or unsettling: it was the same grand interior as before, the same paintings lined the walls and the same shiny marble floor was at her feet. She was even directed to the same uncomfortable wooden bench. But there was something subtly different and Mallory was sure it was related to the thrall's attitude towards her.

She sat on the bench and eyed the Cursed Portrait. This time the moustachioed painting didn't speak, though he did give her a very long, very derisive stare. Hmm.

She was kept waiting far longer than she'd expected. Mallory knew she ought to push back but her earlier irritation had been replaced by a dull numbness as she continued to worry about what she'd say to Alexander.

When she was finally admitted to Chester Longchamps' drawing room, she realised the reason for the delay. His glassy eyes, dishevelled clothes and his perceptible wobble – not to mention the lingering scent of heavy booze – made it obvious: Chester Longchamps was as drunk as a skunk.

'Mallory!' He spread his arms wide as if to embrace her.

Mallory glared and stepped back but the vampire appeared not to notice and stumbled towards her. With a flicker of nausea, she noted splatters of blood on his pristine white shirt.

She knew how the vampires worked: to get to this state of inebriation, Chester must have got all of his blood donors drunk before opening their veins and piggybacking off their blood alcohol. She would really rather not have to deal with this right now.

The easiest way to fend him off was to remind him why she was there so she held up the box containing the jug. 'Here,' she said. 'One bellarmine jug in pristine condition, as requested.'

Chester Longchamps clapped his hands like a child. 'Oooh. Goody!' He lurched forward to take it.

Mallory shook her head. He was horribly drunk; if he dropped the damned jug and broke it, she wanted to be sure that their contract was completed beforehand. She wasn't sure there was another bellarmine jug anywhere in Coldstream and she had no intention of searching for one. 'Nicola Sturgess will meet you tonight as soon as it's dark to arrange for transfer of the Clouded Map. You remember the conditions?'

'Yes, yes.' Longchamps hiccupped. 'It's all in hand. I have the preservation spells you purchased. I know I have to return the Clouded Map to Sturgess by August, and then the bellarmine jug to you.'

'Uh-huh.' Mallory gazed at him. 'But there is zero chance that she'll give you the Clouded Map if you're drunk, even if you have a thousand jugs and preservation spells.'

'I'm not drunk!' he protested. She raised her eyebrows. 'Alright,' he admitted, slurring his words. 'Maybe I'm a *little* drunk. I've been celebrating. This map will change everything.' He grinned at her lopsidedly. 'I'll be sober by this evening, I promise.'

She wasn't sure if she believed him, neither was she sure that she cared. 'So we can shake on the completion of our contract?'

He nodded. 'You have fulfilled your obligations, Ms Nash.' He thrust out his hand.

Mallory exhaled. Good. Very good. She carefully lowered the box onto a table then turned and shook Chester's clammy hand. 'Congratulations, Mr Longchamps.' He didn't seem to notice that she didn't call him 'Lord'. 'I'll be in touch about repayment at some point in the future. You can expect to hear from either me or my representative.'

The vampire executed a perfect bow. 'Not a problem,' he said, then immediately turned towards the box.

'By the way,' Mallory said, 'what's happened to Eric?'

'Who?'

She counted to ten in her head. 'Your thrall, Eric. One of the many members of staff whom you promised to stop abusing.'

'Oh, him.' Longchamps paused as if recalling a distant memory. 'Yeah, I dismissed him.'

'What?' she asked, shocked. 'Why?'

'Well, I can't abuse him if he's not here, can I?'

Vampire logic. For fuck's sake. Doubtless the real reason he'd dumped the thrall was nothing more than petty revenge that had more to do with her than it did with poor Eric. 'Is he alright?'

Longchamps shrugged blankly. 'How would I know? He's no longer my concern.'

Mallory shook her head. Although being free of the vampires was a good thing in her opinion, she knew that Eric wouldn't see it that way. 'Goodbye Mr Longchamps,' she said. 'I'll be in touch.'

The vampire barely heard her; his focus was on the box. Mallory's jaw tightened and she left the room.

As soon as she returned to the hallway, she heard the argument. 'I need to speak to her now!' Boris demanded through the small grate in the door.

'You need to wait,' the female thrall said snippily in return.

Mallory's stomach dropped. Something was clearly wrong – there was no reason for Boris to be here now unless there'd been a disaster. What if it was Alexander? What if it something terrible had happened to him?

The Cursed Portrait cackled loudly but she paid it no attention; instead she ran past it to the door. 'What is it, Boris?' she yelled. 'What's happened?'

The relief on his face when he saw her was unmistakable. 'You're still here. Thank goodness. There's a problem, Mal. A big problem.'

Shit. 'Let me out!' she snapped to the woman. 'My business is done and I'm leaving.'

The thrall sniffed. 'Good. And good riddance.'

Mallory met her eyes. 'It's not my fault Eric was thrown out. Blame that on your boss.'

'Eric would still be here if you'd not interfered!'

The woman was probably right – that was something else to feel guilty about. Mallory gritted her teeth and pointed at the door. 'Just let me out.'

'My pleasure.' The thrall unlocked several chains and bolts and the door swung open. As Mallory marched over the threshold, she asked, 'What is it, Boris? What's happened?'

Boris opened his mouth to answer but he didn't get the chance because a blur of fur barrelled down the stone steps and pushed him out of the way. Mallory jumped backwards and the female thrall cried out in shock.

Then the snarling wolf form of Alexander MacTire thundered down the hallway and into Chester Longchamps' drawing room.

TWENTY-FOUR

The thrall went into complete panic mode; she pressed herself against the far wall and immediately started babbling. 'I don't ... wolf ... attack ... help ... what do I?... No...' Then she clamped her hand to her mouth as coherent speech failed her completely.

'He was early,' Boris said. 'I let him into the flat and he found a note on your coffee table from Mr Longchamps and then—' He gestured helplessly.

Mallory knew exactly which note he meant: it would be the one on headed paper that mentioned roasting her entrails, which she'd been too busy to discard properly. Uh-oh.

She tightened her toes and spun around, then pelted back in the direction of the drawing room past the Cursed Portrait, which was now shrieking, 'Alarm! Intruder! Help!'

Thankfully blood hadn't yet been spilled. Chester Longchamps had jumped onto the sofa, as if that would somehow protect him from the snarling wolf that was facing him. He was clutching the unwrapped bellarmine jug. 'We're under attack!' he shrieked. 'That's a fucking werewolf!'

Mallory darted into the space between Alexander and the vampire and spread her arms out wide. 'Let's all calm down!'

'Eat *her*!' Longchamps shouted. 'Attack *her*!'

For a Preternatural who would probably heal and regenerate from any but the worst of werewolf attacks, the vampire was being something of a prick; then again, he *was* being attacked in his own home. And it was daylight outside so he likely already felt vulnerable. Alexander had no right to be here and they all knew it.

She turned to face the werewolf head on and injected as much cold authority into her voice as she could. 'Stand down.'

He deepened his snarl. In return she put her hands on her hips and glared. 'You heard me. Back off.'

His narrowed eyes flicked to her. Good: at least he'd heard her. The veil of misplaced alpha fury that had brought him here must be starting to dissipate. 'Everybody needs to take a breath,' Mallory said.

Alexander's ears twitched and she thought she was getting through to him, but then a shaky voice trembled from the doorway, 'Wh-wh– what's happening?'

She allowed herself a quick side-glance to assess this potential new threat: a vampire she'd never met before. Chester Longchamps knew exactly who it was, though, and was clearly emboldened by the fact that he was no longer alone.

'Alan! We're under attack from the werewolves! Get into the Understream and sound the alarm! Get everyone here!'

Oh no. Mallory's stomach dropped sickeningly as she realised just how much danger they were suddenly in. The vampires would see this as an act of war. They'd maintained cordial relations with the werewolves for decades, beyond the odd light skirmish here and there, but this wasn't a daft brawl or a silly argument. Alexander had broken into Chester Longchamps' home and violence was vibrating through every shred of his lupine fur. If she didn't stop this now, it could spell disaster not just for everyone in this room but for all of Coldstream.

'Wait!' She flung out her hand towards the vampire. 'Everyone wait. That means you too, Alan!'

Alexander growled again and his hackles rose still further. Frozen in the doorway, Alan squeaked. Chester Longchamps stiffened. Goddamnit.

'That is not a werewolf,' Mallory said. 'It can't be.'

'Are you mad?' Longchamps bellowed. 'Look at it! Of course it's a fucking werewolf!'

She prayed this would work; if it didn't there would be war. 'It's not the right time of the month – that's been and gone. I might be a squib but I know that werewolves can't transform unless it's the full moon.' Apart from Alexander MacTire. But as long as Longchamps wasn't aware of that fact, they might get away with it.

'She's right,' Alan said.

'I know she's right!' Longchamps thundered. 'But look at that thing! That's a fucking werewolf!'

Alexander bared his teeth as if to agree. Not helpful, not helpful at all.

'It must be a wild animal,' Mallory said. 'Magical, sure, but still an animal. It can't be a werewolf!'

'Alan, forget the Understream for now,' Longchamps snapped. 'There's wolfsbane in the storeroom. Go and get some and we'll find out the truth quickly enough.'

Alan nodded and disappeared and Mallory's stomach tightened further. She'd bought them some time, but it was minutes at best. Her only chance to remedy the situation was to talk to Alexander and force him to get out of here before World War III was invoked. But she'd have to talk to him alone.

'Leave the room,' she said to Chester. 'I'll deal with this.' She turned her head to look at him and realised abruptly that his shock was wearing off.

Longchamps was preparing his own attack, mirroring Alexander by baring his vampiric fangs. There was a steely look in his eye that promised predatory violence, spilled blood and absolute vengeance. Unfortunately Alexander had exactly the same look in his eyes.

Shouting wouldn't help. 'Chester.' Mallory softened her voice. 'I will sort this out. Wait outside and I'll deal with it.'

Another figure appeared in the doorway – thankfully it was Boris and not Alan with wolfsbane. 'Lord Longchamps.' He beckoned to the vampire who frowned.

'Go,' Mallory urged. 'I've got this.'

'I am not responsible for your safety here,' the vampire said stiffly.

For goodness' sake: a moment ago he'd wanted to throw her into a werewolf's snapping jaws. 'I know,' she said. 'Now get out of here.'

Still clutching the bellarmine jug, Longchamps stepped down from the sofa and edged towards the door. Alexander growled and Mallory glared at him. 'Enough,' she hissed.

Longchamps sidled further away – but when he was little more than a metre away from the hallway – and just as Mallory was starting to breathe again – Alexander chose to be an idiot again.

He feinted a lunge towards the vampire and snapped his jaws, even though he was too far away for his lupine teeth to connect with flesh. It was nothing but posturing but unfortunately Chester rose to the bait. Without thinking, he threw the bellarmine jug in self-defence. It smacked into Alexander's snout and bounced off, then crashed to the floor and smashed into several pieces.

Mallory and Longchamps stared at the shattered jug.

'Oh shit,' the vampire muttered.

Mallory ran a hand through her hair. 'Leave,' she said dully. 'Please, Chester. Just leave.'

Thankfully, for probably the first time in decades, the vampire did as he was told.

As soon as he'd left the room, Mallory stared at Alexander. He was no longer growling or snarling, he was simply looking at her.

She didn't have any experience deciphering a wolf's facial expressions and she wasn't going to try now. She walked up to him and crouched down until their eyes were level. 'Do not shapeshift,' she told him. 'If you do, Chester Longchamps will find out exactly who and what you are and this won't end until one of you is dead.'

Alexander snorted.

'If he dies, what do you think will happen?' she hissed. He looked away. 'Yeah. You *know* what will happen. You *knew* what would happen when you came here. For fuck's sake, Alex! You're an intelligent person, you know what the consequences could be. Every vampire in Coldstream will be gunning for every damned werewolf, regardless of who they are. People will *die*.'

He dipped his head forward to nudge her with his nose but Mallory drew back before he touched her. 'Don't,' she warned.

She inhaled deeply, aware that her breathing was shaky. 'You saw the note from Chester and you thought you'd come and save me, but I've told you that I don't need you to be my hero. I don't need you to save me. I might be just a squib but I'm perfectly capable and I don't belong to you. I'm not your responsibility.'

She paused. 'I don't even work for you anymore. Our agreement was only until the night of the Wolf Ball and that's over. I failed to find you a First Mate and now you're on your own. You have no further obligation to me and I have none to you.'

He neither blinked nor made a sound. She had no idea what was going through his head but she couldn't stop now; she couldn't allow herself to weaken.

'You have no idea what you've ruined by coming here and doing this.' Her gaze drifted to the shards of the bellarmine jug. 'No idea at all.' She sighed heavily. 'Don't interfere in my work ever again. Right now, you're going to walk out of here as a wolf. You're not going to look at Chester Longchamps, you're not going to look at anyone. You're going to leave very, very quietly.'

Alexander's body slumped and she knew he'd do what she needed him to do. Thank heavens. 'Come on,' she urged. 'You must go now.' She stood up and turned to the door but before she could step towards it, Chester Longchamps reappeared.

'Alan couldn't find any wolfsbane but that's alright because he's gone one better.' He displayed the crossbow in his arms. 'It's been a while since I fired one of these but I'm pretty sure I remember how to do it. And look!' He grinned coldly. 'Silver bolts. These will kill a werewolf stone dead, so I guess we'll know the truth of the matter either way in about three seconds' time.'

Oh God. Fear ripped through Mallory. She began moving towards him. As he raised the crossbow and aimed, she panicked and threw herself at him, knocking the crossbow to the side at the very moment he fired.

Time seemed to slow. She was aware of the silver bolt leaving the crossbow, and she was aware of the air rushing past her as it flew by her ear. And she was very aware of Alexander's howl of pain as it slammed into his flank and he collapsed.

He was already on the floor writhing in agony as she ran to his side. In truth it was little more than a flesh wound but the silver would be seeping into his blood and poisoning him. If he didn't receive medical treatment very soon he would die. Horribly.

And Chester Longchamps was already re-loading the crossbow and preparing to fire again. 'You made me miss,' he spat. 'That won't happen again.'

No. She had to stop him. She couldn't allow a world where Alexander MacTire didn't exist.

'He's definitely a fucking werewolf.' Longchamps sniffed derisively. 'He wouldn't be in such agony right now if he weren't. But you were right that it's not the full moon so that means this bastard is strong – likely an alpha, probably from one of the more powerful wolf packs. The Fergusons, perhaps. Or the Stewarts.'

He paused. 'I heard rumours a while back about the MacTires, and their alpha in particular. I didn't believe them at the time.' He smiled nastily. 'Well, well, well. It appears those rumours were true.' He reloaded the crossbow and pointed it in Alexander's direction.

Mallory felt sick. 'Stop!' she said, her voice ringing out. She'd kill Chester Longchamps before she'd let anything else happen to Alex, even if she *was* just a squib and even though the vampire could snap her neck before she managed to even bruise him. 'Don't shoot. You can't do that.'

The vampire laughed. 'I can. This is my home, my domain. I can do whatever I want.'

'I will release you from all your contractual obligations to me if you let the wolf go.' The words fell out of her mouth in desperation. 'No favours and no secrets.'

'No fucking Clouded Map either,' Longchamps spat. 'He destroyed my only chance of getting hold of it by destroying that jug.'

That wasn't actually true because Alexander hadn't

smashed the jug, but Mallory wasn't going to argue about it, not right now.

'Handy for you that we closed the contract only moments ago,' Longchamps continued. 'One might almost think you planned for this to happen.'

Hardly; she hadn't told him to throw the damned jug at Alexander. 'Our contract is officially over, but if you let this go I will get another bellarmine jug for you.'

'How?'

'I will find a way. Just give me time.'

Alexander's breath was already ragged, his eyes were closed and he appeared to have lost consciousness. Mallory started to shake with fear for him. 'I will get you what you need free of charge. I promise.'

'And if you don't?' Longchamps sneered.

'Then my blood is yours,' she said simply. 'You can drain me of every drop.'

'You're just a squib. Why would I want your blood?'

'Chester,' she pleaded, 'nobody else can find you a bellarmine jug. You know I'm your best chance. It's only March and we have until August. Give me another eight weeks then you'll still have the entire summer to use the Clouded Map. There's still time.' She tried to keep her voice steady. 'You know there's nobody else who can help you. Let me do this.'

'Why do you care so much about one wolf? Werewolf, or otherwise?'

Because I love him, she thought. But she only stared at the vampire and said one word: 'Please.'

He stared back with hard, unfeeling eyes. 'Four weeks.'

Mallory swallowed. What if that wasn't enough time? 'Six. Just in case.'

'Fine,' he muttered. 'But if you don't come up with the goods by then, I'll drink you dry.' He pointed at Alexander. 'And then I'll find this bastard and end him, too.' He laughed. 'Assuming the MacTire alpha lives beyond the end of today, that is.'

He lowered the crossbow. 'Now all of you need to get out of my fucking house.'

TWENTY-FIVE

The hospital was small but efficient. It was the nearest werewolf friendly establishment that Mallory knew of and it had a good reputation, but even with Boris's help it hadn't been easy to get Alexander there. They'd done it, though. What happened next was out of their control.

She was sitting with Boris at one side of the waiting room with Samantha, Nick, Hannah and various MacTire werewolves opposite. There had been no news from the surgeon since Alexander had been wheeled into the operating theatre.

Nick couldn't sit still. He stood up, then he sat down, then he stood up again and paced, circling the room like a caged tiger. When he sat down again, he leaned back as if to settle but started jiggling his legs. 'He's always telling me to think before I act,' he said finally. 'To consider the consequences.'

Nobody said anything.

Nick continued, although Mallory wasn't sure if he was speaking to the room or to himself. 'So why the fuck would he force his way into a vampire's house? A vampire! I don't get it.'

Samantha's eyes flicked towards Mallory then slid away again. 'He had his reasons,' she said.

'What reason could there possibly be?' Nick's voice grew louder with every word. 'If he dies, Sam, if he leaves me alone after what happened to Mum and Dad and...'

'He won't die.'

'You don't know that!'

She lifted her chin. 'I do. He's too stubborn to die. He's too strong.'

'Nobody is too strong for death. My dad was strong and so was my mum, and they were both killed in a freak accident.'

'This is different. He'll recover.'

'You don't know that, Sam,' Nick repeated. She sighed but didn't argue. Nick raised his head, his expression ravaged. 'Mallory, why did he go there?'

She had no idea what to say. 'I ... he ... uh...'

'Tell me!' he demanded as anxiety got the better of him

Samantha put her hand on his arm. 'Nicholas,' she said sharply. 'That's enough.'

Mallory was already shaking her head. 'No, it's alright. I understand how he feels.' She passed a hand across her face. 'Alexander was in my flat waiting for me. He found a note from the vampire that was – threatening.'

'Threatening?' Nick looked confused. 'Towards you?'

'Yeah, but it was just bluster. The vampire was a client who was frustrated at my lack of progress. It was an old note and I'd already dealt with it, but Alexander read it and must have thought I was in danger. He went to the vampire's house and...' She sighed. 'You know the rest.'

Nick stared at her. 'No,' he said after several long moments. 'That doesn't make sense. I understand that he'd want to help you if you were being threatened or hurt, but he still wouldn't be so reckless as to burst into a vampire's lair.'

Samantha's expression darkened. 'It doesn't matter why he did it. It won't change anything.'

Nick barely heard her. 'Wait,' he said suddenly. His eyes widened. 'He was in wolf form.'

'Yeah.' Mallory nodded.

'And he thought *you* were in danger.'

Samantha stiffened. 'Nicholas.' Her voice was filled with warning.

He ignored her. 'He went to save *you*. His wolf had taken over and he went to save *you*. That means...'

'Enough, Nick!' Samantha snapped.

'What?' Mallory asked. 'What does it mean?'

'He thinks you're going to be his mate.'

'Goddamnit, Nick,' Samantha hissed.

Mallory blinked rapidly. 'What? No! No, he definitely doesn't think that.'

Nick was nodding. 'Now it makes sense.'

'You have it all wrong.' Mallory shook her head.

'I don't.' He smiled sadly. 'I get it now.'

'But...'

'Has he shifted in front of you before now?' he asked.

Their session in the gym flashed in her mind. 'Uh...'

'I knew it! That proves how much he cares about you.' Nick leaned forward. 'Uncle Alex shapeshifts when it's the full moon, which is what the rest of us do, but he also does it when his emotions are high. *Very* high. He was scared for you, and maybe angry, too. That's why his wolf took over.'

'That part might be true,' Mallory said gently. 'But the rest isn't. It can't be.'

'It has to be.' Nick glanced at Samantha. 'There are lots of problems during the full moon when werewolves are in love but they've not yet staked an official claim on their partners. Right, Sam? Didn't that McTavish beta almost kill the Bradley kid because he thought that he was threatening that female were-wolf? And isn't he now officially mated to her? Even when I was kidnapped Uncle Alex didn't go full wolf – usually only part of him goes furry when he's upset. But he's gone full wolf for Mallory and that can only mean he wants her as First Mate.' He whistled. '*Want* is probably the wrong word. He *needs* her as First Mate.'

Mallory expected Samantha to tell Nick that he'd got it all wrong, but she didn't. She simply exhaled loudly. 'He was planning to tell you at your flat today,' she said to Mallory.

Boris, who'd been silent until now, chuckled. 'I knew it!'

'In fact he was supposed to tell you before today,' Samantha continued. 'There were lots of times when he was supposed to tell you.' She exchanged glances with the other MacTire werewolves and they all nodded encouragingly. 'Until you came along, I'd have confidently said that the only person Alex has ever been afraid of was his father, but he's much more afraid of you than he was of that old bastard.'

'I'm a squib,' Mallory whispered.

'A squib who he's in love with but who he doesn't believe feels the same way. And a squib who regularly puts herself in harm's way.'

'I'm very careful!'

'I'm sure you are, but that doesn't stop Alexander being terrified that something might happen to you.'

Boris nudged Mallory. 'It won't be so bad once you're his actual mate. You'll have the protection of his name so clients like Longchamps will be more respectful. And Alexander will be more relaxed. So will his inner wolf.'

Mallory stared at him. 'Wh-what?'

Boris grinned at the werewolves. 'She's in love with your guy but she can't admit it because she's supposed to be helping him find a mate. She thinks it would be unprofessional to nominate herself for that position. And she doesn't think he really wants her.'

'Of course he wants her,' Nick said. 'I should have seen it before now.'

'None of this would have happened if the two of you had spoken more honestly to each other,' Samantha muttered.

Hannah intervened. 'You've never been in love, Samantha. You've never felt the fear that you'll be rejected by the only person in the world who makes everything right.'

Mallory's mouth was wide open as her gaze travelled from face to face. 'This is all my fault,' she said, horrified. 'It's my fault he's here and suffering so much.'

Samantha frowned. 'Whoa. No, that's not—' She was interrupted by the door opening to reveal the doctor who'd been working on Alex.

Mallory started to tremble. She stumbled to her feet, as did everyone else. When the doctor smiled and said, 'He's okay,' her knees buckled and she sat down, gulping in air. *Oh thank God. Thank everything and everyone.*

'It's going to be a long road to recovery,' the doctor warned. 'He's not completely out of the woods yet. He'll be weak for a long time, and silver is still poisoning his blood. He'll need several transfusions and he's going to experience a lot of pain. But he will be okay.'

'As long as he's not attacked by any revenge-seeking vampires in the near future,' Boris said as a casual aside.

Mallory stiffened then nodded at him. She would fix this; she had to.

'Can we see him?' Nick asked.

'Yes. He's still sedated but you can pop in for a few moments,' the doctor said. 'One at a time, though, and only a few of you.'

Nicholas went first, followed by Samantha. When the beta werewolf returned she looked emotional but there was also relief in her face. 'You should go in, Mallory,' she said.

'Yep,' Nick said. 'Definitely.'

Mallory got shakily to her feet and followed the doctor to Alex's room. 'Only a minute or two,' he warned. 'And keep your voice low and calm. Although he appears unconscious, he may be able to hear you.'

She swallowed hard then walked into the room. The bed was in the centre with Alex laying prone on top of it, no longer in wolf form. He was covered to his shoulders with a white sheet that was almost as pale as his skin, but his chest was rising and falling regularly. She closed her eyes with relief then went to his bedside and took his limp hand.

His skin was hot, which was probably one of the many side effects of the silver poisoning. She rubbed the base of her thumb against his palm and smoothed back his hair from his forehead with her other hand.

'You stupid bastard,' she whispered. 'You almost got yourself killed. If you wanted me to experience the same fear that you were feeling, then congratulations. Because now I'm bloody terrified that something will happen to you.'

Alexander didn't so much as twitch but she continued regardless. 'You're going to be fine. You have to be fine so I can come back and kick your arse for putting me through this. You have to be fine so that I can tell you that I love you. I love you, Alexander MacTire, with every part of my being.'

Her mouth curved into a sad smile. 'You're handsome, charming and definitely sex on legs, and I want you to be mine. Forever.' She dropped her head and kissed him briefly on the lips.

'I'm going to deal with Chester Longchamps and make sure he doesn't come after you. I'm going away for a while to find him a bellarmine jug but I'll be back. I promise you that. I'm just a squib – but if you want me, I'm all yours. Always.'

MALLORY'S FEET felt leaden with exhaustion as she plodded upstairs with Boris on her tail. She passed the map detailing all her current clients and knew she ought to update it to reflect current circumstances, but she couldn't muster up the energy. Instead she headed into the small flat.

Her gaze fell on the screwed-up piece of paper on her living room floor and she picked it up and smoothed it out. It was Chester Longchamps' note, the note that had sent Alexander storming off to rescue her. She tore it into tiny pieces then dropped them in the wastepaper basket and sat down heavily on the sofa.

What a gigantic cock-up – but Alexander was still alive and he would be okay. That was all that really mattered. She thought about Nick's revelation and hugged herself. Did Alexander really feel that way about her?

'Now what?' Boris asked, sitting beside her and twisting his fingers together. For probably the first time since she'd known him, the spriggan appeared tense and worried. He knew what was at stake. Chester Longchamps was suddenly a very real threat; after all, Alexander had forced his way into the vampire's home and such an invasion couldn't be ignored. Mallory had to find a replacement bellarmine jug to appease him before he went after Alex again.

'You moved hell and high water to get that bellarmine jug the first time around,' Boris went on. 'How on earth will you find another one and keep that silly werewolf safe?'

Mallory rubbed her forehead. 'Vanessa Pitcairn mentioned that some of the renegade covens that don't live in Coldstream might have spare jugs, and so did Salty Miller, for that matter. I'll leave the city and try to contact them. I might get lucky.'

He pulled a face. 'Those covens are crazy. They keep themselves to themselves and they don't like anyone from Cold-stream. If I tried to talk to them, they'd probably kill me before I finished saying hello. And they think anyone who's not magical but who chooses to live here has a screw loose. It'll be a miracle if they even agree to talk to you.'

Mallory shrugged helplessly. 'I have to try. What else is there? I'll pack a bag and leave tonight.'

'Tonight?'

'Longchamps has given me another six weeks. It sounds like a long time but if I can't find a bellarmine jug quickly it'll seem like no time at all. You'll have to stay here and keep everything ticking over.'

'Thank goodness!' Boris shuddered. 'I hate travelling anywhere non-magical. It's all so cold and mechanical and... Ugh.' Unfortunately she knew what he meant. 'Are you sure about this, Mallory?' he asked.

'What else can I do?'

He sucked on his bottom lip and nodded. 'You're going to have to be the one to play hero now.'

Mallory thought about Alexander lying frozen in that hospital bed. 'There's no playing about it.'

TWENTY-SIX

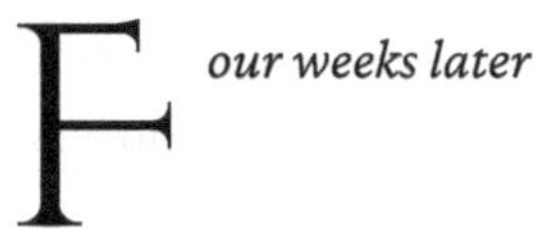

EVEN AT ELEVEN o'clock at night there was still traffic in a small city like Inverness. Mallory might have spent her formative years living in places with buses and trains and cars galore, but now she was used to Coldstream where it was rare to see any vehicle apart from the magically run trams. Only the likes of Alexander, whose wealth enabled him to own a car despite the city's inherent magic that fought such technology, bucked the trend.

It wasn't just the traffic; everything was annoying her. She'd left home almost a month ago and not only did she have nothing to show for her efforts – not even a whisper of a bellarmine jug – but there was also a constant ache in her heart. It was partly due to homesickness and partly due to anxiety that she would fail.

She'd spent six days in Edinburgh navigating her way into

the coven that called the Scottish capital city its home. She'd worked hard to gain their trust, promising to help them with their supply route and trade runs to Coldstream, and using up several favours that her other clients owed her. In the end it had all been for nothing: they didn't have any bellarmine jugs and they couldn't help her find one.

The Glaswegian witches had been slightly easier to talk to. After a couple of days Mallory had learned that an old school friend of hers knew them, and she'd been able to speak to their High Priest without too much faff. He'd been kind and incredibly apologetic, but he couldn't help her. Any valuable historical items had long since been sold because money was king outside the magical boundaries of Coldstream. Decades earlier, when they'd left Coldstream, the Glasgow coven had bartered away their important artefacts. Even their magic was dwindling now because they'd spent too long away from the magical properties bound into the earth in their old hometown.

Mallory had genuinely been shocked at their lack of witchery power and even more aghast when they'd told her they were happy about it. They'd left Coldstream for a reason: they didn't want to be surrounded by magic and they preferred not to wield spells unless they were absolutely necessary.

'We don't understand why you would leave a comfortable, happy life as a non-magical entity to go there,' the High Priest had told her. 'Just as you don't understand why we left Coldstream for the bright lights and technology of Glasgow.'

Perhaps, Mallory reflected grumpily, everyone wanted what they didn't have regardless of whether they were witch, werewolf or human.

It had been a similar story in Dundee, Aberdeen and John O'Groats, where she'd been viewed with such mistrust that she'd double-bolted her door and checked beneath her bed before she went to sleep each night. She'd struggled to get anyone from the covens to speak to her, let alone trust her, and when she did talk to them it quickly became clear that none of the renegade witches had bellarmine jugs.

Only the Inverness coven was left. She crossed her fingers. Tonight would be the night, she told herself. The Inverness witches would be able to help. *Please* let them be able to help.

A large truck trundled by, choking the air with its exhaust fumes. Mallory checked the road again, then crossed and headed for the car park where she was due to meet two of the coven. She had plenty of time because they weren't due for another thirty minutes or so. She had planned to arrive early; she wouldn't let anything derail this meeting, and that included unforeseen delays.

Although summer was beckoning, at this time of night it was still chilly this far north. There was a cold breeze that rippled Mallory's hair and tugged at the collar of her shirt. She zipped up her jacket and moved faster before nipping through a ragged hole in the chain-link fence. On the edge of a busy industrial estate, the car park was filled with all manner of vehicles during the day but now it was devoid of cars, although there were a few darkened vans branded with the names of local businesses.

Nobody came here at night, which was why the Inverness coven had suggested it as a venue. Either that or they thought it was a good place to set a trap for the annoying squib who kept bothering them. Both were possibilities.

Mallory circled the perimeter. She could see other gaps in the fence, as if the area had been attacked by a savage animal rather than the more likely culprits: local teenagers armed with bolt cutters and cheap bottles of Buckfast fortified wine. She spotted a scorched oil drum that had obviously been used as a fire pit, beside which were several empty bottles and some empty sweet packets. Hopefully these teenagers wouldn't appear tonight; she already had enough to deal with.

There was a prefabricated warehouse on the left side of the car park. Mallory had already checked it out and discovered it was owned by an electrical-tool company. Behind her a food company that specialised in jams and chutneys was using another smaller building. They were different to the tool company in that they traded with several Coldstream businesses, but Mallory had checked them out and was certain that the Inverness coven had nothing to do with them. Neither did they sell honey. She was pretty sure that this was neutral ground.

She didn't want to surprise the witches or give them any reason to back away, so once she'd checked out the car park she strode to the centre and waited. It was important to show that she had nothing to hide.

She'd expected the two witches to arrive late in a bid to exert authority and display their power. She knew that the coven was concerned that she posed a threat, even though they knew she was a squib. They didn't often deal with anyone from Coldstream because they believed that the Witches Council would take any opportunity to either stamp them out or force them back to the border city. Mallory was pretty certain that the Witches Council never gave the renegade covens a second thought, but telling the Inverness coven that would probably cause more problems than it would solve. Nobody wanted to believe they were inconsequential.

She was pleasantly surprised when a small car appeared and headed towards the car park a few minutes early. It pulled up outside the fence and stayed there with its headlights on and its engine running. Mallory couldn't tell how many people were inside.

She waited, her hands hanging loosely by her sides, until

the witches decided it was time to make their appearance. She didn't have to wait long. Her watch buzzed, indicating it was bang on eleven-thirty, the rear passenger doors opened and two figures stepped out.

The car's bright headlights prevented her from seeing their faces but their silhouettes were clear; although the two witches were dressed for the cold breeze, they were empty handed. Obviously witches didn't need weapons to instigate an attack but the fact that they weren't carrying anything threatening made Mallory relax slightly. She still had a few fading bruises from an encounter with one of the hot-headed bastards from the Aberdeen coven.

The two figures turned to each other, hesitated, then walked towards the fence. There was a locked gate to their right and Mallory watched as the shorter witch used a blast of controlled magic to pop the lock. Presumably the gate was there to add to the illusion of security. At least there was no sign of any CCTV cameras. That was another possible reason why the witches had elected to meet her there.

The pair walked across the car park, their steps synchronised as if they were part of a miniature army. Mallory waited, doing her best to appear calm. When they were ten metres away, they stopped. They didn't speak.

Mallory supposed that the ball was now in her court. 'Good evening,' she called out. 'Thank you for agreeing to meet me. I promise I won't take up much of your time.'

Neither witch said anything.

She drew in a breath. 'As you already know, my name is Mallory Nash. I am a squib and I live in Coldstream.'

The short witch hawked up a ball of phlegm and spat it on the ground at the mention of the magical city. Mallory didn't react; nothing would change their minds about Coldstream and it was pointless to try.

The second witch, a woman, lifted her chin. 'We don't like Coldstream folks,' she said in case Mallory hadn't yet realised that. 'You all think you're better than us.'

The male nudged her. 'She's just a squib.'

'Doesn't matter. She's still Coldstream.'

Mallory knew she had to gain control of the conversation. 'I wouldn't be here if I thought I was better than you. I'm here because I need your help.' Appealing to their better nature would only take her so far but it suggested she was weaker than them. She was prepared to play along if that was what it took.

'You want a bellarmine jug.'

'Yes.' She licked her lips nervously. 'Do you have one?'

The tall witch shrugged. 'Maybe we do, maybe we don't. Let's hear what your offer is first.'

Damn it. Mallory cursed inwardly but knew better than to argue. Besides, no matter what these witches told her, she wouldn't get too excited until she saw a damned jug with her own eyes. 'I deal in favours and secrets. There are any number of things I can offer you from Coldstream in return for an intact jug.'

'We need nothing from that godforsaken hellhole,' the woman snarled.

Suddenly Mallory was on surer ground. She'd been in Inverness for almost a week now and, while there were very few Preternaturals living there, the small renegade coven weren't the only residents with magic powers. Mallory had found both a troll and a dryad who, in return for future favours, had given her a lot of information about the Inverness witches. Despite their bluster, there were several items they desperately needed to maintain their coven's power – items that were only obtainable from Coldstream.

'Well,' she said, 'I could procure the file that the Witches Council has compiled on your coven.'

Both witches stiffened – even though Mallory had no idea whether such a file existed. 'We don't care what they say about us!' the man hissed. 'We don't care what they know. They can't hurt us.'

She doubted that was true. 'Or,' she offered, 'I could locate some spell books for you if there are any gaps in your knowledge.'

The answer was swift. 'There are no gaps.'

Mallory shrugged before she pulled out the big guns. 'Or I could give you this.' She held up a small silver spoon. 'It's fully charged.'

The female witch made no attempt to disguise her shock. 'That's a spell stirrer!'

'Yep. It's from Mystical Forces and comes with a twenty-year guarantee.' Mallory had arranged for special delivery for the spoon direct from Alison Cole and it had arrived this morning, thank goodness. It wasn't a particularly expensive item but it was necessary to mix powerful spells.

Thanks to the dryad, Mallory knew that the coven's own magicked stirring spoons were failing and their spells were being adversely affected as a result. From the witches' expressions, the dryad hadn't lied. The Inverness coven desperately needed a spoon like this, but for some reason they weren't willing to visit Coldstream to get one.

She added an extra enticement. 'Mystical Forces is prepared to deal with you in future. They can arrange shipping for most items as long as you are willing to pay.' She smiled. 'But such an arrangement will only be possible if you're prepared to trade. Give me a bellarmine jug, and the spoon and trade agreement are both yours.'

They stared at her, then they stared at the spoon. 'We will need to discuss this first,' the male witch said stiffly.

Mallory inclined her head. 'Take all the time you need.'

The two witches marched purposefully back to their waiting car. Mallory crossed her fingers, tightened her toes and held her breath. From the way they were acting, they had what she needed; if these two had a bellarmine jug and were willing to hand it over, the last four weeks would have been completely worth it.

'Please,' she whispered. 'Oh god. Please.'

The witches didn't get into the car; instead they went to the driver's door. Mallory saw the window being lowered but she couldn't make out who was sitting there and she couldn't hear what they were saying. All she could do was wait.

Seconds ticked by, then minutes. Mallory shuffled her feet. The witches continued their discussion. Under any other circumstances, she'd have pressed the matter by starting to walk away but she couldn't afford to. She needed the jar. Alexander needed the jar. And bloody Chester Longchamps needed it, too.

Eventually, the two witches straightened. Mallory watched them, trying to judge by their body language what was happening. Then, to her surprise, whoever was in the driver's seat opened the door, got out and walked around the car to the boot. She swallowed hard as they pulled out a box. It was the right size for a bellarmine jug. Her skin was already tingling.

The driver passed the box to the short male witch and returned to the car. It seemed to take an age for the two witches to stroll back through the gate towards her and she wanted to yell at them to hurry up. She told herself to breathe normally; she couldn't appear too excited, not when she was this close. She stayed firm and waited – but it took almost everything she had to stay where she was.

'Alright,' the woman said. 'We'll trade our only bellarmine jug for a deal with Mystical Forces and that stirring spoon. And we want that file from the Witches Council, too.'

Uh-oh. Mallory shook her head; to succeed now, she had to play hard ball. 'Either the file *or* the spoon. That's my final offer.'

The witches exchanged glances. 'Then no deal,' the male one told her.

Mallory managed to maintain her expression and nodded. 'That's a shame,' she said. 'Thank you for your time.' She turned and started to walk away. Shit. Shit. Shit. She kept walking. What if this was it? What if she'd just blown it?

'Wait!'

She stopped and looked over her shoulder. 'What?' she asked, hoping that her voice didn't betray her emotions.

'The spoon and the trade agreement,' the woman called. 'We'll accept those terms.'

Mallory's knees felt weak and she closed her eyes briefly with relief. She turned to face the witches yet again. 'Alright,' she said. *Alright.*

She closed the gap between them. With her right hand she held out the spoon and with her left she waited for the box. The woman sniffed then took the spoon as her companion passed the box to Mallory. Almost immediately, both witches strode away but Mallory barely noticed. She placed the box on the ground and opened it up, with her heart in her mouth.

TWENTY-SEVEN

The instant she lifted out the jug, she knew. She hefted it in her hands then she dropped the damned thing and ran after the departing witches. 'Hey!' she yelled. 'You fuckers! Hey!'

They simply walked faster. Mallory gritted her teeth and sped up. 'This isn't the right jug!'

The witches paid her zero attention. They passed through the gate and started to close it but, before they could, Mallory put on an extra burst of speed and caught up with them. 'Out of our way,' the male witch growled.

Mallory straightened her shoulders and drew so close that they were almost touching toes. 'Not until you give me the real bellarmine jug.'

'We gave you a real jug,' the woman said, although there was a faint tremor in her voice. 'We kept our end of the bargain so piss off.'

'What you gave me is a tourist knock-off worth about ten quid. If that. I might be a squib and I might choose to live in Coldstream, but I wasn't born yesterday. Either give me back my spoon or hand over the real thing.'

The witches exchanged glances then the man's hands sparked with blue magic and he threw out a blast that knocked Mallory off her feet. As both witches ran for the car, she scrambled to her feet and pulled a pocket knife out of her pocket. She was winded but unhurt – and this was far from over.

As the car's engine revved, she flung herself towards its back wheels and plunged the knife into the nearest tyre before rolling to the side. A second later the car took off leaving her in a cloud of choking exhaust fumes. Unsurprisingly, it didn't get very far.

It was the driver who climbed out to confront her, a thin, middle-aged man with a lot of scarring down one side of his cheek. Thanks to the troll she'd spoken to earlier, Mallory knew this was the High Priest of the Inverness coven.

'Thomas MacAuley,' she muttered. 'At least you've decided to show your real face.' She brushed the dirt from her clothes. 'I'd advise against any further magical attacks. You'll only be sacrificing temporary gain for long-term pain.'

'Is this where you tell me that you have friends in high places and I ought to watch my back?' he asked sardonically.

Mallory regarded him coolly. 'I'll leave you to decide that for yourself.' She folded her arms. 'You didn't really think could pull this off, did you? That I'd let you walk away after scamming me? Best-case scenario, I'd have ensured that the deal with Mystic Forces was cancelled.'

She tilted her head as anger coursed through her body, much of it directed at herself. She'd broken her own cardinal rule of always enforcing a blood contract; even straightforward transactions needed an insurance policy to back them up. 'Worst-case scenario? Well, that remains to be seen.'

'Are you threatening me, Ms Nash?' MacAuley spoke quietly but there was an edge to his words.

Screw him. Mallory met his gaze. 'When I threaten you,

you'll know about it,' she told him, trying to sound far harder than she really was. She examined his face and then laughed coldly. 'Oh, I see. You thought I'd accept that piece of ceramic tat because I'm just a squib who doesn't know any better. I have to say I'm getting mighty tired of people underestimating me because I don't have Preternatural blood running through my veins. I'm also getting mighty tired of being in a bad mood.'

She sniffed. 'I'm usually a very happy person – my glass is half full and my days are filled with sunshine. But during the last few weeks I've lost that feeling. Frankly, Mr MacAuley, I've been pissed off for about four weeks now and you're making it worse.' She stepped towards him. To her surprise, he flinched.

Mallory doubted she'd scare a Coldstream witch so that was curious, but then she realised – somewhat belatedly – that she was the one with the real power because she could make the coven's life unpleasant. The trio of idiot witches didn't pose a real threat. None of them had hurt her; even the bloke who'd knocked her down hadn't caused much damage and she doubted she'd even find any bruises.

But she didn't want MacAuley's fear because fear made people act out of character. Fear encouraged unpredictability and, in Mallory's opinion, that was something to avoid. Besides, at any moment he might remember that it was three witches against one squib, and if they killed her and disposed of her body there'd be nothing she could do about it. She needed to do some very quick and very clever thinking.

'Here's what is going to happen,' she said. 'I will not inform the Inverness police that you have attempted to defraud me, and neither will I remind the Witches Council in Coldstream of your existence. I will not tell anyone that you attacked me with magic, and you can continue your self-imposed exile for as long as you wish. In return you will give me a real bellarmine jug.'

Just to show that she wasn't a complete monster, she smiled. It almost reached her eyes.

Thomas MacAuley flinched again. Oh dear; that hadn't been her intention. She paused and examined his face more closely, then her heart sank and nausea swirled up from the pit of her belly. *No. Oh no.*

'You don't have a real jug, do you?' she whispered.

MacAuley's eyes dropped. He turned and called softly, 'Mikey, bring me that spoon.'

The right-hand passenger door opened and Mikey heaved himself out looking sullen. 'But...'

'Just give it to me.'

The spoon caught the moonlight and glinted as MacAuley turned it in his hands then held it out. 'Here,' he said. 'With my deepest apologies.' There was a catch in his voice and Mallory realised that the Inverness coven was simply doing the same as she was – trying to survive in the best way they could. They really needed that magicked spoon.

Her shoulders sagged and she sighed. 'Keep it,' she said. 'Keep the damned thing.'

There was a brief flare of relief on the High Priest's face before he masked his expression.

'Coldstream isn't a bad place, you know,' Mallory went on. "The covens there do alright. Even if you don't want to live there, you can—'

MacAuley didn't let her finish her sentence. 'We can't.' His tone brooked no further discussion.

Mallory sighed and nodded. If he didn't want it to be her business then she wouldn't pry. 'The trade deal also stands,' she told him. 'Although in truth that has little to do with me. Mystical Forces do deals with many Preternatural beings who live outside the city.'

He nodded but didn't speak. Mikey, still huffing, opened the car boot. 'Good thing we have a spare tyre in here,' he muttered. He reached inside to pull it out.

Another voice drifted across the darkness. 'I'll help you change it. Unless you want to do it, Mallory?'

She went rigid. She was dimly aware of Thomas MacAuley freezing and his eyes darting nervously back and forth, but she wasn't interested in the witch any more. Her focus was on the dark shadow of a man standing less than thirty metres away.

'You had a werewolf as back-up all along?' The High Priest sounded shaky. 'You could have told him to tear us apart whenever you wanted!'

'I wasn't planning to involve myself,' Alexander MacTire said as he approached them. 'I knew that Mallory would have everything under control.'

She stared at every inch of him. He wasn't smiling, and there was an odd, anxious quality about the way he was standing, but he looked well. His skin had a healthy glow, his hair was neatly brushed and his amber eyes were bright and alert.

Mikey, who had moved away from the car boot, huffed grumpily. 'I don't think we need be concerned about a werewolf wearing a sparkly unicorn T-shirt.'

Mallory glanced down. The witch was right: Alexander wasn't in one of his immaculately tailored suits, he was wearing snug-fitting jeans and the glittering T-shirt that he'd told her had been a present from his sister. Her mouth dried.

The female witch got out of the car and stared at him. 'Shit,' she muttered. Moving to the car boot, she lifted the spare tyre and heaved it towards the damaged wheel. 'You lot stand around and stare at each other,' she said sarcastically. 'It's super-helpful. I'll sort the car out. Let me know who blinks first.'

'Me,' Alexander said, his gaze trained on Mallory. 'That will be me.'

IT DIDN'T TAKE LONG to change the tyre. Mallory sensed that all three of the Inverness witches wanted to say more, and Mikey even mumbled something about going to the pub for a drink before MacAuley pointed out that it was now after midnight on a weekday night and there would be nowhere open. Looking at Mallory and Alexander, he said, 'I think we should leave these two alone.' He bowed towards Mallory. 'Thank you. I'm sorry we couldn't help you with a real bellarmine jug.'

Mallory bit her lip, then stood back as the witchy trio piled into the car and drove away. It was only when they were out of sight that she turned to Alexander. 'How did you know I was here?' she asked.

'Boris,' he replied.

It figured. The spriggan had stayed in close contact with the MacTires so that he could keep her updated on Alexander's recovery; he wouldn't have hesitated to tell them where she was. She shuffled her feet. 'How long have you been here?'

'I arrived five minutes before you.'

'So you saw everything?'

'Yes.'

'You didn't get involved. You didn't even show yourself.' It sounded faintly accusatory although she didn't mean it that way.

'I was here if you needed me but I knew you'd manage fine without me.' He was watching her like a hawk, taking in every nervous twitch and tic.

'I'm just a squib,' Mallory said quietly.

A rueful smile crossed his mouth. 'It turns out that squibs can be incredibly powerful. Some of them can even save alpha werewolves from vampires, silver bolts and, most importantly, themselves.'

Her breath caught but she felt a surge of heaviness pressing down on her despite Alexander's words. 'I haven't saved you from anything. If I can't find a bellarmine jug for Chester Longchamps, he'll come after you because of what happened at his house. Nobody will be able to stop him and if anyone tries it could start a war.'

Alexander reached out and pulled her against his broad chest. The heat of his body warmed her and she relaxed against his reassuring solidity. 'A bellarmine jug?' he asked. 'That's all we need?'

All? Mallory no longer trusted herself to speak properly. 'Mmm-hmm.'

'I know someone back in Coldstream who might help us with that,' he murmured. 'Travel back with me and we can talk to them together.'

Mallory's heart skipped a beat.

CHAPTER
TWENTY-EIGHT

Mallory had visited the riverside market in Danksville on several occasions; she couldn't recall shopping there because it was out of her way, but her work had brought her into contact with people who frequented the area. However, she was certain that she'd never spoken to the slightly odd creature wearing a narrow-brimmed hat that was turned up at the back.

She examined the eclectic variety of bits and pieces for sale on the stall, then picked up a small glazed jar that appeared to contain silvered clover leaves. She replaced it and gazed at the stallholder.

'Mr MacTire,' they said. 'It's been a long time since you've honoured us with your presence.'

'Hello, Trilby.'

The stallholder doffed their hat and glanced at Mallory, who smiled nervously. 'I'm Trilby,' they said. Their eyes twinkled and Mallory immediately felt more at ease.

'Mallory,' she said, 'Mallory Nash.'

Trilby's smile broadened. 'Ah! *You*'re Ms Nash! I've heard about your exploits.' Mallory steeled herself for the inevitable squib comment. 'You're very skilled and incredibly powerful. There is much to be admired about your work.'

She felt her cheeks turning pink. 'Thank you.'

Alexander took her hand. 'I certainly admire her a great deal,' he said softly and Mallory felt her stomach flip.

Trilby smiled, as if they expected nothing else. 'Well, what can I do for you today?'

The warmth she was feeling faded, replaced by anxiety. 'I desperately need a bellarmine jug.'

'A real bellarmine jug?'

She nodded. 'One that is empty and can still be used effectively. It's really important.'

'Indeed.' Trilby stroked their chin and considered the matter. 'Alas, I don't have any in stock.'

Although Mallory wasn't surprised, she still felt deflated. 'I figured.' Alexander's hand tightened around hers. 'Do you know anyone who might have one? Someone who would be willing to part with it for a fee?'

'I'll pay whatever it costs,' Alexander added.

'I don't believe that will be necessary,' Trilby told him. They looked at Mallory. 'I can tell you where to find a bellarmine jug but I will ask for a boon in return for this information.'

'Anything,' Mallory said. 'Anything at all.'

The stallholder raised an eyebrow. 'That's a rather dangerous promise.'

'I know,' she replied. 'I don't care.' Mallory meant it. Finding a bellarmine jug meant much more than fulfilling her favour to Chester Longchamps; it meant she could guarantee Alexander's safety – at least from the vampires.

Trilby gazed at her. 'Well, I don't expect this will be dangerous to fulfil. It should be rather easy, given your contacts.'

'Go on.'

'There is a ban sith who is having some … difficulties. She needs somewhere safe to stay for an undisclosed period of time.'

Mallory blinked: that *was* easy. 'No problem. She can stay with me. I have a sofa bed and…'

Trilby was already shaking their head. 'No.'

'I have plenty of room,' Alexander said. 'She can come to the MacTires.'

'No,' they said firmly. 'That won't work either. The ban sith requires space and privacy. It would be preferable if you were to call in a favour with another client who has a self-contained flat to rent.' They shrugged. 'Or something like that.'

There was something that Trilby wanted specifically, but they weren't willing to say aloud. 'There's an ogre on my books who owns several properties in Bellsworth,' Mallory offered.

'That's an option,' Trilby said. 'But I think this particular ban sith is keen to reside somewhere here in Danksville.'

Kit McCafferty immediately flashed into Mallory's mind. 'Does this ban sith like cats?'

Trilby smiled. 'Doesn't everyone?'

'I'll see what I can do,' she said.

'That's all I can ask.' They returned a satisfied nod. 'Very well. I can tell you both that many moons ago I sold a number of magical items to a werewolf. One of those items was a bellarmine jug.'

Alexander was already leaning forward. This was good news. He was perfectly placed to strike a deal with any werewolf in Coldstream. 'And you think this werewolf still owns it?'

'The werewolf in question is now dead.'

Goddamnit. What use was that? Mallory ground her teeth in frustration.

Trilby hadn't finished. 'As far as I'm aware, his heir has not sold any of his father's items. He likely doesn't realise what he has.'

If that were true, it would mean that this unnamed werewolf probably didn't care about the jug. He might be persuaded to part with it.

'Who?' Alexander demanded. 'Who are you talking about?'

Trilby's smile widened. 'That part's easy. I'm talking about you.' Alexander rocked back on his heels as the stallholder continued. 'I sold your father a bellarmine jug almost eighteen years ago. Unless you've sold it after his untimely death, Mr MacTire, it should still be in your main residence.'

BACK AT THE MacTire stronghold they burst through the gates, past the guards on duty in the courtyard and ran inside. Hannah was in the main lobby. 'Is everything alright?' she asked.

'Fine,' Alexander said. 'Hunky-dory.'

She glanced at Mallory, undisguised hope flaring in her eyes.

'We're heading to the basement,' Alexander told her.

Her optimistic expression faltered. 'The basement? But...'

'It's fine, Hannah,' Mallory said.

'Should I come with you?'

Alexander and Mallory glanced at each other then simultaneously shook their heads. 'No,' Alexander said. 'In fact, some privacy would be welcome.' He pointed to an unobtrusive door behind the grand staircase. 'It's this way,' he told Mallory.

She smiled uncertainly at Hannah and followed him. It seemed too much to hope that there really was a bellarmine jug in a dusty old box in the MacTire basement, but she felt hope all the same.

The stairs leading downwards were rickety, and their creaks bounced off the old walls until it sounded as if they were listening to an orchestra of strange sounds. On another occasion Mallory might have paused to enjoy the oddly melodic cacophony but today she simply stayed hot on Alexander's heels.

At the bottom he led her down a dusty corridor. 'The wine cellar is that way and that room to the left has all sorts of old crap in it.' They passed it. 'This one is where all my father's stuff was stored after he died. I don't normally come in here, but I did last month when his study was finally cleared out.'

Mallory nodded mutely. He turned to look at her. 'You do realise that I only changed the décor to impress you?'

'You don't have to do anything to impress me, Alex,' she said softly.

His eyes darkened. 'Yes, I do.' He turned into the old store room and flicked on a light.

Mallory's mouth dropped. She'd been expecting a lot of boxes but the piles of them were innumerable.

'Yeah,' Alexander said. 'My father liked owning things. He saw everything as a possession, and the more he owned the happier he felt.' He cast a critical eye around the room. 'It might take a while to find the jug. Maybe I ought to get the others down here to help.'

'No.' Mallory couldn't say why but it was important that she and Alexander completed this search. 'Let's do this together, just you and me.'

His eyes gleamed suddenly. 'As you wish, honey.'

For a moment, they gazed at each other then she turned to the first box. 'Come on,' she whispered. 'Where are you?' She flipped open the lid and started to rummage.

The box was full of random objects. Mallory found a pair of antique candlesticks that appeared to be hundreds of years old and fashioned using druidic magic. They were nestled next to a grubby teddy bear with glass eyes that certainly possessed no magic properties whatsoever. There was also a collection of old coins in a battered tin.

'I'd forgotten half this stuff existed.' Alexander's head was buried in another box. 'I should have got rid of it all years ago.'

'I'm glad you didn't.' There was no guarantee that they'd find a bellarmine jug – it might have been broken or sold off by Alexander's father – but she felt deep inside that they would, and it would be intact. Everything was going to be fine.

She moved to the second box. Nothing there. She pushed it aside and grabbed the third one: again, no jug. She was stretching up to pull down a fourth box when Alexander cleared his throat. 'Here,' he said. 'Here it is.'

Mallory turned. When she saw the jug in his hands, she closed her eyes for a second then she gently took it and turned it over to examine it. It was, without doubt, genuine.

'You found it,' she breathed. 'You did it. It's going to be a happy ending.'

'No. Not yet.' He took the jug from her, wrapped it carefully and placed it inside a smaller box. 'For one thing, *I* didn't do it. *We* did it.' He put the box on the floor.

She smiled happily as the pain and trauma of the last month slid into oblivion. 'It's almost impossible to believe that jug was hiding in your basement all this time.'

'It's amazing what can hide in plain sight.' Alexander wasn't smiling; in fact, there was an intensity to his gaze that spoke of serious matters. He reached out and cupped her face. 'I'm sorry, Mallory. I'm sorry for so much.'

She opened her mouth to speak but he shook his head. 'I'm sorry because I knew I'd fallen in love with you the first time I saw you with that bastard Ferguson, and I didn't tell you.'

Her breath caught. He'd said the words and made it real.

She didn't trust herself to react and instead seized on the one thing that didn't seem important. 'Liam's not a bastard, Alex.'

'I know that, too. That's what makes it worse.' He stared into her eyes, his gaze gentle and fierce at the same time. 'I tried so many times to tell you how I felt, but every time I got close you mentioned that damned contract! You were helping me to find my fucking First Mate when all I wanted was for *you* to be my mate. Everyone thought I was nuts for not telling you. Even Cathy West told me to man up.'

Mallory stared at him. 'She did?'

'I spent the whole date with her talking about you. I couldn't tell you, though –I couldn't bear the thought of scaring you away. There was so much to lose. What if I told you and then I never saw you again? What if it was my alpha arrogance that made me think you might feel anything at all for me?'

His voice dropped. 'What if I was too much like my fucking father and thought that I could own you in the same way I might own a damned magical jug?' He shook his head. 'And when you kept putting yourself in danger and my wolf kept appearing because I had to protect you...' He ground his teeth. 'And it turned out that you were the one who had to protect me.'

'I thought you saw me as weak and you'd never think I'd be suitable,' Mallory whispered. 'After all, you told me yourself you didn't want love.'

'It turns out I don't have a choice. You're all I want. If you don't want to be First Mate, if you don't want that responsibility, I'll step down as alpha right now.'

Her heart thudded against her ribcage. 'I would never ask that of you.'

'I know, but I'll do it. I want you more than I've ever wanted anything or anyone.'

Mallory shook her head. 'No. You're a werewolf alpha – it's

who you are. I'm a squib and that's who *I* am. And I love every part of you, Alex. I think I always will.'

He reached for her, wrapping his arms around her waist and pulling her against him, then he dropped his head and the tip of his nose brushed against hers before his mouth descended. He kissed her with aching tenderness.

Mallory raised her hands and ran her fingers through his hair. His spicy cinnamon scent enveloped her as she dropped one hand to tug at his T-shirt, pulling it up until she could feel the heat of his skin.

Alexander growled in response. 'Be mine,' he murmured in her ear.

She moved a step backwards and started to unbutton her blouse, exposing herself to his greedy gaze. 'I already am,' she said. 'But I'm happy to prove it, if you like.' She kicked off her shoes, then unfastened her trousers and slid them down over her hips until they joined her blouse on the floor. She hooked her thumbs around her bra straps and lowered them an inch, her eyes dancing.

'Tease.' Alexander's breath was ragged.

'You're not going to turn wolf, are you?'

'Not if we hurry this along.'

Mallory laughed. She stepped towards him, licked her index finger then raised it to his mouth and traced the shape of his lips.

'I think,' he said hoarsely, 'that my heart is beating so fast it's going to burst out of my chest.'

'Show me.'

He peeled off his T-shirt and placed her hand on his bare chest, covering it with his own. She placed his other hand over her own heart and they stood together, marvelling at every thrum and thud.

Alexander leaned towards her again and kissed her more urgently.

Mallory reached down to unzip his jeans, but when she tugged them down they tangled with his ankles. He stumbled slightly, half-gasping, and they went down together onto the floor. 'Ouch!' she exclaimed, sitting up abruptly.

He froze. 'Are you hurt?'

'Yes!' She pointed to her mouth, unable to hide her grin. 'Right here.'

Alexander reached for her. 'I'll kiss it better.'

Mallory tapped her neck. 'It hurts here, too.' His lips descended as he pressed butterfly kisses against her skin. She moaned briefly and reached behind her back to unclip her bra. 'Lower,' she breathed. 'It hurts lower. So very, very sore.'

His hands cupped her breasts, his thumbs brushing her nipples. 'Here?'

She gasped. 'Y–yes.'

His head lowered again, his mouth closing around one nipple while his hand teased the other.

'God, Alex...' she whispered. Mallory's entire body was shaking now, trembling with need and desire.

He pulled back just enough to look at her. 'I love you, Mallory Nash.'

'I love you, too.'

And that was when the tide broke and their movements became frantic with need. Her fingers slipped beneath the waistband of his boxer shorts, pulling them down and out of the way. She had barely a moment to admire the hard length of him before he reached for her pants, ripping the fabric in his haste. He tossed her underwear aside. Then, with his eyes on hers, he moved his hand between her legs and circled the nub of her clitoris.

'Please, Alex.' Her voice was strained.

His answer was rough. 'Please what?'

'I need you now.'

'In that case, I suppose I'd better oblige. You are a powerful squib, after all. There's no telling what you might do if you don't get what you want.' He moved slightly and thrust inside her, groaning as she clung to his shoulders.

He pressed his sweat-slick forehead against hers. 'Tell me, Mallory,' he said. He thrust once more and her hips rose to meet his, then again and again and again.

Her breath was coming short and fast as their rhythm speeded up and she felt the power building to a crescendo inside her. 'Now,' she gasped.

Alexander pushed even deeper inside her and Mallory cried out. A second later he did the same, his body shuddering until they collapsed together, hearts pounding, limbs entwined.

Several long, glorious seconds passed as the last of their tremors ebbed away.

Alexander cupped her face. 'Now it's a happy ending,' he murmured huskily.

Mallory wrinkled her nose. 'No,' she disagreed. 'As far as you and I are concerned, this is only the beginning.'

His eyes danced. 'That might be the cheesiest thing you've ever said.' He stroked her cheek with his thumb. 'And that's saying something.'

'Shall I retract my statement?'

'Absolutely,' he breathed, kissing her once more, 'definitely not.'

EPILOGUE

Lord Chester Longchamps was dressed to the nines but not in a top hat and tails, nor in a custom-made kilt or a sharp suit delivered direct from Savile Row. He was wearing the best, the strongest, the most magically enhanced armour that money could buy. A bulging backpack rested on his shoulders and in one hand he carried a gun loaded with poison-tipped bullets. In his other hand, he cradled the bellarmine jug.

The silly squib woman had been almost giddy with delight when she'd passed over the jug. She'd couldn't keep that ridiculous grin off her face even though it had been her fault that he'd had to wait so long for the damned thing. Lives had been lost because of the delay, though thankfully not vampire lives.

The new system was working well and no-one with fangs had died since it had been implemented, but that wasn't the point; it was the principle that bothered him. Besides, it was only a matter of time before one of the other Preternatural groups noticed their missing brethren. The new system was a stop gap, not a permanent solution. Some of his less sensible peers were growing suspicious and their delicate sensibilities and overly liberal attitudes would soon be a problem. The Clouded Map was the only way to put an end to this dreadful palaver once and for all.

It wasn't lost on Chester that there was something going on between Mallory Nash and that mange-ridden excuse for a werewolf who'd dared to force his way into his house and launch an unprovoked assault. Once this gruesome business was dealt with, he'd take his revenge on the MacTire bastard *and* the Nash squib.

He smiled. He'd told them that everything was over and done with, and that he wouldn't seek further retribution; he'd even signed a second blood contract to that effect – but he'd not given his spoken vow. After Nash had scammed him with her contract the first time around, he'd taken care to look for loopholes and exit strategies. He could break the contract without consequences for an eye-wateringly expensive fee, but it would be worth it. Nobody made a fool out of Lord Chester Longchamps. *Nobody*. Those two would learn that the hard way.

'Do you have enough spare blood with you?' Alan asked him, pawing anxiously at the ground. The fool was more skittish pony than powerful vampire.

'Yes, yes.' Longchamps dismissed his question and ignored the gnawing worry that was settling deep in his bones. 'I'm carrying enough to last me until August. In any case, I doubt that this will take me more than a couple of days now I have the Clouded Map.'

Alan swallowed. 'Are you sure you're happy to do this alone?'

Longchamps stared down his nose at him. 'You're welcome to join me if you wish.'

The other vampire blanched and Longchamps snorted.

'That's what I thought.' He turned towards the entrance. 'It takes a great man – a great *hero* – to put their life on the line for others. Somebody has to step up and take control, to stand up and make sure the Understream is kept safe for the generations of vampires who...'

He stopped and glared at the group of people standing to one side. 'You are supposed to be filming this!' he snapped. The anxiety he was trying to disguise was getting the better of him. 'How can my exploits be recorded for posterity if nobody is fucking recording?'

There was a scramble and eventually somebody produced a small camcorder. Longchamps huffed. This would be a lot easier if smartphones worked in Coldstream. Somebody ought to do something about finding a way to blend the new technology with the old magic. Perhaps he'd give it a shot when he returned from the maze. Maybe it would be worth keeping the Nash woman alive for a bit longer so he could get her to work on the problem. He'd think about it; he could always drain her blood at a later date. She'd proved easy enough to manipulate and she'd gotten hold of a second bellarmine jug when he'd been almost certain that she would fail. Longchamps caressed the jug almost absent mindedly.

'Adieu, my fellow vampires,' he declared. 'I leave you now not because I want to but because someone must save the day. Many of you do not yet perceive this threat as real, despite the blood that has been shed on our doorsteps, but it is as real as I am and far more dangerous. Be thankful that I am prepared to deal with it on your behalf.'

He smiled, displaying his sharp white fangs that had been polished for this very occasion, then turned on his heel. With a swagger perfected over many decades, he entered the Night Maze.

His mission would be successful. He'd made every possible preparation. He could do this.

It was relatively easy to begin with because there were few choices to make and the Clouded Map soon proved its worth. Every time he came to a crossroads, he took out a preservation spell, cast it and unstoppered the jug in order to slide out the map. It revealed the surrounding area and indicated which path Longchamps should take and which he should avoid.

Although he would never have admitted it out loud, he was nervous about what the centre of the maze would reveal but he'd have the element of surprise of his side. He would do this and those other vampires in the Understream would thank him for it. If they didn't, he'd be sure to let them know the error of their ways.

Ambling along a long walkway, he registered a junction up ahead with five possible exits. When he cast the preservation spell and extracted the Clouded Map from the jug, it indicated that the third exit was the correct one. He returned the map to its magicked container and turned, but he'd barely taken a step when there was a loud chime followed by an odd rumbling noise. It sounded ominous.

The ground trembled beneath his feet and a faint smell of musty cobwebs and stone dust tickled his nostrils. He hesitated then plunged down the third path.

Easy, he thought. It might have been a ball-ache getting hold of the bellarmine jug and the Clouded Map, but his efforts had clearly been worthwhile. He turned the next corner.

He didn't get very far. When he saw what was waiting for him his steps faltered. What the hell was it – and why was it there? There had been nothing on the map to indicate...

Chester Longchamps didn't get the chance to complete his thought or to work out what was happening. The sealed bellarmine jug containing the Clouded Map tumbled onto the dark ground. This particular jug was sturdier than the last one but even so it was surprising that it didn't shatter.

Unfortunately that didn't matter to Chester Longchamps, not anymore. He was beyond caring.

About the Author

After teaching English literature in the UK, Japan and Malaysia, Helen Harper left behind the world of education following the worldwide success of her Blood Destiny series of books. She thanks her lucky stars every day that she's able to do so.

Helen has always been a book lover, devouring science fiction and fantasy tales when she was a child growing up in Scotland.

She currently lives in Edinburgh with far too many cats – not to mention the dragons, fairies, demons, wizards and vampires that seem to keep appearing from nowhere.

Acknowledgments

As always, there are many thanks to be made. First of all, to Karen Holmes for her continuing and superlative editing. Her enthusiasm for this series is a genuine thrill and she's a true joy to work with. Jay Villalobos created the cover design for both this book and the series as a whole and has captured both Kit's spirit and that of the cats' with such clarity that I can't wait to see what he comes up with next. I'm also particularly happy to be able to express my gratitude to @chrissyofthevale who has been working on some immense illustrations for The Cat Lady Chronicles and whose inspiring ideas and drawings amaze me every time.

I have a long running relationship with Kara Stebbins and the rest of the Tantor audio team who all deserve mention - and especially Ruth Urquhart who does such a sterling job with her narration and who is so wonderful and picking up loose typos and inconsistencies that have been missed. I'd also like to thank the lovely authors who I meet with online and who always inspire me to do and be better, especially Heather G Harris, Debra Dunbar, Lauretta Hignett, Annabel Chase and Deborah Wilde.

Last, but certainly not least, a special thank you to Scout, Mavis and Lara. Your furry company is always welcome, even when you fall asleep on top of my keyboard.